modern ages of magic

THE FAMILIAR

For information contact;
Address
www.jbrafferty.com

Book and Cover design by John Rafferty
Photo credits — iStockphoto.com
  steve-goacher
  Dmitriy83
  klyaksun
  Pituk Loonhong

Fonts
  Angelic Peace
  Angelic War
  Times New Roman
  Tw Cen MT Condensed

ISBN: 978-0-9966027-5-4
First Edition: October 2024

10 9 8 7 6 5 4 3 2 1

This book is dedicated to
my Michele who reminds me
every day that
magic is indeed real.

Tovenaar's aerial view of
Crab Meadow Beach and Saltmarsh

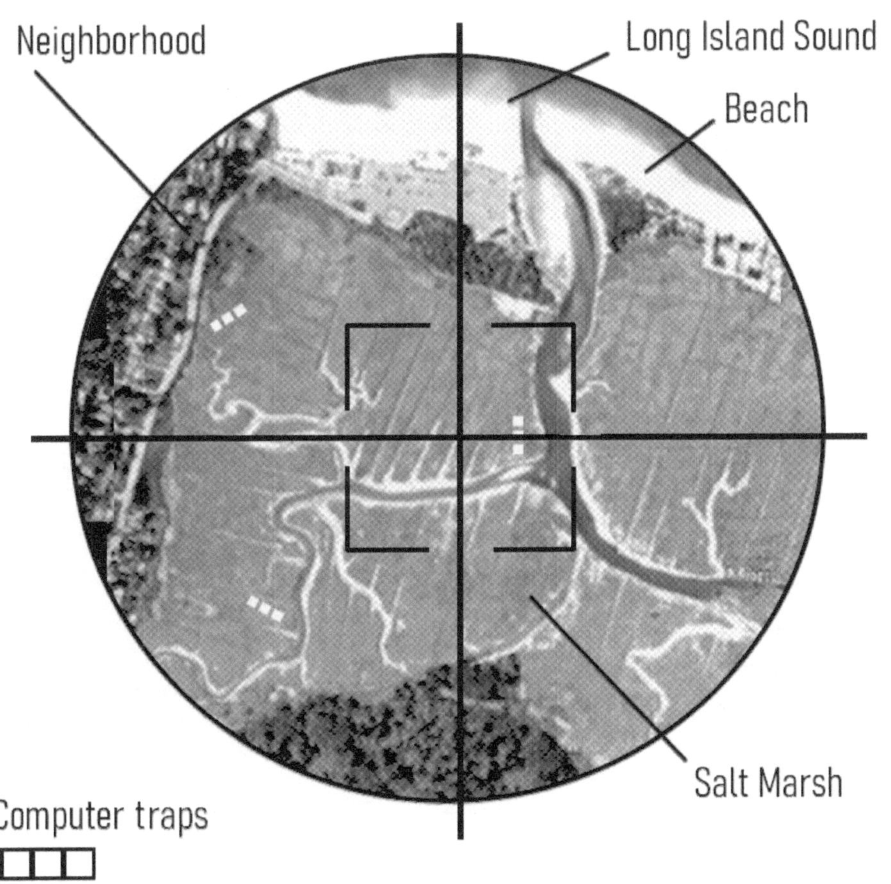

THE FAMILIAR

John Rafferty

BRRAAAP...BRRAAAP. The grim metallic scream of two-stroke engines cuts through the oppressive heat and humidity that blankets a dense forest in Rabun County, Georgia. Soft flashes of heat lightning radiate above the thick canopy of trees. Birds and squirrels scatter frantically from this unnaturally aggressive noise. BRRAAAP... BRRAAAP...BRRAAAAP.

Three motocross bikes burst through the brush, racing along a narrow switchback trail bounded by steep ravines. Faded paint and overgrown vines render the old trail markers useless.

Two young men and one young woman, twenty-one years of age, speed past trees at an alarming rate. They skid-turn around tight bends and jump over obstacles, all while up and downshifting gears as skillfully as seasoned professionals.

The race is against the very forest itself that has come to life with a malicious fury. Tree roots burst through the hardtack dirt, grabbing at the spokes of their wheels. Boulders tumble haphazardly into their path. Tree branches sway and swipe at them furiously, tearing at the protective pads sewn into their now-tattered nylon racing jackets.

Leanne McCurry's fiery red hair spills out from the back of her badly scraped black motocross helmet. She defiantly pulls up her scuffed goggles for a clearer view, leaving her intense hazel eyes precariously exposed.

"Off-trail!" She calls out and swerves to avoid a large tree crashing down ahead.

Calvin Monroe, whose chiseled features make him quite the head-turner, follows closely behind Leanne. He pulls back on his handlebars and expertly pivots after her. "I knew we should have taken trail bikes!" He yells.

Their trail bikes are equipped with shields that would have safeguarded their gloveless hands and the engines from the treacherous elements. The motocross bikes they ride now offer no such protection.

The third rider is Terrence Stokes. His wiry build and long dirty-blonde hair give him the look of a musician in a Southern rock band. He wears a perpetual squint, even when it's cloudy. It was Terrence who insisted on using the lighter motocross bikes.

All three riders have cell phones duct-taped three deep across their handlebars. With every swipe of their screens, powerful flashes of pixelated energy burst forth enabling the riders to clear obstacles from their path.

Leanne deftly swipes at one of her cell phones. A brightly colored blast of reddish plasma, swathed within a fine coating of electricity, decimates a tree stump leaving a pile of wood chips.

Terrence rolls back on the throttle and watches his friends disappear around a bend. He glances back nervously at the unnatural force that is animating the forest. The mayhem continues along the riders' original path, as if unaware its prey has strayed off course.

The aggressive force abruptly settles down.

A cloud of dust thins, and leaves settle gently to the ground, revealing a grotesque humanoid silhouette standing atop a downed tree. It wears a black satin robe, much like that of a boxer entering the ring at a prizefight. Its sickly yellow eyes glare down at Terrence from its cloaked head.

Terrence breaks eye contact with the creature and takes off after his friends.

*

Leanne realizes Terrence is no longer with them and motions for Calvin to stop. "Where the hell is Terrence?" Her heart is pounding.

Calvin shrugs and lifts his dusty goggles from over his eyes. "The dumb ass must have spilled."

Calvin's deep brown eyes regard her protectively, "It's going to be okay. We just need to stick to the plan," he reassures her.

"Maybe," Leanne replies quietly. She turns away so Calvin won't see the tears welling in her eyes. The tenderness in his voice makes her feel vulnerable. She takes a deep breath and slowly exhales, regaining her cool composure. "Why did it suddenly get so quiet?"

They cautiously look over their shoulders. Although neither will admit it, both are painfully aware of how inadequate their newfound powers are for defeating a creature that can control the forces of nature. But they did not choose this fight. It chose them.

"And where the hell is Archibald?" Calvin shows his frustration.

"Archibald bailed." Leanne reminds him.

She is relieved to hear the sudden squeal of Terrence's engine. *Thank God.*

Terrence finally rounds the bend and speeds toward them.

"Let's go!" Calvin kicks his bike into gear taking the trail to the

3

right. Leanne quickly follows.

Terrence shakes his head and cuts down the left fork.

Calvin glimpses Terrence from the corner of his eye, now speeding down the wrong trail. He quickly loses sight of him as the forest between them grows denser. "Dammit, Terrence!" The engines drown out his yell. He rolls off the throttle and comes to a harsh stop.

Leanne brakes hard and pulls alongside Calvin. She balances precariously on the ravine's edge. "Why isn't he following us?" She exclaims breathlessly.

"I don't know. Let's just keep going and hope he finds his way to the old well in time to help spring the trap." From Calvin's vantage point, he sees the trail ahead leads downhill in a meandering of twists and turns, only to wind back up again just fifty feet to the right across a small ravine. The top of the old stone well is faintly visible.

Calvin considers it would save them time if only they could jump across the ravine. He has an epiphany and guns the engine. Just as he approaches the edge, he swipes quickly across all the phones on his handlebars. Green plasma flies out like a glowing wave rapidly forming into a crude but serviceable ramp that extends over the ravine. He hits the ramp and flies in a graceful arc.

"Oh, crap!" He realizes he overshot the distance. Two uncontrolled bounces later, Calvin ends up prone in a bramble next to his bike. Without wasting time to brush himself off, he springs back up and onto the saddle.

Leanne shouts excitedly, "Hell, yeah!" She charges the ramp and easily clears the distance. She quickly catches up to Calvin, who is now doing a slow roll only fifty yards from the old well.

"You made a ramp!" She exclaims incredulously. "How did you do that?"

"I just thought it and it happened," Calvin explains with an oddly distracted tone. He can almost feel his mind expand as his psychokinetic prowess increases. "No! No!" He quickly launches blasts of plasma toward the old stone well.

"Stop! You'll ruin the computers!" Leanne cries out. Then she sees it. The dark shape of the strange creature darting through a cloud of plasma dust from one tree to the next, somehow avoiding Calvin's persistent blasts.

It has beaten them to the well and has already destroyed the laptop computers and the generator the trio had concealed under a pile of brush. A stack of batteries and hard drives are still intact. Powerful computers can explode plasma like artillery blasts. Or so they hope.

With their trap in shambles, their only chance is to strike quickly and hope to land a lucky shot that will destroy the creature. Leanne speeds recklessly past Calvin while swiping furiously across the line of phones on her handlebars. A wide arc of plasma flashes forward and conjures a ramp resembling the one Calvin created. She takes it fast and catches big air, like the jumps that made her a fan favorite at the motocross circuit. She stares down at the old well from high above and pictures in her mind an explosion that will put an end to this terrifying ordeal.

Suddenly from below, one of the computers reacts and emits a massive pulse of plasma. The other computers follow suit and strafe the area like a virtual air strike.

I just thought it in my mind and the computers reacted! Leanne sticks the landing, and skid turns to a halt. She looks back, feeling confident her assault was a success. A thick cloud of smoke and dust prevents her from confirming a kill.

Calvin slowly cruises past her and circles around the remains of the old well.

"Where is it?" Leanne has an uneasy feeling. She does not plan to let her guard down until she sees a corpse.

Without a word, Calvin pries a cell phone from his handlebar and tosses it like a hand grenade into the well's shaft. He gestures with his hand and a series of explosions descend deep into the earth. "Just in case," he smiles at Leanne and winks.

She returns his smile, letting herself relax enough to suck in a deep breath.

An unexpected blast of blue-tinged plasma blasts Calvin from his bike. His head slams against the trunk of a tree. Through the pain of broken ribs and a possible concussion, he tries to stand up, only to fall back down.

Terrence has finally arrived and wears a satisfied grin as he watches Calvin struggle. He swipes another blast at Calvin's bike for good measure. He laughs as it flips in the air from the explosion and lands in a broken heap. He dismounts from his bike and smirks at Leanne with a crazed smile.

Leanne's wide-eyed stare of disbelief at Terrence's attack turns into one of rage. She revs her engine and races her bike at Terrence then coolly dismounts, allowing it to speed riderless in his direction. She runs and slides on her knees to Calvin's side. He is sitting on the ground with his back propped up against a tree. She gently removes his damaged helmet. "Are you okay? Can you stand?"

Calvin's eyelids flutter as he struggles to remain conscious.

Terrence effortlessly dodges Leanne's bike, which has now come to a crashing halt against his. He springs over to Leanne and grabs her by the shoulders, dragging her away from Calvin.

She falls back and manages to avoid striking her head on the ground.

Terrence positions himself between her and Calvin. He looks down at Leanne triumphantly. "It's over. It's just you and me now."

"You asshole!" Leanne screams. She pulls off her helmet and

tosses it aside. The mad universe of freckles that cover her beautiful face is even more striking from the flush in her cheeks "Archibald warned us what would happen if we betrayed one another!"

"Archibald doesn't know shit," Terrence laughs cruelly.

Leanne shifts her attention to Calvin. She kneels beside him and urgently squeezes his arm "C'mon Calvin, shake it off!" She whispers harshly.

"I knew you would choose him," Terrence sneers and spits on the ground.

Leanne springs up in anger. "How can you be so stupid? We had it beat!" She throws a punch at Terrence, but misses. She follows with her left hand, this time hitting him square in the face.

Terrence yelps out in pain and stumbles back, mortified that she would strike him. He wipes blood from his nose with the back of his hand.

Suddenly, the air around them quivers with a low pitch rumble. The creature that has been chasing them appears out of nowhere and stands only feet from them both.

Leanne jumps back, both in fright and to distance herself from its offensively oppressive odor.

It pulls back the hood from its head to expose a face covered with row after row of shimmery black scales. Random clear patches of skin and tufts of blond hair, not hampered by the scales, reveal that this creature may have once been human. Unsightly lumps occur where the scales grow too dense.

Leanne recalls when Archibald had first warned the three of them about this creature. A "familiar," he called it. An apprentice who betrayed his master and is now bound to serve the Wizard of the Industrial Age. It has existed for hundreds of years. She throws up a little in her mouth, repulsed by the sight of it.

"Nice," the familiar remarks in a gravelly voice regarding the silly girl nearly vomiting at the sight of him. "You thought you had me beat?" He mocks. The familiar flashes a smile filled with contempt, "As if."

Leanne notices Terrence standing proudly next to the familiar and calls him out on it.

"Why?"

Terrence defends his betrayal. "Cristobal was right. He knew you would choose Calvin over me."

Leanne struggles to keep her balance as a wave of nausea shudders through her. She feels weak, but not weak enough to give up. "Oh, so you're on a first-name basis?" She regards them both with disgust. "You two deserve each other."

Calvin struggles to his knees. Sweat runs down his face as he fights against the pain. Leanne rushes over to help him up, but he collapses back against the tree.

An amused Cristobal observes Calvin's misery and speaks in an odd singsong tone, "Always it begins with three and forever ends with one. I only needed to convince one of you to betray the other two." His yellow eyes twinkle with glee as he gloats over Calvin and Leanne. "You are betrayed. You are no longer magically adept. Only useless humans."

Leanne attempts to throw a bolt of energy from her smart watch just to prove the familiar wrong. It sizzles ineffectively and splats into the dirt.

The familiar giggles gleefully.

Terrence nervously rubs his cell phone. To his relief, plasma arcs and sizzles around his thumb. He will do anything to keep his new powers. Unbeknownst to him, a thin line of black scales grows along his left cheek. Terrence looks down at Calvin and smiles victoriously. He always hated the pretty boy and is glad that he will no longer be in the picture. He leans in toward the familiar and says under his breath,

"You promised me she would live."

Cristobal frowns. "Trust me, it is best for everyone if they both perish," he informs his new accomplice, and snickers as Terrence's face grows red.

BAM!

Cristobal shrieks in skull-pounding pain as Leanne's well-aimed motocross helmet strikes his temple. His knees buckle and he falls to the ground. "Are you...AHHH...kidding me?!"

Leanne reaches for a large rock to throw next, but Terrence quickly reacts and restrains her wrists. "Stop it. I am trying to save you! Just come away with us," he pleads.

Leanne spits in his face. "You disgust me."

The familiar staggers to his feet. He rolls his two fists against each other, cracking every knuckle. Ripples of energy pulsate from his fingertips.

He questions Terrence, "Do you *still* want me to spare her?"

In her last moments, Leanne wants nothing more than to hurt the one that betrayed her and Calvin. She kneels and tenderly places her hand on Calvin's cheek. She speaks softly, yet loud enough for Terrence to hear, "It was always you."

Calvin smiles through his pain, "I never doubted you, Matchstick." Matchstick was a nickname he teased her with in grade school because of her long skinny legs and fiery red hair. It used to push her buttons, and she hated him for it. In her last moments of consciousness, she finds it to be endearing.

The display of affection nails Terrence right through his ego. "Do what you got to do," he informs the familiar.

The fury and pain of the welt growing on his temple prevent Cristobal from considering even the slightest bit of mercy. He once again raises his arms. His body convulses as an overwhelming force of energy wells inside him.

Calvin calls out weakly, "We aren't a threat to you now. Please don't hurt her!"

The familiar's hands swing forward and come together like a thunderclap. Visible energy surges forward and engulfs Leanne and Calvin. Every molecule in their bodies screams against the unnatural changes the magic is forcing upon them.

Leanne clings to Calvin in a spasm of sheer agony. As he pulls her close in a protective embrace, their cries of pain are choked off as their skin dries and becomes increasingly rigid. Salty tears thicken into sap. Their torsos lengthen and twist together. The bones of their feet sprout forth as roots that sink deep into the soil. Arms elongate and replicate into branches. Their fingers multiply and sprout leaves.

Calvin and Leanne can no longer breathe. Their lungs and other organs cease to function humanly, stretching and hardening to become the long grain of living wood. Their bones break and regrow grievously to re-purpose for a new existence. Sense of smell, taste, sight, hearing, and touch blur into a lumbering numbness.

Leanne's life force is altered into that of a twenty-foot-tall red maple tree with smooth bark and crimson red foliage.

The malevolent sorcery simultaneously transformed Calvin into the form of a honey locust tree. Rough bark covered with long sharp thorns.

Both trees have twisted together in an anguished embrace that will last for decades.

Cristobal's callous attention to detail has ensured that Calvin's piercing thorns will forever tear at Leanne's smooth bark with even the slightest breeze. She will not physically feel the pain as a human would, but consciously, her soul will be fully aware.

Calvin's soul is also aware of the continual damage he is inflicting on Leanne.

Cristobal staggers back, exhausted from his vengeful altering of the laws of nature and the adepts' new realities. He takes a moment to catch his breath and calm the hell down. He offers his adversaries a parting thought, "Live long, you two."

Terrence stares at his friends' transformations with a slack-jawed expression. He considers that it could have been him being turned into a freaking tree. Thankfully, he was smart enough to take up Cristobal's offer to join forces with the Wizard of the Industrial Age. He unconsciously uses a fingernail to scratch at the small cluster of black scales that now blemish his face.

Cristobal snaps at him. "Stop picking! They do not come off!"

Terrence gives one last scratch and dumbly asks, "So, what now?"

The air around them sizzles and sparks with energy. Cristobal and Terrence vanish.

*

The soft glow of twilight settles over the now tranquil forest. A gentle breeze rustles the leaves of the two new trees. Already, thorns have left scratches on the tender bark of the maple tree.

A tricolored foxhound bursts through the brush and skids to an abrupt stop. It is fiercely out of breath and turns sharply to look in every direction. The hound's body quivers and magically morphs into the form of a slender man with wispy hair and a thin scraggly beard. He wears an old wool coat.

The strange man studies every aspect of the scene where the battle took place. Scorched earth and vegetation scarred from explosives. Mangled motorbikes lie in a heap. The remains of an unusual ramp dissolve and crumble like a sandcastle in the rising tide.

His head turns quickly to the oddly entangled trees. "Oh, no." He recognizes that the two trees are what remain of Leanne McCurry and Calvin Monroe. "Terrence what have you done?"

He looks at the trees and apologizes. "You must believe I did everything I could. If I could undo this unspeakable spell, I would!" He picks up a dead cell phone. "It's *not* my fault!" He cries out in despair and smashes the phone against a large rock.

Whoooomph. He disappears.

Chapter 1

An unwashed pearl-colored SUV towing a vintage silver Airstream motor home plods along the passing lane of the eastbound Long Island Expressway. The message *Bite Me,* that some joker scrawled into the grime on the back window at the used car lot, infuriates impatient motorists. They express their displeasure with vulgar hand gestures as they hurry past the slow-moving vehicle. They just want to get to where they are going and enjoy the last weekend of summer.

What kind of dumbass drives like this?

Said dumbass is Carmine Blakely, a sweat-stained-white-tank top-wearing citizen in his early fifties who is oblivious to other motorists. He is exhausted from packing his family's possessions for the big move.

Riding shotgun is his high school sweetheart Agnes Blakely. She is overdressed for the occasion wearing a black cocktail dress and high heels. Agnes is determined to make a good first impression on their new neighbors.

She tries her best to ignore the rude behavior of the other drivers but is appalled. She frowns and informs her husband, "Carmine, I don't know if you are paying attention, but that is the twelfth bird that's been flipped at us. Do something about it...Now!"

Carmine grunts. He flips up his turn signal and hits the gas pedal hard. The trailing mobile home leans precariously as it careens across three lanes of traffic. Horns blare and brakes screech.

"Must have zoned out," he mumbles. Carmine has been in a funk ever since bidding farewell to their rent-controlled apartment in Queens, New York. He reluctantly agreed to move when Agnes insisted their son attend a quiet school in the suburbs.

He peers into the rear view mirror at his son, "We will not be hearing any more excuses. Ain't that right, Shea?"

The back seat is piled high with boxes and black plastic bags, leaving only enough room for one person to squeeze in. It has not been an exceptionally long drive, but for 17-year-old Shea Blakely, it feels like an eternity.

Shea was named after Shea Stadium, the home of the New York Mets. Ironically, he is not the least bit interested in sports. He blows his shaggy blond hair from his eyes, which he has been growing out ever since he learned of the move. The peach fuzz hint of a goatee and a mustache still have a way to go.

His guidance counselor, for once, gave him valuable advice. *Fake it until you make it.* His plan with this fresh start is to shed his lackluster image and put out more of a bad boy vibe.

It is hot in the car, even with the windows open. His dad refuses to run the A/C to save on gas. Shea pulls at the front of his faux vintage Doctor Who tee shirt that is now damp with sweat. He has mixed feelings about his family's move to the burbs, though he will use it to his advantage. He has always wanted to get a car, but never needed one in his old neighborhood. Everything was within walking distance, or a subway stop away.

He likes the idea of a fresh start but is a little apprehensive about starting his senior year in a new school. Shea has always had a laid back attitude toward most things. He has friends, but also does not mind being by himself. He could be found reading a book under a shady tree in the schoolyard or sitting in front of his computer at home.

Last semester he had become the target of some jerks on the school bus when he was spotted casually minding his own business. They followed him off the bus and taunted him. He never considered himself much of a fighter, but when a rock was thrown at his head, it was a local politician's son who suffered a black eye.

His father continues, "You have a fresh start at this new school. No more bullshit. No more fighting. No more video games. I want you to concentrate on your studies and do your homework."

He cuts the wheel to avoid a pothole but manages to hit it anyway. "And if you must hit someone, be sure to not leave a mark. Are you hearing me?"

His mother chimes in, "How are you going to become a doctor if you keep behaving like a hooligan?"

"Your mom and I are counting on you to supplement our retirement," his father adds, only half-kidding.

Shea leans back against the headrest and closes his eyes. He cracks a thin smile when his father mentions homework. The truth is, he has been using his homework time programming his own video game. He spends the rest of his time reading sci-fi and sword and sorcery novels, like the one on his lap.

His left hand clutches a smartphone and the fingers on his right are sticky from the candy he has stashed in his jeans pocket. If his dad knew he had jellybeans, he would eat all the red ones. Shea has resorted to sneaking them one at a time while trying not to be too obvious with his chewing.

His mom smells the candy, but to her credit, she does not betray Shea's secret.

Something in the sky catches Shea's attention.

"Stop the car!" He blurts out.

Carmine locks the brakes. The mobile home begins to jackknife. He instinctively steers the SUV into the skid and screeches to a halt onto the dusty shoulder of the road.

Agnes shrieks and braces her hands against the dashboard.

"What are you crazy?" Carmine spins around in his seat. "What the hell is wrong with you?"

Shea already has the door open and is getting out of the car. "Look at that! I must get a shot." He has finally perked up since the start of this trip.

Up ahead in the distance, a lone dark cloud floats ominously in the otherwise clear blue sky. It emanates continual flashes of purple, green, and yellow-colored heat lightning.

Shea frames the shot with his cell phone and videotapes footage of the crazy phenomenon.

Back in the car, Carmine argues with Agnes, "That son of yours is going to catch a beating."

"He's your son too." She frowns as she watches Shea taking pictures of the sky with his phone. "I just hope that moving out of the city is going to straighten him out."

Shea slides back into the car and slams the door shut.

"Let's roll," he commands.

His father stares him down in the rear view mirror with displeased eyes. "Don't you ever pull that crap when I'm driving. We could have been roadkill."

"Sorry pops, but this will be perfect for my video game. I needed a reference shot."

"What did I tell you about wasting time on video games. And don't think I don't know about them jellybeans."

His mother chimes in, "Honey, you should spend your time reading biology books. Doctors do not waste their time photographing stars and such."

Quick wits have always been one of Shea's strong suits. He has the perfect comeback, "They do if they're a plastic surgeon in Hollywood."

This idea nails Carmine Blakely in the cranium, "Do you hear that, Agnes? The kid is finally thinking. That is one hell of a lucrative line of work. Movie stars don't even use HMOs. They pay cash."

"My little boy, plastic surgeon to the stars! Maybe we will get invited to gala events!" Agnes shrieks with excitement at the possibilities.

Carmine likes the sound of this and is more than happy to play along with this line of thought, even if it is just a fanciful distraction. "We could hobnob with the upper-crusters like we belonged, couldn't we Agnes?"

Carmine finally gets an opening to merge back into traffic and hits the gas.

Agnes asks excitedly, "Do you think I will meet Brad Pitt?"

Shea ignores them both. His video game will be completed before his first year of college is over. *Hopefully they will get off my back after I make my first million.*

He reviews the footage he shot of that crazy cloud and smiles.

Chapter 2

Huntsport is a bustling town on the north shore of Long Island.

Seventeen-year-old Marion Grey ignores the trendy clothing shops and salons as she posts "lost dog" flyers onto telephone poles with a staple gun. She sports an old pair of loose-fitting khakis, a seriously wrinkled tee shirt, and stained canvas sneakers. An attentive observer might look past her unkempt brunette hair and be rewarded with the discovery of a stunning pair of amber colored eyes. But Marion does not care to be noticed. She is more comfortable being invisible.

She looks like she just washed a dog. In fact, she washed seven dogs earlier in the day. Marion is a bleeding heart who prefers the company of animals to humans. She dedicates her free time to caring for abandoned puppies and kittens at the local animal shelter.

A young man on a skateboard with an athletic build wearing board shorts and a black tank top cruises by Marion and snatches one of the flyers from her hand.

"What's up Chainsaw?" He grins as he rolls past her.

Marion calls after him, "Jerk."

Chainsaw is a terrible nickname that was given to her when she wore traditional metal braces in middle school while most of her peers wore clear ones. It has been a few years since the braces were removed, but the name has stuck and continues to push her buttons.

Tonio gets a kick out of pushing people's buttons. His dark slicked-back hair and hazel green eyes give him a roguish allure that he often uses to his advantage. He carries his athletic build with a relaxed indifference.

Lawrence Brown, also on a skateboard, struggles to keep up. A cell phone strapped to his shoulder blares out an aggressive death metal tune. His curly blond locks stick out like a mop, and he suffers from an implausible combination of being overweight and having a high metabolism.

He mimics Tonio's lead and says, "Sup, Chainsaw?" He clumsily grabs at the stack of flyers in Marion's hand and loses his balance. He slams into the side of a parked utility repair truck.

The flyers scatter to the sidewalk along with his phone.

"Watch it, spazzymoto!" The technician calls down in a mocking tone from atop the cherry picker bucket. The telephone line that he is repairing emits strange purplish sparks.

"Stupid place to park a repair truck," Lawrence says in his defense. He gets up rubbing his shoulder and looks at the scattered flyers with a comically pained expression. By way of apology, he stammers, "Sorry Chain...I mean...well, um, I..." He quickly grabs up his board and trots across the street to catch up with Tonio.

*

The tricolored foxhound from Marion's flyers peers at the traffic from within a tight alleyway between two stores. It turns its head from one direction to another and seems to be equally intrigued by Marion, Tonio, the man in the cherry picker bucket, and the Blakely's approaching SUV.

*

Shea is unaccustomed to being favored by good fortune. He blurts out with an uncharacteristically enlivened tone, "We're moving here?" He sees teenagers everywhere and shifts quickly to peer over the boxes that block his view of the other side of the road.

"Hey, there's a bookstore. And that's like the third pizza place I've seen," he gushes. Huntsport is more happening than he could have hoped for.

Carmine watches his son via the rear view mirror. Except for his recent bizarre photo shoot, it has been a while since he has seen Shea this excited about anything.

As the SUV approaches a busy intersection, the cherry picker holding the technician unexpectedly swings down and drops directly in front of them.

"Watch it!" Agnes yells.

"Holy crap!" Carmine slams on the brakes and screeches to a halt, narrowly avoiding a collision.

Brakes screech successively from the line of cars behind them.

"What do you want me to do, dumbass?" Carmine's temper flares as drivers blare their horns at him.

Agnes loudly shushes him. "Do not make a scene! They might be our new neighbors!" She quickly rolls up her window and dons her sunglasses.

A low-pitched hum causes everyone in town to stop what they are doing and look for the source of the disturbing resonance.

Visible sparks sizzle along all the electric wires. Then, without warning, every traffic light and streetlight explode successively in a five-block radius.

Pedestrians on the sidewalks shield their faces from flying shards of glass.

The engines of every car in the vicinity go silent.

Shea is overcome with the sudden urge to step out of the car and into the street.

"Get your ass back in this car!" Carmine roars.

Shea barely hears his father or the panic-stricken pedestrians shrieking as they duck for cover. Or even some weirdo yelling something about alien pulse rifles. He perceives his surroundings as if he is underwater, both audibly and visually.

Shea's eyes focus solely on the beautiful girl holding a staple gun and flyers who stands diagonally across the street from him. He is mesmerized by the way she returns his stare.

His heart sinks when her gaze turns from him to a skateboarder who stands on the opposite corner from her.

For a moment, Shea locks eyes with that guy. They regard each other with glares of suspicion and animosity.

His attention snaps back to the girl when he sees a translucent panel of energy emanate from her and rush directly towards him.

A second panel of energy leaves the girl and connects with the punk holding the skateboard.

Is this a sick dream? Shea wonders. He feels like he stepped into a cheesy nineties video game.

Is she doing this? How is this possible?

Another thin line of energy leaves the skateboard punk and comes straight for him.

"No, gross!"

It hits Shea and creates a perfect equilateral triangle. The vibration is intense and tingles every cell in his body, though it does not alarm him. It somehow feels okay.

A mad blur of scattered computer-like imagery races along the three panels. Every sound from the highest pitch to the lowest bass hums and vibrates through their cores.

Time stands still. Their senses of reality shift. No one else exists. They regard each other coolly and marvel at the impressive display of power that drives through them.

The mop-haired kid who is yelling about alien pulse rifles stumbles into the line of energy that connects Shea with Tonio.

The energy fields instantly dissipate, and the three teens snap back to real time.

All the stalled car engines simultaneously restart themselves. Horns blare as drivers try to maneuver their way out of the gridlock caused by the busted traffic lights. People straighten up and brush themselves off.

The foxhound that was hiding in the alley lets out a long forlorn howl that gives Marion an excuse to escape the madness to chase after it.

Tonio hops onto his skateboard and heads off in another direction.

"Shea...SHea...SHEa...SHEA..." His father's incessant yelling finally gets his attention, but not before he notices one of Marion's flyers has blown against his leg.

"Get in the car now!"

Shea ignores his father's command long enough to grab the flyer before stepping back inside the SUV.

Mr. Blakely guns the pedal and maneuvers wildly through the intersection.

"Calm down, Carmine! You're going to get us killed!" Agnes clamors.

"When the shit hits the fan, you get the hell away from the fan," Carmine conveys a life lesson to his son.

Shea looks back as they race out of town trying to catch another glimpse of the mysterious girl. He suggests to his parents, "Maybe we should go back and see if anyone needs our help," half hoping his father will make a U-turn.

His mother replies, "Cut and run, honey. Cut and run."

What just happened? Shea is more taken by that brown-haired beauty than with the strange phenomenon he just experienced. Her image is etched on his mind. He has had strong feelings for girls before, but nothing this intense. The very thought of her makes his stomach flip.

He is too absorbed in his thoughts to realize that they are now well out of town and passing through suburban neighborhoods. Shea starts to notice that the further they go, the more modest the houses become.

Mr. Blakely has finally calmed down and is doing the speed limit. He looks in the rear view mirror at Shea, "Back in the day, these houses used to be vacation cottages for folks who wanted to be close to the beach." He hangs a right into a neighborhood with small homes.

"You don't even like the beach," Shea remarks still distracted. "I don't see a beach."

Carmine hangs a left. "About two miles north." He points north with his thumb. He cruises midway up the block just past a tiny, weathered cottage with peeling yellow paint. The yard is overgrown with weeds and tall grass.

Whew, I am glad it's not that one, Shea thinks. *I would never stand a chance with that girl if I lived in that shack.*

Shea's father does the unthinkable. He stops the car and then backs the trailer into the driveway of the paint-peeling, weed-infested tiny house.

"Now get out and unhitch the trailer," he instructs Shea.

Shea groans and lets himself out. He slowly takes inventory of his new home. A picket fence that looks like it will blow over with the next gust of wind. A yard in need of serious landscaping. A house in need of at least two coats of paint. At least the roof looks new. *Who is going to do all this work?* Reality quickly settles in. "There go my weekends," he unintentionally mumbles aloud.

His father playfully smacks the back of his head. "Enough with the self-pity kiddo. The inside is already finished, and your Uncle Tony is going to help us with a lot of the outside work. We're going to pay him in meatballs and cheap beer."

"You can hardly blame him for fearing the worst," his mom teases Carmine.

Thank God for Uncle Tony, Shea thinks with a sigh of relief.

But his father is not finished, "Now hurry up and unpack the trailer."

"What's the rush?"

"Go ahead, Agnes. You tell him."

His mom shows a look of concern but steps up to break the news.

"Well Shea, as you can appreciate, this is a very small house, and we, your father and I, we feel we need the space, and so..."

Shea stares back expressionless waiting for it.

His mother continues, "...we decided, and this could be pretty cool if you think about it, that the trailer would be your bedroom."

Mr. Blakely quickly adds, "It's not like we aren't going to hook you up with electricity and whatnot."

Shea is thrilled with the idea but keeps his composure. *I will not have to hear their constant jabbering. I can work on my video game without interruptions. I don't even have to sneak out at night. I am already out. Psych!* He frowns outwardly and says, "I guess we can give it a shot."

Chapter 4

Huntsport High School stands unoccupied. A length of chain secures the entrance to the empty parking lot. It is the last Saturday of summer vacation before the new school year begins. The mercury in the thermometer creeps upwards of 95 degrees.

The rumble of two motorcycles increases as they approach the school. One is a black cruiser-style BMW ridden by a lanky male dressed in an oversized tee shirt and ripped jeans. He wears aviator sunglasses and sports a psychotic-looking bowl haircut. His outstretched legs give him a relaxed, easy-rider vibe.

The other motorcycle is a black and yellow street racer with a severely scraped paint job. Its sinewy, long blond-haired rider straddles his seat in a more aggressive forward-leaning position.

Both young men's faces are dappled with black scales.

They ignore the unimposing chain and jump the curb to the sidewalk and casually cruise across the freshly lined football field toward the rear of the building. The riders roll to a stop and set down their kickstands.

The biker with the bowl haircut looks to be about 21 years old. He dismounts and strikes a match across a patch of scales on his chin to light up a cigarette.

His cohort calls out with a slight southern drawl, "Hans, Cristobal said to be discreet." He motions with his head toward a security camera.

"Chill, Torrence. Alles ist gut," Hans replies in a mix of English and German. He pulls a cell phone from his back pocket. With a quick swipe of the screen, a glowing mass of purple and red plasma flies from his phone and strikes the camera with an audible splat, effectively obstructing its lens.

Hans grins, "Are we learning yet, Torrence?"

"Say my name wrong again and see what happens," Terrence warns.

Hans steps up to the school door. He places his cell phone against the key-less lock and swipes the screen. The keypad lights up and numbers flicker in random patterns on the red display finally settling on 7777. The door unlocks with a click.

The pair enter the school and make their way down a dimly lit hallway toward the faculty offices. They reach a door with a plaque that reads "Principal Skinner" and enter.

Hans hop-slides over the desk and helps himself to a seat. He powers up the computer and takes one last drag of his cigarette before grinding it out on the carpet with his boot. The startup screen finally launches but requires a password. He then executes the same trick he used outside to crack the door's password.

Terrence removes a phone from his pocket. "I can't believe this communicates with that antiquated rotary phone Cristobal insists on using."

"That is how it is with magical beings from a previous age," Hans replies dryly without looking up from his nimble typing. "They are incapable of utilizing computer technology."

Terrence instructs his phone to "Call Cristobal." He sets the phone to speaker mode and studies the computer screen over Hans' shoulder.

Cristobal's sphincter-clenching voice projects through Terrence's phone. "Let's make this quick," he calmly demands.

"I am accessing the school records as we speak," Hans replies obediently, his fingers typing faster. Student records fly across the computer monitor. Hans studies them intently until he spies one that emits a faint blue glow. He selects it.

A yearbook photo of Marion Grey fills the screen. Hans recites aloud the student's information. "Marion Grey, not *mein* type, but not *brutto*. She carries an A-minus grade point average. No allergies or medical issues, *ya ya ya*. Wait, was *ist das*? *Mein frauline* has dropped out of the orchestra, *und* mathletes, *und* drama class, *und* field hockey. She does charity work at an animal shelter though," he rolls his eyes.

"Piece of cake," Terrence blurts out, then quickly shuts up. He pops a piece of chewing gum in his mouth that he found in the desk drawer.

"Number two, please." Cristobal is already anxious to move on to the next adept.

Hans taps a key with his finger. More records scroll across the screen. He stops once again when he detects a blue glow. "Antonio Marcantonio" he snorts. "Who named this joker?"

He continues, "This one excels at nothing. C's and C-minuses for all his classes. No wait, he earned a D+ in computer science. No records of participation in sports or extracurricular activities." He peers closer at the monitor. "A note from his athletics teacher reads, 'Antonio Marcantonio is a regrettable waste of talent.'" He slaps the palm of his hand on the desk and bursts out laughing. "What a loser!"

"Well, at least he *has* talent." Terrence laughs along with Hans.

"Marcantonio is a *dummkopf*," Hans concludes his narration. "He has been disciplined on many occasions."

"And the third?" Cristobal's hard-gravel voice prompts from Terrence's phone.

More records flash across the screen before coming back full circle to Marion and Antonio.

"There does not appear to be a third adept" Hans replies nervously.

From the phone a low growl, "There is always a third."

"Give me a moment." Hans deftly taps at the keyboard. "Dropouts? *Nein*. School transfers? *Nein*. Death records? *Nein*. There, um, *ist* no record for a third adept."

Cristobal's irritated silence is followed by a rude slam of his rotary phone.

"Really, Hans! Why didn't you just make up a third name?"

The air in the room quivers and a pungent smell assaults their nostrils.

Cristobal materializes dressed in a filthy pink terrycloth bathrobe. His feet are bare and his gnarly toenails are long overdue for a clipping. He holds a half-empty cocktail glass and wears an irritated scowl on his scaly face.

Hans jumps up from the chair.

Terrence bites his tongue to keep from laughing.

"Show me." Cristobal hisses.

Hans does a double take of Cristobal's attire before retaking his seat behind the computer. He clicks the mouse and images of student records once more dance across the screen. Only two records have the telltale blue halos that mark them as potential wizards. They are Marion Grey and Antonio Marcantonio. There is no third record.

Cristobal does not appreciate the interruption of his nighttime activities. "Tovenaar does not respond well to inconsistencies." It has become Cristobal's nature with age to vent his anger when dealing with frustration.

He gestures wildly with splayed fingers. File cabinet drawers fly open and expel paper records into the room with the effect of a ticker tape parade. Two of the fluttering files glow with an aqua blue hue, but still no third. The papers pick up speed and swirl even faster resembling a small tornado.

Hans and Terrence use their arms to shield their faces, but still receive their fair share of paper cuts. The storm subsides and the papers flutter quietly to the floor, except for the ones that are stuck in the ceiling tiles.

"Very well," Cristobal announces in an unexpectedly calm voice. "I will deal with this abnormality. You two can get to work on the delinquent Marcantonio."

Hans and Terrence bump into each other as they hasten to the door.

Cristobal calls after them with a warning, "Do not overstep...yet."

The blazing sun is getting the best of Tonio. He pauses under a shade tree and gulps from a water bottle before heading home to chill out in the AC. Lawrence's incessant chatter is beginning to give him a headache.

Lawrence follows Tonio under the tree and continues to ramble on. "It must have been aliens, man. Aliens were shooting pulse rifles at us from up in the ozone layer. They circle the earth and watch us, man. Haven't you ever seen alien movies? I bet we don't even have the technology needed to..."

Tonio cuts him off mid-sentence, "Can you just shut up for a minute, Lawrence?"

"I told you to call me Lasagna," Lawrence snaps back.

"You can't give yourself a nickname, idiot. That's not how it works."

Tonio's thoughts stray back to the events that unfolded earlier. He questions Lawrence, "What exactly did you see this morning?"

"Are you kidding me?" Lawrence replies incredulously, "I saw the same shit you did."

Tonio tries again, "But what did it look like? Did you see the laser beams and sheets of color?"

Lawrence laughs at his friend, "Are you tripping, dude?"

"So, you didn't notice anything strange connecting me to Marion."

"To Chainsaw?" Lawrence wrinkles his nose in distaste finishing Tonio's sentence.

"Yeah, connecting me to Chainsaw." Tonio hopes Lawrence will confirm what he is convinced occurred earlier.

"No, I didn't see anything like that," he snorts. "All I saw was the streetlights blow up and shit." He cranks up the death metal music on his phone and pumps his fist to the beat.

Tonio normally shares Lawrence's musical tastes, but now it irritates him. He is becoming frustrated with this conversation. He knows Lawrence will take it the wrong way, but he does not care. "Lawrence, why don't you take off? I need to think."

Lawrence throws his skateboard to the ground, "Smell you later ass wipe." With that, he jumps the curb into the street and lands directly in front of a moving convertible.

The driver blares his horn and swerves to avoid him.

Lawrence yells after him, "Watch it, douche bag!" He heads off in the opposite direction.

Tonio grabs his skateboard and squeezes through an opening in the chain link fence surrounding the school grounds where large trees line the perimeter providing patches of shade.

His thoughts return to Marion Grey and the weird phenomenon that took place earlier. He knows what he saw. He just cannot understand exactly what occurred. *And who was that loser staring at Marion?*

He kicks at a golf ball lying in his path. *And when did I get feelings for freaking Chainsaw, of all people?* He always found her goofy smile to be off-putting, but now, if the word endearing existed in his vocabulary, it would be the perfect time to use it. But he does not know that word, so he leaves the thought hanging. Yet, he cannot get the image of Marion's face out of his head. He feels an inexplicable desire to protect her. He wants to hold her. He wants to...

"There he is." A voice pulls him from his thoughts.

"Yo, Antonio! Hold up."

Being preoccupied with his thoughts, Tonio has not noticed the pair of motorcycles keeping pace with him on the opposite side of the chain link fence. He glances over and does not recognize either of the riders. *No one ever calls me Antonio,* he thinks suspiciously. He quickens his pace ever so slightly.

A voice with a slow southern drawl calls out, "Don't even think to ignore us when we're talking at you, son."

Tonio stops walking and turns to face them. They look to be older than him. Neither wears a helmet. *A couple of bad asses daring the police to issue them a summons.*

He initially mistakes the strange markings on their faces for tattoos, but decides they look more like scabs. He smirks at the thought of them riding too close behind a gravel truck.

"Is something funny?" The one with the Southern accent squints his eyes and spits his gum in Tonio's direction.

"*Ach,* he knows nothing. Just a guppy," the other rider says to his cohort in a mix of English and German. Then to Tonio, "Ist das nicht, Kleiner fisch?" *Isn't that right, little fishy?*

Tonio quickly sizes them up. He decides he can take either in a fair fight but would need a pile of luck to beat the two of them. He notices up ahead that the fence that separates him from the two freaks abruptly ends, so he stands his ground.

The rider with the blond hair dismounts and approaches the fence. The cell phone in his hand glows intensely with a pulsating green and purple.

"Don't be nervous. We just want to show you something," he looks back over his shoulder at Bowl Cut and grins. He turns his attention back to Tonio, "Check this out."

He drags his phone across the chain link radiating sparks of sizzling plasma that crackle and charge across the metal. He repeatedly strikes the fence with his other hand for good measure creating mini explosions.

"You, Hans and me, we're gonna be tight," the blond rider declares.

Hans remains straddled on his bike and strikes a match. "*Ya, mein freund.* We will teach you the power," he proclaims enticingly, his unlit cigarette dangling between his lips. He discharges a green and red plasma bolt from his cell phone. The plasma strikes a section of the fence followed by a flicked match. Green and yellow flames burst dramatically into the crude form of a grinning skull.

Tonio keeps his cool. He reassesses his chances against these two and concludes that he is out of his league. Their show of power is imposing, though he is not sure if they are trying to intimidate or impress him. He now regrets sending Lawrence away. Lawrence sucks as a fighter but is surprisingly good at creating chaos. Chaos that Tonio has learned to use to his advantage.

"Nice trick," Tonio sneers and turns to walk away.

"Where are you off to?" Hans calls after him while revving his motorcycle.

"We are friends of Marion. Don't you remember us?" The blond lies. He mounts his bike and kick-starts the engine.

Tonio stops dead in his tracks and spins around to face the duo. *Marion would have nothing to do with the likes of these two.* He becomes angry that they have dragged her into this and is suddenly in the mood to kick ass.

"You losers don't look familiar," he yells over the incessant revving.

Both riders regard each other with startled expressions. The only word they heard over the engine noise was *familiar*. They let their bikes idle and lean in and converse with one another, feeling a little less confident than they did a moment ago.

"Can it be he knows das we are familiars?"

"He knows more than he is letting on."

"You think he *ist* being sneaky?"

"Sand-bagging-son-of-a-bitch." Terrence yells.

They peel out leaving tire tracks on the pavement.

Tonio watches as they ride off past the fence that is now adorned with a menacing black skull burned into its silver paint. He takes his cell phone from his back pocket and regards it with renewed interest.

Marion Grey walks through a working-class neighborhood lined with modest homes. Trucks and vans bearing business logos and phone numbers occupy driveways.

It is late Saturday afternoon, and clouds begin to cover the sky providing relief from the late day sun. A lawn mower drones in the distance. An ice cream truck blasting a ragtime piano tune slowly cruises by. Children are shouting boisterously, "Marco!" and "Polo!" from a backyard pool.

Marion hears none of it. She is deep in thought. *When did I develop feelings for Tonio? Eeeeew, and why now? And who was that other hot guy staring at me earlier? Why can't I stop thinking about him either? This is so senseless.*

A commotion up ahead snaps her back into the moment. A utility truck idles at the corner surrounded by a small crowd of curious neighbors. They are staring up at a telephone pole that is buzzing with vivid multicolored currents of electricity that spark and dance along its protruding wires. The bystanders theorize as to what could be causing this strange sight.

"That is static electricity I tell you. Nothing to worry about."

"I'm guessing solar flares or sunspot activity."

"It's the damn government installing more spyware on our internet."

"But the colors. There shouldn't be colors."

One of the neighbors addresses the utility worker who has been sitting in his truck the entire time, "Shouldn't you be up there getting a closer look?"

"This shit is above my pay grade," the utility worker mumbles before driving off.

The strange colorful electricity reminds Marion of the event she experienced earlier in town. Although she knows the neighbors, she does not feel confident enough to join the conversation. Instead, she cuts across a brown lawn, which is in serious need of watering, and walks past a sporty white Fiat convertible parked in the driveway.

The house is still the same faded off-yellow color it was when her mom first rented it. *This is just a temporary place, so do not get too comfortable*, her mom warned her four years ago.

She swings open the front door and steps inside the shoe-cluttered foyer. "Mom?"

Her mother answers from another room. "I think we got another damn virus on this damn computer."

Marion steps into the kitchen and finds her mother seated at the table hunched over a laptop. She gives her mom a peck on the cheek and peers over her shoulder at the profiles of available men frozen on the computer screen.

"You know mom, I think some of those dating sites are where the viruses come from."

Angela Grey swivels in her chair to face her daughter. She looks youthful for fifty-three with a deeply tanned complexion and long blond hair pulled into a high ponytail. Her black dress is low cut and form fitting. Her appearance is a stark contrast to Marion's.

"Hey, I'm not getting any younger, kiddo. I do not plan to leave any stone unturned when it comes to finding a new husband." She winks at Marion and attempts to take a sip from her empty champagne flute.

Marion sighs and changes the subject. "Mom, have you ever seen–I don't know–strange colored beams of light where there shouldn't be?"

Angela snorts, "I grew up in the eighties, hon." She then eyes her daughter suspiciously. "Wait, what are you saying? Should I be concerned? Have you been smoking...?"

Marion interrupts, "No, I'm not smoking anything." She regrets bringing it up and realizes she cannot describe what took place that morning without coming across as a complete stoner. "It was just something weird that happened in town earlier."

She watches her mother reach across the table for the bottle of prosecco. "Mom, I thought you were going out. Why are you drinking already?"

"Oh honey, relax. It's Sharon's turn to drive. I'm just pre-lubing." Angela giggles and takes a sip. "Just so you know, men my age don't tend to be very generous when it comes to buying drinks for a lady. And you can just forget about dinner. You should remember that." She sighs and takes a slug of her prosecco.

Marion rolls her eyes and leaves the kitchen vowing, *I will never need a man to make me feel complete.*

Chapter 7

A cell phone alarm rings with a harsh Radar sound.

Shea awakes with a start forgetting momentarily where he is. He relaxes once his new living arrangement re-establishes itself in his consciousness.

"Mom? Dad?" He smiles at the silence. "I can get used to this."

Shea's bed is at the front end of the Airstream and the bathroom is at the back. In between is a galley kitchen with a mini fridge and a large cabinet for storage. There is also a narrow table where he has already set up his computer and a small folding chair.

For now, his father ran an extension cord from the house to the trailer for the bare necessities. His mom promised him the cable installer was coming today to hook up the television and internet.

The mystery girl's dog flyer lays atop one of the moving boxes next to his bed. He grabs it and looks it over for the hundredth time.

Shea lays his head back down on the pillow and closes his eyes.

He can picture every detail of her as if she were lying next to him. The way she gazed at him through strands of long brown hair. He recalls every curve of her body, every feature of her face.

Meeting her is his top priority of the day.

Shea springs out of bed and rips open a cardboard box labeled "clothes." He rummages through and pulls out a pair of camouflage shorts and a plain black tee shirt. Black canvas sneakers complete the look.

He showered the night before at his parents' house since the water in the trailer still needs to be taken care of. A splash of bottled water on his face followed by a quick brushing of his teeth, and he is good to go. He finger-combs his hair since he cannot find his hairbrush.

It is already beginning to heat up inside the trailer, so he grabs his wallet and phone then heads outside. It's only 8:00 a.m., but the sun is already beating down. He walks across the lawn to the cracked cement pathway that leads to the front door of his parents' house. It's Sunday and he knows they like to sleep in. Shea slowly turns the doorknob and finds it conveniently unlocked. He quietly steps inside and heads to the kitchen.

The house reeks of fresh paint and new carpentry. Shea takes a moment to appreciate the light blue walls, bright white cabinets, and shiny appliances. He opens the fridge and is pleasantly surprised to find it well stocked.

Yes! They must have gone food shopping last night.

He pulls out a carton of orange juice and looks over his shoulder to see if the coast is clear before chugalugging. He returns the half-empty juice container to the fridge before rifling through the cabinets.

"Nice," he says under his breath when he spots a box of strawberry Pop-Tarts.

Odd sounds coming from his parents' bedroom startle Shea. He grabs the untoasted Pop-Tarts and drops them to the floor with a slap. *Busted.*

His father calls out, "Who's there?"

Shea hurries out the front door letting it slam behind him.

Once on the street, he turns left and commands his phone to, "Take me to the Huntsport Animal Shelter."

A female voice with an Australian accent politely responds, "Make a U-turn and head south for a quarter of a mile. Then turn right onto Wilson Street."

Shea changes direction and begins his 3.2-mile trek to the animal shelter so he can properly meet his future girlfriend, under the guise of searching for a dog for his mother.

*

Shea has walked only one mile, yet his tee shirt is already showing signs of puddling around the pits. He now regrets selling his bike for money to buy a new gaming computer. As he turns the next corner, he cannot help but admire a freshly washed, mint condition 1932 Ford Roadster hotrod. It is candy apple red with a black rag-top roof. Painted across the door in gold leaf lettering outlined in black are the words *Low Brow Legacy.*

Shea cannot believe his eyes when he sees who is kneeling next to the hotrod wiping it dry. It is none other than that boot licker from yesterday who was also caught up in the weird energy grid.

Tonio notices Shea and stands to face him. With clenched fists, he stares down Shea with narrowed eyes.

Shea stops in his tracks and stares back with a deadpan expression. He recalls his father's advice, 'Next time don't leave a mark.'

"Tonio!"

A fifties-looking greaser type steps out from the garage. From the sound of his voice, he is not happy. "What did I tell you about my car?"

Shea is relieved the car doesn't belong to Tonio. He could never compete with that.

"Relax. I only washed it." Tonio replies without breaking eye contact with Shea.

His father reaches through the driver's side window and turns the ignition. The engine misfires and does not start. "Every time! Tell me then. Why doesn't she start if you only just washed her? Look at me when I talk to you!"

Shea almost feels bad for Tonio. He knows from experience that you do not want witnesses when your old man is chewing you out. He does the kid a favor and walks away.

It takes a block and a half before he can no longer hear the father's yelling.

*

Shea finally spots the sign for the Huntsport Animal Shelter in the distance. He stands under a shade tree to allow his armpits to dry, and to bolster his nerves. After twenty minutes, he starts up the long driveway.

Shea's heart skips a beat when he sees the beautiful girl from yesterday standing in the entranceway. He summons his courage and walks over to her.

"Hi, I'm Shea," he smiles warmly.

She stares at him with a blank expression.

Shea can't help but feel disappointed by her lack of enthusiasm, "Um, Are you okay?"

She snaps to attention and smiles apologetically, "Hi, Shea. I'm Marion." She extends her hand, which Shea eagerly takes in his. He notices how soft her skin feels and lets the handshake linger a little too long.

Marion pulls away and nervously runs her hand through her hair. She looks around avoiding eye contact with Shea.

He senses something is bothering her. She seems distracted. Shea decides to just get to the point. "So, um, the weirdness that happened yesterday...I mean, is that a Huntsport thing?"

Marion laughs anxiously, "Yeah, it happens all the time."

Shea is relieved to hear her laugh at his joke.

Her face grows serious, "Would you believe me if I told you it's going to get even weirder?" She realizes she must sound like a complete idiot, but she is off her game. As if she even had game.

"Weirder than yesterday?" Shea's curiosity is piqued. "What do you mean?"

Marion looks away, uncertain how to respond.

They fall into an uncomfortable silence.

This is not how Shea imagined their first conversation would progress. He struggles to think of something clever to say, but his mind is uncharacteristically blank.

Marion finally speaks, "Why did you come here?"

"Well, my parents moved here from Queens and they kind of expected me to come along, so...," he rambles.

"No, I mean, why did you come *here*?" Marion clarifies her question.

"Oh, well to, um, to see if there are any, um, dogs my mom might like," he lies. "She said she wants a small dog or a wiggly puppy or a...," His voice trails off when he catches her doubtful stare.

"Is it because you wanted to see *me*?" She looks intently into Shea's eyes.

Her directness takes Shea by surprise. "Well...yes," he mumbles. He can feel his face grow hot.

"He said you would say that." Marion pushes herself from the wall to stand straight.

"Who said I would say that? I don't even know anyone here."

In the past, Shea would have quickly bailed on a conversation long before it got as awkward as this one.

"I can't believe I'm doing this," Marion says quietly. She turns away for a moment as if contemplating what to do next. When she looks back at Shea, he is startled to see tears welling in her soulful eyes.

She pushes the door to the shelter open wide for him. "Take a look inside. Let me know if you find anything wiggly enough."

Shea is confused, but relieved to escape inside, if just to clear his mind.

Marion watches the door swing shut behind him and whispers, "I am so sorry."

chapter 8

The heavy door closes behind Shea with a solid thud.

What was that? He stands there stupefied by what just took place. *This should have been easy. How did I screw this up!*

Shea imagined they would be making plans to go to the movies later or maybe out for coffee. There is really no reason for him to be inside the shelter, but he decides to look around anyway. He needs time to come up with a clever way to connect with Marion.

An overwhelming scent of wet dogs assaults his nostrils. Dozens of chain-linked pens illuminated by dim fluorescent lighting line each side of a long hallway.

A seventy-pound mutt in the first pen on the left is growling at his upside-down water bowl. A handwritten note on his cage reads "Buddy."

Shea gently taps the pen, "Hey, Buddy, whatcha doing" he asks softly.

Buddy snaps his head up at the sound of Shea's voice. He snarls ferociously and hurls his body against the cage to get at Shea.

Shea jumps back and knocks into the pen behind him. The beagle in that pen howls loudly then abruptly cowers in the corner.

"C'mon guys," Shea pleads, "What the hell?"

A tin bowl with dry kibble mysteriously flung itself at the beagle, but from Shea's perspective, he assumed it was the dog that knocked the bowl over.

As he continues down the hallway, the occupant of every pen acts out with similar aggression. Water bowls splash violently. Dry dog food is sprayed everywhere. The mind-numbing sound of incessant barking and growling grows deafening. A large dog with teeth bared is psychotically staring him down.

Shea does not believe it could be his presence that is causing this pandemonium. Animals usually respond favorably to him. An unseen force is agitating them.

Through the commotion, his mind drifts back to Marion. For a split moment, he wonders what she must be thinking. *Will she blame me for this ruckus? Why did she want me to go inside the shelter when she knew I wasn't serious about wanting a dog?*

At this point, he doesn't care. "Screw this." He hightails to the front entrance only to suddenly face-plant onto the dirty floor. It felt suspiciously like someone intentionally kicked his right foot behind his left foot.

As if a switch flipped, the room is suddenly quiet. The just-crazed dogs now sit calmly panting with their tongues hanging out the sides of their mouths and happily wagging their tails.

Shea pushes up off the floor and finds himself face to face with a dog that must have escaped from its pen. He recognizes it as the dog from Marion's flyer. He slowly rises to his feet, his hands held in front of him in a defensive posture.

"Hey there, fella. Good doggy."

The dog eyes him curiously and lets out a soft woof. As if on command, the lights turn off and all goes dark. A thin line of sunlight from under the door is all that illuminates the room.

Shea can only see the stray dog in silhouette. He blinks his eyes to better focus, but the silhouette now is that of a man standing before him.

"Who's there?" Shea calls out uncertainly.

"We have to talk," a man's voice replies.

As Shea's eyes become accustomed to the dark, he is alarmed when the silhouette of the man morphs back into a dog again.

"What the..." Shea steps back, not trusting his eyes.

He hears the man's voice behind him now, "Be warned. You are in grave danger."

Shea spins to face him but sees only the dog. He stares in disbelief as the dog transforms back into a man. Then back into a dog. And so on until he achieves a virtual strobe light effect of dogMANdogMANdog....

Shea had always assumed he would be chill if he ever crossed paths with something supernatural, like a poltergeist or an alien. Unfortunately, his imagination falls far short of reality.

"Di...did did...did?" He just can't seem to get the words out.

The man reappears again. "A sorcerer of the Industrial Age has sent familiars to hunt you down. Once they find you, they will terminate you along with your two friends." He disappears again only to reappear as a dog.

Despite the weirdness, Shea scans his mind wondering who his "two friends" could be.

Inexplicably, food bowls, loose kibble, and a yapping Chihuahua rise and circle around Shea's head. He struggles to keep his center of gravity. Shea yells to be heard above the yapping Chihuahua. "Stop it! Why are you doing this?"

The Chihuahua suddenly stops yapping. The flickering dogMANdogMANdog settles for the form of a man. "It is imperative that you trust that magic exists. I am here to help you."

"Why would someone want to kill me?"

The man responds, "I will get you and the two others up to speed tomorrow. I must go now and lead the familiars on a merry chase. Until then, stay away from people who are marked with strange black scales."

"But, but...I... wait, what?"

"Tomorrow!" The odd man vanishes with a quiet whoomph.

Metal bowls and kibble clatter to the floor. Shea has the presence of mind to catch the little Chihuahua before it falls to the ground.

"Freak!" He yells after the vanishing enigma.

*

Outside Marion leans against the shelter. She listens as the dog food bowls clang to the floor followed by Shea yelling "Freak!"

I met this cute guy and the first thing I do is set him up for a dreadful experience. She looks to the sky and prays aloud, "Please don't let him hold this against me."

The door swings open. Shea steps outside shielding his eyes with one arm against the bright sunlight and holding the Chihuahua with the other.

"I am so sorry," Marion apologizes. "If it is any consolation, he pulled the same stunt on me just an hour ago."

Shea quietly hands Marion the Chihuahua before leaning against the wall next to her. He is still trying to mentally come to terms with his bizarre experience. "When we moved out here, I half expected to see a UFO, or a mermaid. But a talking man-dog?"

"Kind of lame, right?" She smiles shyly, relieved he has a sense of humor about the situation.

Marion takes a leash from a hook and clips it to the Chihuahua's collar and begins walking him down the long driveway. She turns and motions with her chin for Shea to walk with them.

He follows.

Moments pass before either speaks. They are not used to each other's company.

Marion breaks the silence, "I mean, he said that a magician wants to kill us."

"He told me it was a sorcerer," Shea corrects her.

"Whatever," Marion says under her breath.

"There *is* a difference, you know. A magician pretends to do magic with illusion and sleight-of-hand tricks. A sorcerer has actual powers. He can turn someone into a toad or change the direction of the wind to thwart off a navy of invaders or create potions that can..." Shea becomes aware of the amused expression on Marion's face. "I read a lot of books," he explains in his defense.

"That's cool. I wish I had time to read." Marion glances back over her shoulder.

"What are you looking for?"

"The strange gentleman. Is he still inside the shelter?

"If you mean the sideshow freak, he said he would meet with the three of us tomorrow. Then poof. He vanished." Shea frowns, "Who is the third person?" He has a sinking feeling he already knows who it is.

"He means Tonio," Marion informs him. "Tonio was the third point in our triangle yesterday." She rolls her eyes, "He's, well, he's kind of a..."

"An asshole?" Shea finishes her sentence.

"Not exactly an asshole, but yeah."

Shea is glad to learn she doesn't think much of this Tonio jerker.

Despite her failure to warn him about his impending encounter with the freak show, his attraction to Marion has intensified. "I passed by Tonio's house on the way here. There is nothing passive about his aggressive."

Before yesterday, Marion would have happily continued to badmouth Tonio, but everything's changed. After being caught up in that mysterious force field, she feels oddly drawn to both Tonio and Shea. She pushes those thoughts from her mind.

"Anyway," Shea announces, "what happened yesterday is the only thing keeping me from dismissing this situation as some kind of con job." He watches Marion as he speaks and feels an overwhelming urge to take her hand or drape his arm around her shoulders.

She catches Shea studying her. Marion uncharacteristically wishes he would kiss her already. She decides it would be best to cut this conversation short before she does something she may regret. "I bet he left a terrible mess inside. I should be getting back."

Shea is not ready for his time with Marion to end so abruptly. "I will be happy to help clean up the mess," he offers.

Marion quickly refuses, "I've already put you through enough for one day."

"Will I see you at school tomorrow?" He asks hopefully.

Marion surprises him with a brief hug. She pushes away from him and hurries toward the shelter. The Chihuahua's little legs move quickly to keep up with her.

Shea watches Marion until she and the little dog disappear into the shelter before heading home.

chapter 9

Principal Pamela Skinner makes it a point on the first day of each school year to greet the students with encouraging words and light conversation. She decorates the lobby with inspirational quotes and cheerful messages displayed on colorful poster boards. It is her favorite day of the year, followed closely by the first day of summer break.

Principal Skinner almost didn't make it to school on time today. Her cell phone did not charge, and the alarm feature never went off. She woke with a gasp when she heard the sanitation truck rumbling down the street.

Straight out of bed she threw on the white blouse and charcoal gray pencil skirt she laid out the night before. She pulled her unwashed hair into a tight bun. No time for breakfast. A quick dab of clear lip gloss and she dashed out the door.

Ms. Skinner beat the school buses by minutes and rushed into the building to take her post just inside the front entrance. She had just enough time to catch her breath and wait for the students to crowd into the now empty lobby.

Barbara Fox hurries over to her side, "Something has happened, Ma'am."

Principal Skinner sighs and glances at Barbara with a look of annoyance. "What is it this time, Barbara?" She returns her attention to the front doors and flashes a smile.

"We've been vandalized."

"What! Are you certain? Let's make this quick." Principal Skinner leads the way to the administration offices. Everything appears to be in perfect order. She looks at Barbara questioningly.

"I'm afraid it's just *your* office, Ma'am."

Principal Skinner crosses to her office and swings open the door. She sees the contents of her filing cabinets strewn over every square inch of space. "Who would do this?" She demands.

Barbara gripes. "It will take weeks to put all these files back in order."

"Barbara, you scanned all these files into the mainframe last spring, correct?"

"Yes, but the council requires that we keep hard copies for ten years."

"As I recall, the council was not too specific about how we should store the files." The principal has an easy solution. "See if there are any trash bags in the janitor's closet in the basement."

Barbara flashes a relieved grin. "Yes, ma'am," and scurries out of the office.

Principal Skinner walks over to her desk and brushes off papers. She notices a new black leather chair. Oddly, no paper covers it.

"Who ordered this?" She wonders aloud and runs her hand across the scaly-leathered armrest and wrinkles her nose. "This is foul."

She reluctantly sits down and wiggles her butt to sample the chair's comfort. The chair emanates an odd musky smell.

The phone on her desk rings loudly.

The principal leans forward to reach the receiver but is unable to move her arm.

An oily black texture from the upholstery has secured her wrists. It spreads rapidly up and over her elbows and continues towards her shoulders. Before she can scream for help, it covers her face and seals her mouth. The black slick works its way upward until it saturates her hair. The principal's body contorts in anguish as every inch of her is now coated with the scale-like texture of the chair.

Just as quickly as it appeared, the blackness absorbs into her skin revealing the principal's natural pale complexion. She looks exactly as she did moments ago, with one exception. Her eyelids open to reveal the familiar's sickly, yellow-tinged eyes with their inky blue irises.

Cristobal has successfully taken control of Principal Skinner's body. He smirks with satisfaction as he stretches and makes himself at home. He wills his new body to *relax* and settles back down comfortably in the desk chair, which has returned to its original industrial gray colored pleather.

The telephone continues to ring.

Cristobal cracks the principal's knuckles before lifting the receiver. He listens for a moment before responding in an impatient imitation of Ms. Skinner's voice.

"Forget the trash bags. I changed my mind. I need you to alphabetize all the papers in my office and return them to the file cabinets before the end of the day." He listens. "Yes, today." He smiles wickedly with his borrowed face. "If you can't complete this simple task, I will question whether you are the right person for this job." Cristobal slams down the phone in glee.

He wills the principal's body to stand from the chair and walks tentatively over to a full-length mirror that hangs behind the office door. He shimmies his shoulders to get the feel of his new body.

"I look like a prissy librarian," he mocks his reflection. Cristobal returns to the desk and grabs a mail-order fashion catalog and cackles with delight. He thumbs the pages and settles on a photo of a woman wearing a skintight, black spandex jumpsuit that laces up the front.

When he touches the photo, Principal Skinner's conservative attire transforms into the smoldering outfit depicted in the photograph. Cristobal sashays about the office like a model on the catwalk. He pauses and once again thumbs through the catalog and taps on another photo. Principal Skinner's conservative flats transform into black over-the-knee stiletto boots.

He removes the clip from the principal's tidy bun and lets her hair spill out carelessly. As he backs away from the mirror to blow himself a kiss, his heel snags the carpeting. He tumbles backward with a shriek.

As it often occurs on Long Island, Labor Day marks the end of summer with a noticeable change in weather. Hazy, hot, and humid are replaced by clear, cool, and crisp. Students pour onto the school grounds from buses and cars, with mixed emotions. Sadness that summer is over, yet excited for the start of a new school year.

Shea is no exception. He would have liked more time to explore his new surroundings. Maybe even check out the beach. But realistically, his brain is tuned to only one channel. The 24/7 Marion Grey station. If anything, his infatuation has become all-consuming and even more distracting. He doesn't even notice the stares from the other students wondering who the new kid is.

Shea's eyes light up when he spots Marion across the parking lot, but instantly narrow when he sees her chatting with a male student. Luckily, the kid gets called away by his friends.

Shea cuts between parked cars to intercept her on the sidewalk.

"Hi, Marion," he waves and calls out.

She smiles and waits for him to approach.

"I'm glad you found me," Marion says shyly. "Archibald said to meet him later at the ball field."

"I thought his name was Tonio," Shea replies distastefully.

"Archibald is the magic guy, silly," she giggles. Marion has never been the flirtatious type, but her attraction to Shea has affected her personality. She finds herself enjoying Shea's obvious jealousy of Tonio.

"I take it you saw the freak show again," he comments.

"*Mister* Freak Show came back to the pound to spend the night."

Shea snorts back a laugh, "Tell me the dude slept on the floor." He finds the thought of this Archibald curled up on the dirty floor amusing.

Marion giggles again, "Of course not, silly. I put a mat down for him." She feels her face flush when she realizes she called him silly for a second time.

Shea shakes his head, "So weird."

Marion grows serious. "He was acting nervous. I think he is hiding from someone."

"Maybe he is being hunted by the same homicidal clown he warned us about?" Shea says sarcastically.

"Let me finish," Marion smiles and lightly smacks his arm. "It was crazy. He reached out and his hand disappeared into thin air. When he pulled it back, he was holding a paper bag." She studies Shea's face, wondering if he believes her. "The bag contained a deli sandwich and a carton of milk."

"Did he have anything to say?"

"Not really. He seemed exhausted. All he said was 'Round up the other two and meet me during lunchtime at the school field.' Then he ate and went to sleep."

"Unbelievable," Shea is still having doubts about the entire situation.

They linger just outside the school's front entrance. Both are reluctant to step inside and part ways.

"I'll admit that guy has moves," Shea says, stalling. "I mean that trick with the flying taco dog and water bowls was impressive. I'll give him that." He looks around to see if anyone is listening before speaking in a hushed tone. "Let's just be careful we aren't being scammed."

Marion purses her lips at the thought. "We should at least hear what he has to say. No harm in that, right?"

Shea shrugs his shoulders.

They finally step inside the lobby when the bell to begin homeroom rings.

Marion doesn't want to be late on the first day. "Don't forget to meet up at the football field at noon," she calls back over her shoulder.

"I'll be there. Hey, which way to the principal's office?"

Marion pauses and points, "The administration offices are right down there." She smiles and speaks in a playful tone, "Why is it I always seem to attract the bad boys?"

"Let's make a date and try to figure that out," Shea grins.

Marion laughs and runs off.

Shea heads down the hall with a new air of confidence in his step. He finds the door with a brass plaque that reads Principal Skinner and knocks.

"Come in," a voice says sweetly.

Shea steps inside, "Hi, I'm looking for..."

His jaw falls open when he sees an attractive woman in a spandex jumpsuit sitting atop the desk. She is adjusting the zipper on her thigh-high leather boot.

The principal at once hops off the desk as if startled. Cristobal was not expecting an adept. He sees the confused look on Shea's face and relaxes a bit.

Shea stammers. "I...um...I think I am in the wrong office. I was looking for Principal Skinner." He turns to leave.

"You found her. How can I help you, Hon?" The principal has regained her composure.

"Oh, sorry, I'm Shea Blakely. I'm new here. My parents spoke with you about..." His voice drifts off as Principal Skinner walks towards him with a tantalizing stride. Her approaching cleavage distracts Shea from noticing her sickly yellow eyes. He bashfully looks away and notices the papers strewn about.

"Did a bomb go off in here or something?"

"Never mind that." The principal is now only inches from Shea. "Do you have something you want to give me, sweetie?" She asks in an alluring tone.

"What? No!" Shea takes a step back.

"The envelope in your hand. Is that for me?"

"Oh, sorry. Yes," he mumbles, handing it over.

"Thank you, darling," she says seductively.

Shea is overcome by a wave of nausea when he finally notices the principal's disturbing eyes. "Okay, well, I guess I'll be going." He fumbles for the doorknob and dashes from the office.

The principal calls after him, "Young man! Come back here!" She steps outside the office to see Shea jogging down the hallway.

WHOOOMPH. Principal Skinner's body vanishes along with her possessor, Cristobal.

WHOOOMPH. Her body reappears, still possessed by Cristobal, now accompanied by the familiar Hans.

Hans is confused. "Is das you, Boss?"

"Don't be an idiot," Cristobal hisses. He plops down on a sofa with an exasperated huff.

"The energy it takes to possess a person's body is more taxing than it is usually worth."

"Why did you bring me back here?" Hans stares at Cristobal's newly acquired physique.

Cristobal hands over the manila envelope that Shea gave him. "This is the third adept's information. Tell me what you can find out."

Hans slides behind the desk. As he waits for the computer to power up, he can't help but steal another glimpse at Cristobal's sexy attire.

Cristobal catches Hans staring at him. "If you saw what this woman was wearing, you would understand." He leans back on the couch and closes his eyes.

"Whatever you say, boss." Hans inserts the thumb drive from the envelope into the computer. He reads from the screen.

"Shea Blakely. Perfect attendance. Straight As in math, English, and computer science. No sports. What a shmuck."

Cristobal speaks from the couch, his eyes still closed. "I knew he was the third adept the moment he walked into the room with that offensive blue aura."

Hans peers at Shea's class photo and smirks. "He doesn't look like much. Nothing to worry about."

"He may look harmless enough, but never underestimate an adept. Any one of them has the potential to become the Prime Wizard of the Computer Age."

Hans says nothing and continues staring at Cristobal's reclined body.

"We are going to move quickly on these three. Give them just enough time to learn the fundamentals of *the craft* before we strike."

"Why ist that, Boss?"

"Tovenaar wants the betrayer to be of *some* use once he becomes a familiar." Cristobal remembers to finish zipping up his stiletto boot. "You said the other kid, the delinquent," he wearily swings the principal's legs from the couch and stands, "may have figured you for a familiar?"

Hans shrugs, "Maybe. I don't know."

Cristobal is unhappy with Hans' ambiguous answer. "Beat it, kid. Your services are no longer needed."

Hans whines as he steps out from behind the desk. "But my bike ist five miles from here."

Cristobal escorts Hans by the elbow towards the door. He snatches the sunglasses off the familiar's head before kicking the door shut.

*

Second-period class is in session. The once crowded halls are now empty.

Under Cristobal's control, Principal Skinner patrols the school's corridors. She wears the scowl of a strict disciplinarian, rather than her usual warm and inviting expression. Dark sunglasses camouflage Cristobal's filmy eyes.

He intends to interact with the three adepts while safely under the guise of Principal Skinner. Adepts of the Computer Age are a threat to him.

Although Cristobal has tried in the past, he learned that as a magical being from the Agricultural Age, he is unable to harm a magical being from an ensuing age, such as the Industrial and Computer Ages. Through trial and error, Cristobal discovered a surprisingly easy solution. The three adepts can only wield magic if the bond between them stays unbroken. All he must simply do is convince one adept to betray the other two. The betrayed would lose their powers and revert to mere humans. The betrayer will keep his magic at the cost of selling their soul and serving as a familiar to the Prime Wizard of the Industrial Age.

The easiest way for him to do this is with deception and mind games. But first, he must decide which is the weakest link.

A bell rings to signal the end of the second period. Students spill noisily from classrooms, using this precious little time to socialize.

The real Principal Skinner has regained consciousness and is alarmed that she has no control over her own body. She is forced to go along for the ride and watch helplessly as students give her a wide berth and stare with expressions of surprise and amusement. Catcalls and laughter follow her down the hallway. *"Why are you doing this to me?!"* she whimpers in her mind.

Cristobal ignores his host's pleas as he scans the crowd. A faint blue halo surrounding a student catches his attention. "Ah, the girl. What was her name again?" He puts a finger to Principal Skinner's temple. *Ah, yes.* He calls out, "Marion Grey."

"You leave her alone!" Principal Skinner yells in her mind. Her fear turns to anger. She desperately focuses her brain to control the muscles that move her mouth.

"Shut up in there," Cristobal speaks aloud.

It takes Marion a moment to recognize the principal. She approaches her with caution.

"Principal Skinner?"

"Umm mph." Cristobal attempts to answer but realizes that the principal has willed her lips tightly shut. He bites the inside of her lower lip until he tastes blood. Once her lips loosen, he questions Marion, "So, two boys, huh?"

Marion feels her cheeks flush. *How could the principal know I am attracted to Tonio and Shea?* She does not know how to respond to such a rude question from an authoritarian.

"Um, I'm going to be late for gym." Marion picks up her pace and rushes towards the gymnasium. To her dismay, Ms. Skinner follows and is not ready to abandon the subject.

"I imagine the local boy deserves the first go around." Cristobal continues, "He has dibs, so to speak."

This is none of her freaking business! Marion keeps her head down and quickens her pace.

Cristobal keeps his stride despite his five-inch heels. "Although I will admit there is a certain thrill to be had when lying with a stranger." He flashes a blood-tinged smile. "You know what I mean."

Marion cringes. She cannot believe what she is hearing, or seeing. She is relieved when she reaches the locker room door and prays that the principal will not follow her inside.

"Oh, for pity's sake. What kind of ridiculous advice am I giving you? I apologize for being such a bore." He places the principal's hand on Marion's shoulder. "Of course, you will take them both for a ride. It really is the best way to make an informed decision."

Marion rushes through the doors.

"Never had much luck with prudes," Cristobal murmurs under his breath. "Not impossible, though." He spins on his heels and heads in the opposite direction. He enjoys corrupting young minds. Jealousy and lust are two of his favorite motivators. He will concentrate his efforts on persuading the two young men to fight for Marion's affections. "One down, two to go," he announces to the emptying hallway.

Principal Skinner screams at Cristobal in her mind. *Why are you doing this? Please get out of my body! I promise I will not call the authorities.*

"Chill out, Hon. You never looked so good," Cristobal says aloud. "Now be quiet or I'll cut you."

Cristobal spies a telltale blue glow emanating from around the corner. He picks up the pace and spots Shea fidgeting with the lock on his locker. "Mr. Blakely, there you are," he calls out breathlessly.

Shea grimaces at the sight of the principal.

"You departed my office before I could finish our conversation."

"Sorry, I didn't want to be late for class," Shea lies.

"Since you are new to this school, I thought it would be nice if one of the other students showed you around. There's a girl by the name of Marion Grey who I think would be perfect."

Shea's heart races at the mention of her name. "I know her. I mean, I just met her."

"Wonderful!" Cristobal leans a little closer to Shea. "She is quite the little hottie. Who knows? You might even get lucky."

Shea is taken aback. "Are you sure you're the principal?"

Cristobal turns and walks away, pointing a thumb over his shoulder, "I just saw Marion trolling for boys by the gym," he calls back. "Tell her Ms. Skinner sent you. She will know exactly what to do."

Shea stares in disbelief. *WTF?!*

*

The halls are empty. Cristobal's instincts tell him that the third adept is cutting class. He steps outside and walks along the perimeter of the building, keeping close to the brick walls. Around the next turn, he spots Tonio's blue aura. He sits behind an AC unit with his back against the wall. Cristobal hesitates briefly when he notices the delinquent is fiddling with his cell phone.

As soon as Tonio realizes that Principal Skinner has snuck up on him. He stuffs his phone into his back pocket and stands ready to face the consequences of cutting class.

Cristobal asks with an amused tone, "Is it smoking? Drinking? Something a bit more hallucinogenic?"

Tonio shakes his head and replies, "Just needed some time to think."

"Thinking? Doesn't seem to be your style." Cristobal relishes the look of anger in Tonio's expression. *Hotheads are very pliable.* He eases back. "I would rather that if you smoked, drank, or popped pills, that you do it here on school grounds where you'll be safe. Who knows, I might even join you."

Cristobal laughs when he hears Principal Skinner screaming in her head.

Tonio is now more confused than angry.

Cristobal continues, "Your vices are of no concern to me. I came looking for you for a favor."

Tonio cannot imagine what she is going to say next.

"There is a new student by the name of Shea Blakely. His prior school records show he is quite aggressive with the ladies and does not take no for an answer."

Tonio chokes back his laughter at the thought, "Yeah, he looks like a real menace."

"Allow me to finish, please." Cristobal pauses dramatically and continues, "I saw Mr. Blakely talking intimately with Marion Grey near the locker room. From what I could see, he was getting uncomfortably close to her."

Tonio's nostrils flare.

"And we both know Marion has a thing for the intelligent boys." Cristobal smiles to himself.

Principal Skinner's consciousness is horrified. She has had enough. She must get this filthy, foul-mouthed demon out of her body. Even if it means destroying her reputation more than this pig already has. She concentrates hard on relaxing her body while the familiar is conversing with Tonio.

Cristobal continues, "So if I were you, Mr. Marcantonio, I would..." He suddenly feels warm water running down the bottom half of his jumpsuit. "What the?" He reflexively clenches his knees tightly together.

Tonio cannot believe what he is seeing. "I'm outta here." He turns and hurries away.

Cristobal says aloud to the principal, "You couldn't just wait a few more minutes until I finished with the delinquent."

GET THE HELL OUT!!! Principal Skinner screams in her head.

Cristobal has had enough. "Because you deserve it, I am going to leave you with a very special memory of mine." He cackles as his black form steps away from the principal's shaking body, letting her crumble to the ground.

Principal Skinner's mental screams of anguish become vocal as she reclaims her body. She pulls herself into a fetal position and sobs heavily at the horrid memory Cristobal has implanted in her mind. She recalls the event firsthand as if she committed and even enjoyed the unspeakable acts herself.

Cristobal scratches at the tingling sensation of a new scale emerging on his forehead. A shiny testament to his heinous act of cruelty.

He disappears leaving Principal Skinner alone to come to terms with a new and undeserved sense of self-revulsion.

Huntsport High splits the lunch break into two sessions. Half of the student body breaks at noon, and the other half at 1:00 p.m.

At twelve o'clock sharp, Marion and Shea meet at the far side of the field, now occupied by a gym class playing flag football. The two stand and wait at the opposite end from where the gym teacher Mr. Holmes has stationed himself, yet close enough to blend in with the students who wait on the sidelines for their turn to play.

"Technically, we are supposed to be in the cafeteria," Marion informs Shea. "This is my first time breaking the rules." She looks over at him anxiously.

"I think it's probably good to break a rule every so often," Shea reassures her. He too is a little nervous about getting caught but plays it cool. Getting detention on his first day would not go over well with his father.

"Here comes, Tonio," Marion nods across the field.

Shea watches with contemptuous eyes as Tonio ducks under a section of the chain-link fence back onto school property.

Tonio glances over his shoulder at the skull image burned into the fence. He turns his gaze to Marion as he casually cuts across the field of play. He carries two cups of coffee.

"Did *you* tell him to meet us here, or did Archibald?" Shea asks. He can't help but notice Marion's face flush.

Marion shrugs her shoulders. "It wasn't me."

The gym teacher calls out, "Anytime you want to join the team, Marcantonio, I have a jersey with your name on it."

Tonio dismisses the offer with the back of a hand over his shoulder. He continues towards Marion and the new kid who gave him attitude yesterday. He doesn't care for the way the creep is standing so close to her.

Tonio is still not sure how to deal with the situation. He cannot figure out when or why he suddenly developed feelings for Marion. He suspects it had something to do with the weird energy that connected them. He sees her staring at him and feels a warm chill course through his body. *Do not call her Chainsaw*, he reminds himself.

"Hello Antonio," Marion greets her childhood nemesis coolly, and by his proper name.

Shea grins, "Wait. So, your name is Antonio Marcantonio?"

He gets no reaction from Antonio a/k/a Tonio.

"Oh thanks, you shouldn't have," Shea says in a sarcastically sweet tone, holding out his hand in jest, "I take mine with milk and sugar."

Although he has no interest in taking part in organized sports, Tonio is by nature ultra-competitive. He never properly met this new clown, but already he feels a powerful urge to kick his ass. He turns his back on Shea. "Hey Marion." He hands a cup to her. "I guessed almond milk." He smiles and takes a sip from the other cup.

Shea does not mind being ignored by this tool. He finds Tonio's boorish behavior entertaining. What really irks him though, is the attention Marion is paying to him. *There is no way a class act like Marion would be interested in a raging mouth breather like Tonio,* he thinks in disgust.

"Um, thank you." Marion is surprised and pleased with Tonio's thoughtfulness, and yet equally disappointed that he didn't bring a coffee for Shea. Her dubious attraction to this bad boy confuses her. He has a reputation for settling arguments with his fists, and his rude language often lands him in detention. Marion used to hate him for his past relentless teasing of her awkward braces, but something recently clicked like a light switch inside her brain that she cannot turn off. The mere sight of him now makes her palms sweat and her knees weak, but in a weirdly good way.

The three of them stand in silence.

Before it gets too awkward, Marion gestures towards the section of the fence that bears the burnt image of a skull. "That's creepy. I wonder who did that."

Tonio is aware but says nothing.

"Some psychopath," Shea suggests hoping that Tonio is the artist, and is baiting him for a reaction.

A football bounces at their feet.

Mr. Holmes calls out, "A little help."

Tonio stops the ball with his foot. He snatches it up and casually tosses it in the air a few times, to the chagrin of the gym teacher. On his final toss, he gracefully kicks the ball, sending it in a high arc over the field with a slight leftward curve. It heads directly for the canvas ball caddy and nails it with an exquisite direct hit. Four of the extra footballs fly out in all directions.

Mr. Holmes gives Tonio a mock bow with a comically exaggerated amount of flourish to acknowledge a masterful shot.

Tonio turns back to face Marion, pleased to see that she regards his stunt with smoldering eyes and an appreciative smile.

She questions him, "Is that your Like-A-Boss move?"

"Like a Boss?" He scoffs, "Is that still even a thing?" He instantly regrets his words as the smile disappears from Marion's face. Tonio quickly recovers. "Yeah, I guess it is," he agrees with a twinkle in his eye. He is relieved to see her smile return. "How about you? Do you have a move?"

"I do," she answers shyly, "but only my mirror has ever seen it."

Tonio encourages her, "Let's see what you got."

"No."

"Why not?"

"I don't feel like it."

"Just do it."

Marion looks to Shea, hoping he will be chivalrous and provide her with an out. To her dismay, Shea further encourages her.

"A debut performance is in order."

She regards the two of them watching her expectantly. "Oh, why not?"

"It's a good thing I'm wearing my leggings instead of a skirt." She assesses the ground to find a good balance for her left foot. "I cannot believe I am doing this."

Marion slowly raises her right leg. Without bending either knee, her leg swings up like the hand of a clock. Eight, nine, ten o'clock. She deftly leans her torso to counterbalance herself. Her toes point at eleven o'clock and she keeps going.

Both boys gawk at her with captivated attention, along with a good portion of the students who are standing on the sidelines.

Suddenly Marion's right foot is pointing straight up at twelve o'clock. She holds a perfect standing split for a moment until—

PWEEEEEEEEET! --A whistle blasts.

Marion self-consciously swings her leg back down. Her face flushes warmly when she hears a small group of students whistling and cheering.

"That was pretty outstanding!" This time Shea steps directly in front of Tonio. He holds up his hand for a high-five from Marion.

She shyly slaps his hand.

"I don't suppose *you* have a move, Boss," Tonio says snarkily to Shea.

Shea grimaces at the sound of his voice. Tonio is correct in that regard, but he can't let Marion see him for the dud that he feels he really is. Luckily, he can think quickly on his feet.

"I would love to show you, but it requires two snowmobiles and a roman candle."

Marion giggles delightedly at his quick wit. "I would pay to see that."

Tonio calls him out, "So you got nothing. You're just bullshit."

Shea retorts, "Maybe you should chill out, Grover Dill."

Marion lets out a squeal of laughter at Shea's unexpected reference to Tonio being not the bully from *A Christmas Story*, but the bully's toady.

Tonio doesn't pick up on the reference, but senses it's an insult. He steps aggressively toward Shea.

Shea holds his ground and wrinkles his nose from Tonio's coffee breath.

Whooomph.

The Freak Show from yesterday appears out of thin air between the two of them.

They both step back quickly in surprise.

Marion looks around nervously to see if anyone else witnessed Archibald's sudden appearance. To her relief, the gym class is already walking back to the locker room.

The odd stranger addresses the three of them. "If I have neglected to formally introduce myself, I am Archibald Abel."

Archibald Abel looks like an old man that could pass for a twenty-year-old or a twenty-year-old who resembles an old man. Everything about him is a contradiction. His youthful skin is contrasted with tired and baggy eyes. He has thick, wavy brown hair, yet his thin beard is wispy and gray. His voice is clear and youthful, but his tone borders on exhaustion and haunted.

Archibald quietly studies the trio as if adding up numbers in his head. He begins with Shea. "Do you have any skills other than a trick with snowmobiles and fireworks, as glorious as I am certain it must be?"

Shea stammers, "I am developing a computer game and am already halfway to finishing a beta test version." He looks to Marion with a wincing expression as if to say, *why am I even talking to this headcase?*

"That could certainly be useful." Archibald nods his head. "Anything else?"

"I've read a lot of books."

"What sort of books?"

Despite his reluctance to engage in Archibald's inquisition, Shea feels compelled to answer, "Urban fiction, lately. I've also read a lot of science fiction and sword and sorcery before that." He adds defensively, "I'm well-read."

Tonio laughs, "You truly are skilled."

"Shut up."

Archibald rolls his eyes at the two of them. He is used to the love/hate dynamic between adepts, but it gets old. "A powerful sorcerer is coming for your lives. I doubt a bedtime story will be an effective defense."

Shea feels his face grow hot.

Archibald takes a breath. "I apologize, but the Prime Wizard of the Industrial Age, Tovenaar the Nefarious, is as conniving as a reptile and is equally vicious. He controls scores of nasty familiars, and he knows his business."

He continues, "He has likely already sent familiars to assess your weaknesses. The most powerful familiar in history will follow them. You have only days, if that, to figure out a way to survive." He blows out a heavy breath. "You will understand if I occasionally come across as being impatient.

"How do you know all of this?" Tonio asks, "And why us?"

"He has destroyed many before you three," Archibald assures them. "I have been studying him for decades, searching for a way to end his reign."

"Okay, but why does he want to kill us?" Shea is getting annoyed.

"As it turns out, the three of you are adepts. The universe has gifted each of you with the potential to become a wizard of the Computer Age. Tovenaar currently enjoys the benefits of being the Prime Wizard. If he allows even one of you to become a wizard of the Computer Age his reign will end." Archibald shrugs, "So he has determined that he must destroy you."

"How are the three of us selected to become wizards?" Marion sounds dubious.

Archibald considers for a moment. "That is like asking, how big is the universe? What is the color of clear? Why not stronger adepts with grand intellects and useful skills? These questions I cannot answer."

Shea's patience is becoming increasingly thin with this guy's vagueness and lack of genuine answers." He calls him out. "Every con man has a story."

"You think I'm lying to you?" Archibald exhales sharply. "Your mistrust is no different from the scores of adepts I have attempted to help in the past."

"I'm out of here." Shea turns to Marion. "Are you with me?"

Marion grabs Shea's arm to stop him from leaving. "Wait. What if he's telling us the truth?" She implores Archibald, "Please tell us what you do know."

"Very well." He takes a deep breath. "To be clear, the ages reach back to before time was even a thing. The Bronze Age, The Iron Age, Middle Age, Renaissance, Agricultural and Industrial --"

"Space Age?" Marion asks, trying to be helpful.

"No." Archibald continues. "The world requires only one Prime Wizard to serve as a conduit for the infinite flow of its magic. The Prime Wizard is always a representative of the current age." He studies each of them carefully to be certain they are grasping the seriousness of his words.

"What does a Prime Wizard do?"

"Good question, Mr. Marcantonio. A Prime Wizard does not have to do anything. He can simply sit back and allow the world's magical energy to course through his very being. He gains the privilege of having everything his heart desires. The best of everything. Gourmet food, fine wines, and even consorts. He would live the life of a god for doing naught but simply being a conduit."

He hesitates then continues, "A life without purpose, however, becomes boring all too quickly. Typically, a wizard serves in this capacity for a decade or two before passing the torch to a fellow wizard."

"I'm guessing this Industrial Age dude, this Tovenaar, did not sit back and let that happen," Shea interjects.

"From what I have determined, Tovenaar took it upon himself to end every magical being from the Industrial Age, thereby eliminating all possibility of passing it on. Such was his lust for total power.

"He then went on to work ridding the world of every wizard,

adept, and familiar of the Agricultural Age and even a few stragglers
from the preceding ages."

"So, he has been a Prime Wizard for centuries?" Marion questions.

"Yes. He is immensely powerful, extremely dangerous. If even
one of you manages to become a wizard of the Computer Age you will
automatically assume the role of Prime Wizard. Hence the situation you
now find yourself in."

"So, this creep killed everyone with magical ability in the
Agricultural Age, the Industrial Age, and now so far, in the Computer
Age." Shea is even more skeptical. "That is a lot of murders, mister. So
why haven't we heard about them? Or of Tovenaar? There should be
dozens of books, articles, and movies about such a maniac."

Archibald shrugs. "The one thing Tovenaar does not seem to require
is attention. It has been generations since the general populous has seen
a proper display of magic, They no longer believe it exists. The Prime
Wizard of the Industrial Age prefers to be an invisible influencer."

"And now he is coming after us," Marion squeaks with a worried
trill in her voice. "But I don't know any magic. Not even a card trick."

"Don't worry, Marion," Shea consoles her. "This story is
ridiculous and I'm not buying it. Not any of it. First off," he challenges
Archibald, "if you are from the sixteen hundreds, how do you know
how to speak our slang? You don't talk like a person from that age.
How would you know about snowmobiles and computers."

Shea assures Marion, "He's just a magician with a unique version
of a disappearing dog trick."

He turns back to Archibald, "My question for you is why are you
trying to scam us?"

Archibald does not appear to be offended. "So, you think I time-
traveled into the future to trick you out of your allowance?"

Shea snaps back "None of your stories add up. I know fiction when I hear it." He looks to Marion for backup. "I mean, it's obvious we are being played."

Marion frowns and addresses Archibald, "No offense, but Shea is right. It doesn't make sense that I would be caught up in something like this."

"What about you, tough guy? Aren't you the least bit suspicious?" Shea presses Tonio. "Do you really believe this dude when he tells you that you could be a wizard?"

Tonio replies calmly, "I had a run-in with two guys on motorcycles who I'm guessing were familiars. And what about all that crazy shit that happened in town on Saturday?"

"Motorcyclists? They are probably part of the sting," Shea argues. "What makes you so sure they were familiars?"

"It's what they were doing."

"What were they doing?" Marion wants to know.

Tonio removes his cell phone from his hip pocket and rubs his thumb back and forth across its screen until a pool of plasma sizzles from the screen. It glows purple with yellowish tinges and sputters into the palm of his hand. He uses his fingers to urge the globe to float upwards about eight inches where it crackles and explodes like a series of fireworks.

"Shit," Marion says wide-eyed.

Shea gawks at Tonio's display. His arguments against this ridiculous story are suddenly dashed. "Hard to argue against that," he mutters.

From the corner of his eye Tonio sees his friend Lawrence and cuts short his demonstration. Lawrence has been eavesdropping on them.

Archibald also notices Lawrence. "We are attracting unwanted attention." He hesitates before adding, "I would prefer being more discrete, but time is fleeting. Let us take this elsewhere. Shall we?" He raises his shoulders as if to shrug, followed by an odd motion with his fingers, and Whooomph.

The four of them vanish right in front of a stunned Lawrence.

77

chapter 12

Whooomph.

Tonio, Marion, Shea, and Archibald appear from thin air and collapse to the sand of a secluded beach. Archibald is the only one to stick the landing. He smiles as Tonio and Shea attempt to stand. "You'll get used to it," he assures them.

"What the hell was that?" Shea asks pressing his hands against his ears trying to unclog them.

Archibald simply replies, "Travel."

"Okay, I'm in!" Marion exclaims, still sitting on the ground. "I believe in magic now." All concerns that Archibald is *playing them* have vanished. Oddly, the fact that they are in imminent danger is the furthest thing on her mind.

"My ears are still popping," Shea complains as he wiggles his pinky inside his ear.

"Maybe you need to toughen up, cupcake," Tonio grins at Shea.

He glances back at Marion to see her reaction, but she is occupied with her phone.

"Screw you, Marco Polo." Shea turns his attention to their surroundings. "Where the hell are we?"

Tonio answers in an exasperated tone like he is explaining the obvious to a complete idiot, "Crab Meadow Beach, dummy."

"Are we still in New York?" Shea asks. His question goes unanswered.

Marion has been ignoring the conversation. She stays seated with her legs crossed and elbows propped on her knees intently studying her cell phone which rests on the sand between her feet. She frowns intensely at her phone with its blinged-out protective case.

Suddenly the surface of the screen appears to fill with a crackling liquid that flashes with a bright pink and white glow. It begins to spill over into the sand.

Marion gasps and jumps to her feet. She extends her arm and urges the glowing mass to come to her. A translucent glowing pink sphere rises from the phone and floats toward her. Upon touching her outstretched hand, it solidifies into a pliable globe of shimmering plasma.

Archibald watches with rapt interest at Marion's first attempt at wielding her magic. Intrigued as he is, he cannot help but wonder how a pink ball could be of any use against a beast like Tovenaar.

Marion stares mesmerized by the magic that swirls around the sphere and her hand. A sense of euphoria courses through her entire body as she elegantly rolls the apple-sized orb down one arm, across the back of her neck, then down her other arm. She is overcome with joy and uncharacteristically bursts out in song. She sings the lyrics of a Fleetwood Mac tune that her mom was listening to this morning.

"And wouldn't you love to love her?
Takes to the sky like a bird in flight.
And who will be her lover?"

After the last line, she shrieks with laughter. Marion was never brave enough to sing in public, but suddenly she is no longer self-conscious about it.

Tonio and Shea study her as well. She has never appeared as beautiful or as graceful as she does now. If it is even possible, their attraction to Marion has magnified immensely.

Marion senses they are staring at her. With a mischievous grin, she spreads her hands letting the sphere grow to the size of a small beach ball. She blows on it softly and drops it onto the sand where it sprouts animated legs and hops up and down. When she points at the boys, it obeys her command and charges at them like a frantic bunny.

Shea and Tonio scramble backward away from the psychotic pink ball with legs. It chases after them until Marion directs it to bounce into the water where it fizzles and dissolves with a loud hiss.

Shea yells, "That was insane!"

With a wild gleam in her eye, she challenges Shea, "You do it."

Shea exhales deeply and takes a moment to collect his wits. He holds his cell phone with its screen facing away from him and concentrates on creating magic. He feels nothing. He attempts to use *the force*. Again, nothing happens. His palms begin to sweat. *If I can't do this, I will look like a loser in front of Marion. And Tonio.*

Then it happens.

A magical force radiates from the sides of his phone and grows into a three-foot circular disc that continuously changes shape with rotating geometry. Translucent ripples of energy radiate in navy blue with streaks of lime green incandescence. Shea presses his hands together. When he separates them, a second disc of energy radiates from his left hand. The discs of energy continue to multiply out of control. In a moment of panic, he slams his hands together causing the geometric planes to recede back into his phone.

Shea marvels, "All I had to do was think it and it happened."

"Nicely done, both of you." Archibald commends them, "A bit flamboyant, but nonetheless very nice."

Tonio is a little apprehensive. His earlier display of magic was lame in comparison to Marion and Shea's. He challenges Shea, "Think fast, Flam Boy." He hurls a purple zap of plasma at Shea that hits him square in the chest.

"Hey!" Shea looks down to where the bolt hit. "Your stupid purple magic stained my shirt."

Tonio once again aims his phone at Shea.

"Do NOT!" Shea warns him.

Tonio fires.

Shea instinctively creates a plasma shield and effectively blocks Tonio's blast.

"Ha! Bring it, Douche!" Shea eggs him on.

"You're all defense, Citifield," Tonio taunts Shea with the name that replaced Shea Stadium. Tonio unleashes blast after purple blast.

Shea expands his hands wide. Energy shields multiply and surround him like a translucent sphere effortlessly absorbing Tonio's shots.

Tonio grits his teeth and redoubles his efforts.

Shea grins and coolly turns his back on Tonio. He smiles triumphantly at Marion.

Tonio takes advantage and sends a final blast at Shea.

This time the shield deflects Tonio's plasma. It ricochets back striking him square in the face.

"Shit!" Tonio wipes the purple plasma off his face with his tee shirt.

Shea grins and allows his shields to dissipate.

"You're so dead." Tonio rushes Shea.

"Enough!" Archibald yells sharply. He gestures at the gentle waves lapping against the shore. One of the tiny waves rises massively into the form of a rearing water stallion. The wave crashes down giving Shea and Tonio a good drenching.

Both Tonio and Shea instinctively turn their backs on the unnatural wave to protect their phones.

"There is a time for that later."

As the boys shake the water off themselves, Marion asks, "Why weren't we able to do this before?" Marion is still giddy from her newfound powers.

"Nothing can happen without intention," Archibald grins. "Just as you could not write your name until you learned that there was such a thing as writing your name."

Marion purses her lips in thought, "Why is it different for each of us and why the different colors?"

"I venture to guess your magic manifests to how your mind perceives it," Archibald considers. "Your magic expresses itself as pink. Pink symbolizes love and compassion." He turns to Shea. "Blue with hints of green. Blue may mean a sense of calm, and the green, a new beginning, perhaps." He regards Tonio, "Your magic is purple with traces of yellow, like… a bruise, so there's that." He wishes he had a better answer.

"It only left a stain on his shirt," Tonio complains, "Why didn't it--."

"Kill him?" Archibald raises an eyebrow. "Was it your intention to kill him?"

"No. I don't think so..." Tonio's voice trails off.

Shea rolls his eyes. "Why us?" He finger-combs the wet hair from his eyes. "Why can't everybody wield magic like this?"

"Again, I do not have an answer," Archibald confesses.

Tonio continues to focus on the recent sparring match. He narrows his eyes at Shea. "So, tell me. Did you get your magic shield idea from reading fiction books?"

"Sure, I guess. I mean, all stories are different, but the protagonist…" He dumbs it down for Tonio, "I mean the *hero*, always finds a clever way to solve a problem. Using your magic against you was my idea," Shea answers proudly.

Archibald addresses the three adepts, "So, now that you have accepted magic as your new reality, do you trust me?"

Marion stops playing with the magic plasma that radiates from her phone and looks up at Archibald. "We still need to hear *your* story. What happened to you in your past and why are you now helping us Computer Age adepts?"

Archibald scans the beach suspiciously. "Very well, I will tell you my story, but we have been in one place for too long." He spreads his arms wide.

Whooomph.

They all vanish.

chapter 13

Whoomph.

Marion and Tonio brace each other to remain standing.

Shea stumbles forward and falls to one knee. He pretends to purposely mimic a classic superhero landing. He looks around to see if anyone bought it but becomes distracted by the new setting.

Meandering streams of water cut lazy paths through a field of long grasses like a wonderful maze in a happy dream. A pair of snowy white egrets fly overhead. If it weren't for the houses in the distance, he would think he was in a different country.

"It's beautiful. Where are we?"

"Crab Meadow Salt Marsh," Marion laughs and points. "The beach where we just came from is beyond those trees over there. And our school is that way about a mile or two away."

"This looks like something you would see down south or somewhere tropical." Shea looks around in all directions taking in the view. "I expect to see water buffalo grazing," he marvels with childlike innocence. "Wait until my parents see this."

Marion and Tonio have already settled down and are waiting for Archibald to tell his story.

Shea follows suit and nods to Archibald that he is ready.

Archibald begins, "It has been roughly 300 years since the Prime Wizard of the Great Agricultural Age, Magnus Zachariah Llewellyn employed me as a familiar to—"

"—Wait. You're a familiar?" Shea interrupts. "You're one of *them*?"

Tonio moans, "Seriously? Not even a full sentence in."

"Sorry." Shea sweeps his arm with a flourishing gesture for Archibald to continue.

"To be clear, familiars are attendant beings who perform remedial and/or unsavory tasks at the command of their wizard. Some are creatures, such as cats or salamanders."

"I do like cats." Marion whispers to no one in particular.

"Cats have their limitations," Archibald winks at her. "They should only be used for the simplest of tasks."

"A more capable familiar would be an ensnared demon. Demons do as they are told with acute precision," he scratches at a patch of his beard, "but one must be certain they are bound correctly because they will not hesitate at a chance to strike down their captor. Demons are dangerous and wisely avoided.

"It was not uncommon, however, for a peasant boy with latent magical abilities to be considered to fulfill the role of a familiar. I was one such peasant boy. I jumped at the opportunity to escape the slums. The arrangement was for me to work as a familiar for a time to earn my way to becoming a full apprentice."

"Your goal was to become a wizard." Shea clarifies.

"Obviously." Tonio rolls his eyes, even though he was unsure where Archibald was going with this.

Archibald continues, "My quarters were set in the basement of a classic Tudor-style cottage, or so it appeared from the outside. A cottage that was nestled comfortably at the border of an ancient forest that appeared on no map of England proper.

"My master, Magnus Zachariah Llewellyn, was a kind and generous man. At that time, he was already tutoring an apprentice born into wealth.

"The apprentice's parents paid lavishly for him to study under the tutelage of the Prime Wizard. I often imagined they would have paid double for an excuse to send their conceited little son so far away."

"His name was Cristobal Adlay Denison. He was two years my senior. A young know-it-all with three first names. He wore a ridiculous blonde pageboy haircut, and always made certain to overdress for any occasion."

Marion observes, "You hated Cristobal."

Archibald continues, "One day, I was returning from a three-day errand. I had been searching for an untapped source of Sweet Bergamot. Sweet Bergamot was an herb used to concoct many everyday potions. Unfortunately, it had become popular amongst the masses for making tea and it had become quite rare.

"As was my habit, I scanned the area before returning to a state of visibility. I would occasionally use it to sneak up on Cristobal and startle him. Although I despised him, it was all in good fun. Passive/aggressive behavior, I believe, is what they call it these days. Nevertheless, I materialized just behind him, but not close enough that he could strike me.

"'Cheerio, Cristobal!' I shouted." Archibald pauses and laughs. "The daft prick nearly soiled his knickers."

Archibald's face grows serious once again. "Cristobal was furious,

'Damn you to hell, Abel! Didn't I warn you?' He pointed his little finger to scorch me with a blast of energy.

"I transported just in time to avoid the blast and reappeared directly behind him. 'You could have killed me, I protested.'

"'You could have killed me; you could have killed me.' Cristobal mocked me with a whiny parody of my voice. 'What self-respecting familiar does not have bone spurs or talons? I would wager that there is not even one scale on your malnourished body.'

"'Only evil actions mark a familiar with such aberrations,' I replied. Something he would learn soon enough.

"'I know why you don't have scales.' Cristobal continued to insult me, 'You are lazy and are a waste of everyone's time. And the house smelled fresher without your foul presence.'

"I never understood Cristobal's anger. I often considered that he had everything. Born into wealth, the handsome features of a stage actor, an apprenticeship under a truly kind and powerful wizard, and he had good teeth! Cristobal had it all, and yet he was always miserable.

"I turned to walk toward the cottage to deliver a report of my findings.

'Wait, Archibald,' Cristobal called after me in a suspiciously saccharine voice. 'You should stay a bit longer. You wouldn't want to miss something that will occur only once in a lifetime.'

"He had piqued my curiosity, as well as my suspicions. Cristobal never wanted to spend time with me, let alone call me by my proper name.

'Once in a lifetime?' I called back. 'Is the king coming for crumpets and tea?'"

Archibald looks down and sighs. "I was naive, and it was all I could think of."

He continues. "Cristobal rolled his eyes and scoffed, 'You expect the king? You truly are as…' He caught his words before completing the insult. 'It will be even better than the king.'

"It was then that I noticed a faint and unfamiliar rumbling in the distance. 'Do you hear that? What could it be?' I asked. A breeze brought with it an unusual odor that stung my nostrils.

"'You will soon see,' was all Cristobal said. And he said it with great delight.

"Just then, Master Llewellyn beckoned my presence. He did so in my mind so that Cristobal could not overhear it."

Archibald stops talking as he notices Marion fidgeting with the plasma that dances atop her cell phone.

"I'm sorry. I'm listening." Marion looks up. "It's just…"

Archibald shows her his palms to cut her off. "Trust me, I understand. The first time I turned a house fly into a mouse, I couldn't help myself. It got to the point my parents had to bring a cat into the cottage."

"You are one sick puppy, Archie," Marion playfully teases him. She is rewarded with snorts of laughter from Shea and Tonio, as well as a bemused grin from Archibald.

"Maybe so," he admits, "but I am getting to the important part of the story, so please pay attention." Archibald takes a deep breath before continuing. "As I was saying, I teleported straight to my master's side within the cottage. I was uncertain, but I thought I noticed dark smoke just above the tree line.

"The exterior of my master's cottage was deceptively small. However, on the inside, it was a mansion. Cavernous chambers that held esoteric paraphernalia of the craft. Odd vessels full of dark liquids, barrels of exotic herbs, sealed glass urns full of decaying powders, and shelves that held a chaotic array of books and notes. Tables covered with burners for heating, ice boxes for cooling, and other devices for dissolving and trans-modifying.

"Master Llewellyn used his powers solely to benefit the whole of society. A man whose accomplishments would make him a national hero if the general populace knew he existed. But alas, he will go down in history as…. well, he will not go down in history at all. But that is how it is for most wizards. They perform great wonders, yet live thankless lives and are content to do so.

"Llewellyn was not dressed for visitors. Instead, he wore a tattered and stained cotton dressing gown. Something one might wear while practicing new incantations that may incur accidental charring. It was also strange that he looked like an old man. My Master had not troubled himself with spells of youthful appearance that morning. And the shimmering of magic that normally surrounds a Prime Wizard was nowhere to be seen.

"He was staring hopelessly at his gazing spheres, one for each of his colleagues. Most now resembled common gray rocks instead of the multi-hued lucent orbs that I was accustomed to seeing. Only two remained illuminated, when suddenly one of them faded out before my eyes."

Shea interrupts, "Wait, what are gazing spheres?"

"Gazing spheres were a means by which wizards could communicate with one another from great distances. Like your computer phones, which you indifferently take for granted."

Archibald continues. "I asked Master what was happening?

"'The Age of Industry is upon us,' he replied, 'and the new Prime Wizard will not suffer Agricultural Age magic to exist in his new Age of Industry.'

"In that moment, all my hopes and dreams for a career in the magic arts were dashed. I felt dizzy. If I had eaten that morning, I may have regurgitated. *What shall I do? How shall I survive?* My thoughts were as naive as they were self-centered.

"The once Prime Wizard of my Age stood with stoic

determination. His hand gestured at the gazing stones. 'They are all deceased. Macklin, Synthesea, Flane… along with their adepts, all their familiars, and anything else that bears witness to our order of magic. This monster is usurping our friends' very souls to bolster his power.'

"The noise outside steadily increased in volume to a low-pitched staccato, whooghwhooghwhooghwhoogh. It was not a sound I recognized. The cacophony grew louder, now mixed with the screeching and clanging that I later learned was the sound of large machinery.

"'We have been betrayed!' Master Llewellyn informed me.

"I knew at once who the turncoat was. 'We must kill Cristobal before he has the opportunity to gloat,' I urgently suggested, but Master had another proposal."

"He clutched at his chest with both hands and uttered an incomprehensible spell in a shrill language. Great energy coalesced and pulsated as he extracted an orb the size of a melon from his chest. He uttered another incantation that caused the radiant orb to contract to the size of a polo ball.

"He held it out to me. It was his soul stone, the life essence of the Prime Wizard of the Agricultural Age himself. He was surrendering it to me as if it were as insignificant as an apple. 'Take this and run. Destroy it if you must, but do not allow this murderous wizard to take possession of it.' He pressed his soul stone into my hands which I deposited into my wizard's cupboard for safekeeping."

The three adepts exchange quizzical glances at the mention of a wizard's cupboard but hold their questions.

Archibald notices their perplexed expressions but continues his story. "Master Llewellyn's eyes were somber when he said, 'This is the last I will ever ask of you, Archibald Abel. I now release you with heartwarming gratitude for your service.' He had to raise his voice to be heard above the din outside which had become deafening.

"A shadow was descending over the cottage. But Master, I yelled back, if I take your soul stone too far away, you will surely perish.

"Imagine my shock when he told me, 'Then I bid you to run as swiftly and as far as possible.' Those were the last words I would ever hear him speak.

"The front door burst open.

"I ran down the hallway and did not look back as I raced to the basement and took the stairs three at a time. "I could hear Cristobal yelling and swearing after me with deadly threats. The traitor may have thought he had me trapped down there, but I knew of an animal burrow that ended at the far corner of the room. I dove for it as I shifted to the form of a badger and scurried into the narrow tunnel.

"Cristobal would have thought it beneath him to transform into an animal. Instead, he sent fire to chase me down.

"I escaped into the forest with a singed tail and an uncertain future. From there, I teleported to a distant location, and again, and again, and again, shifting into different canine bodies each time. I did not know the abilities of this new wizard, but I transported and morphed enough times to leave Cristobal with a cold trail to curse at."

"Holy crap," Tonio mumbles under his breath.

chapter 14

Archibald is clearly pained by his retelling. He sucks in a deep breath and continues his story.

"Between bouts of crying for the loss of Master, and everyone I ever knew, and of self-pity, I shifted and teleported every day for months. I didn't dare show myself in human form.

"Tovenaar, the Prime Wizard of the Industrial Age, wasted no time using his power to infiltrate and manipulate the cream of society's crop. The guilds, the universities, the financial institutions, and the politicians. He also embraced the dregs of society, from the crime bosses down to even pickpockets and guttersnipes. He had even infiltrated the royal palace, for pity's sake.

"Those were dark days. I resorted to working as a canine, killing rats at local markets to earn scraps of food. In time, I learned of a land across the sea, and of men threatening to abandon king and country for personal freedom. That sounded like a perfect place to disappear.

I stowed away aboard a frigate and worked my way across the ocean with my new career of hunting varmints. I never looked back."

With that, Marion gets up off the ground and wraps her arms around Archibald's shoulders, giving him a long sympathetic hug.

Shea and Tonio watch with unjustified pangs of jealousy.

Tonio loudly clears his throat before asking, "Dude, you've been running ever since? After all this time, you still haven't figured out a way to kill Tovenaar, or at least mess him up? What kind of chance do we have?"

Archibald responds defensively, "What could I do? A familiar cannot harm a wizard of any age. It is as indisputable as the law of gravity. No adept, human, or even an army can harm a Prime Wizard. Only a wizard from an ensuing age can destroy him."

Shea blows an errant lock of hair from his face in frustration. "But *we* are only freaking human."

"Not anymore, my friend. You are adepts now." Archibald studies each of them. "And at least one of you," he pauses dramatically, "must become a wizard if the three of you are to ..." His voice trails off.

"No worries." Shea says disparagingly, "Tonio can kick footballs at him."

Marion giggles more from nerves than from humor.

Tonio scoffs, "You think your loser story books are going to get us through this?"

"At least I know how to read."

"You want to go, Citifield."

Archibald sighs and tells Marion, "Look at these two. They're like roosters scratching at dirt."

Marion inserts herself between the two of them to diffuse the situation and gently pushes them apart.

"Only together do you stand a chance," Archibald warns them

again. "Now allow me to finish."

He eyes the two young men to be certain they are listening. "A year had passed. I felt confident enough in this new land to retake human form. Unfortunately, my peace of mind did not last. Machinery and industrialization were introduced to my new world. Tovenaar's influence had crossed the ocean and had caught up with me. Once again, I resorted to hiding my identity in one canine form or another."

"For how long?" Marion asks sympathetically.

"There are almost two centuries of historical photographs that include the presence of a canine. Many of those dogs were me."

Tonio lets out a low whistle. "You photo bombing sonuvabitch." His comment earns a chuckle from all, easing the tension.

"Not just photo bombing. I was present for significant achievements. Let's just say I couldn't help but employ my magic to nudge things along. For example, Nikola Tesla's experiments with electricity."

"And were you able to help?" Marion inquires.

He shakes his head. "My good-intentioned meddling never quite brought the results I had anticipated," Archibald admits. "It turned out my Agricultural Magic was more of a jinx in the new age. I eventually learned to mind my business."

All three swap concerned glances at Archibald's disclosure.

"I've seen it all, from the American Revolution to building of the railroad, to the Civil War. The invention of the radio. The Great Depression. The invention of television, nuclear energy..."

"Wait," Shea interrupts. "Did you just breeze past two World Wars?"

"I never went back to Europe," Archibald explains. "With the passage of time, existing in human form became a distant memory. I eventually remembered to return to my old self before I slipped too far. I wasn't confident I could pass as a viable man." Archibald scratches at his sideburns. "Fast forward to the sixties. I began traveling from one outdoor music venue to another with the *free spirits*. Vast crowds and loud music make for a brilliant cover. No one would question my mistakes while I was practicing being human again. Many people at those events were, let's just say, under the influence."

Shea and Tonio grin at one another.

"I became quite enamored with rock and roll music and could finally name a benefit of existing in the Industrial Age. Would you believe me if I told you I saw Jimi Hendrix play at a venue right here on Long Island? He opened for the Monkeys. The crowd had never heard of Jimi Hendrix before and was not yet ready. They booed him."

"Wait, are you telling us you were a hippie?" Marion smiles widely.

"Hippies owned little and were happy with their lifestyle. They were thus useless to a greedy sod liken Tovenaar. He wouldn't bother with them.

"By then, computers were just beginning to become mainstream. I hoped that it marked the start of a new age and a natural end for Tovenaar. I was always on the move since I feared Tovenaar still coveted Master's soul stone. It would be a power source that could bolster his already obscene powers.

"It was then that it came to my attention that adepts of computer magic began showing up in sets of three, only to disappear. I investigated and learned to my dismay that Cristobal was hunting and destroying them at Tovenaar's command."

Archibald smiles proudly, "It took me quite some time, but I conjured a means of foretelling when and where adepts, such as yourselves, would likely show up."

Marion opens her mouth to speak.

Archibald holds up a hand expecting Marion's question, "A mixture of what magic I know, coupled with countless mathematical calculations and a dash of astrology. Quite complex."

Marion does not appreciate being silenced, but she lets it slide.

"I tried to help these adepts. I wanted to at least warn them about Tovenaar and give them a brawler's chance to survive."

Shea interjects, "Wait. How long have you been helping adepts?"

Archibald frowns, "I only began reaching them before Cristobal did for about ten years now. At first, I only got to them moments before disaster."

Their disheartened expressions remind him of those he could not help over the decades. "My lead time has improved dramatically," he assures them. "In the beginning, groups of adepts would arrive annually, as far as I could figure out. Gradually, it became increasingly frequent to a monthly occurrence. This is, of course, not taking into consideration the ones who hail from foreign countries."

"Lately, the occurrence of adepts has dwindled back to once every two to three months." He ponders for a moment then shakes the thought away. "To be honest, it took me many years to develop a means of foretelling when and where a trio of adepts would present themselves. Unfortunately, in most instances, Tovenaar and Cristobal were able to find them before me. They have the added advantage of using their newly corrupted familiars as trackers. My chances of reaching any adepts before them is exceedingly rare."

"Did you get to us in time?" Marion asks quietly.

"I can only hope," Archibald answers to her dismay. "I am beginning to fear the Computer Age will pass us by without a hierarchy of wizardry, and that Tovenaar will continue his reign."

Tonio interjects, "Okay, now we know what you know, so tell us what you *don't* know. What *haven't* you figured out?"

Archibald seems startled. "This is the first time someone has asked me that question. You are more intelligent than I anticipated.

Tonio winces at the backhanded compliment.

Archibald scrunches his face. "Let me see. I do not understand your computer magic. I do not know the significance of adepts showing up in groups of three. It is surely not how it worked in the Agricultural Age."

"So, you are telling us we don't stand a chance," Shea impatiently stares Archibald down.

Archibald lifts a finger. "There is something." He considers for a moment. "I believe Tovenaar commands his familiars not to harm adepts until they have gained some semblance of magical power. A familiar without magical powers would serve no purpose in his army. That should give you some time."

"How much time?" Tonio asks.

"I really don't know," Archibald responds. "That is up to you."

Marion is still concerned that one of them will become a familiar. "So obviously the betrayer doesn't know what he is getting himself into." She huffs, "Serves them right."

"What happens to the other two?" Shea is almost afraid to ask.

"The remaining two are killed, or worse."

"There's an, *or worse*?" Shea gulps.

"Yeah, you'll die a virgin," Tonio jokes.

Shea's face reddens. "Out of the three of us, you're obviously the betrayer." He has no clever retort for Tonio's dig.

"Screw you."

Archibald frowns. "If I had to guess, Cristobal would use jealousy against these two."

A LONG-DRAWN-OUT WHISTLE startles them.

Out of habit, Archibald instantly transforms into a dog.

Everyone turns to see Lawrence stepping from behind a patch of tall sea grass with a wide grin on his face. "That is some kooky story, Dog Boy."

Archibald regains human form and raises a hand, fingers splayed for casting a spell.

"No, wait!" Tonio steps protectively between Lawrence and Archibald's fingers. "He's a friend."

Chapter 15

A two-hundred-year-old structure sits nestled deep within a dense South American jungle. Filthy white stucco walls crumble in spots, revealing its natural stone construction. The shuttered windows are decaying with rotted wood slats. Thick, twisting vines cover two sides of this once distinguished hotel. Only the armed men who stand at either end of the flat roof reveal that the property is not vacant.

In an upstairs room, the self-titled El Diablo paces nervously. The barrel-chested wannabe dictator mentally prepares for a dreaded, yet unavoidable, meeting with his benefactor's ominous representative. He watches as his first lieutenant Esperanza Fuentes sews another service ribbon onto his jacket.

Esperanza is a raven-haired beauty he crossed paths with at a cantina in Cartagena. He convinced her to join him as a revolutionary. Esperanza sorely needed something to rebel against, and the high rank of first lieutenant sealed the deal. Ranks and titles, however, are as cheap as the *eye candy* that now clutters El Diablo's military jacket.

"*El jefe* will need a larger chest soon." She holds out the jacket for him to slip into.

El Diablo has come to rely on his capable, and delightfully unhinged, first lieutenant. "The guns are loaded?" He inquires.

"Of course, the guns are loaded," she replies with a hiss. "Cada puto uno de ellos." *Every f*cking one of them.*

"Good," he frowns. "This bastardo that is coming cannot be trusted.

Every encounter he has had with Cristobal has ended with El Diablo feeling the fool. He makes a silent vow that he will not take the bait this time. *I will not lose my temper.*

"Be certain he is the first to speak," Esperanza coaches him. "It will give you the upper hand."

*

The massive interior lobby is unexpectedly elegant with freshly painted walls, gilded trim, and marble floors. Long red velvet draperies cover the windows. Exquisite forms of weaponry decorate the walls. An enormous mahogany table that dominates the large space is covered with firearms of all styles and calibers. Stacks of ammunition are abundant.

Cristobal materializes into the otherwise empty room wearing a well-tailored pinstriped hooded robe. He has brought with him a tall and lanky familiar named Theo Ramirez.

Cristobal knocks sharply on the table three times.

Ramirez takes in the grandeur of his surroundings.

"Tovenaar created this entire compound," Cristobal informs the familiar.

"I dig his style." Ramirez replies admiringly. "Muy machista." *Very macho.*

A large ornate tapestry behind the table is swept aside and El

Diablo, in full generalisimo mode, steps into the room. He wipes a greasy smudge from his lips with a cloth napkin and nonchalantly tosses it in Cristobal's direction.

An expressionless Cristobal subtly raises the tip of his index finger one inch.

The temperature of the room increases dramatically.

Cristobal and El Diablo stand in silence.

A sweat mustache forms on El Diablo's upper lip. He shrugs out of his ornate military jacket revealing a sweat stained undershirt. He drapes the jacket over the only chair in the room and casually sits down behind the table.

The silence between them continues for an uncomfortable length of time.

"Tovenaar asks for too much," El Diablo blurts out. "He will have to be satisfied with ten percent less for a while."

Cristobal responds by rolling his fists together. His popping knuckles are reminiscent of a twenty-one-gun salute.

El Diablo mumbles incoherently under his breath. He cannot believe he lost the upper hand so quickly. He waits morosely for Cristobal's response.

"Tovenaar has fulfilled his end of the bargain," Cristobal's eyes narrow. "You think it was a simple task to build up a low-level gun runner to the status you now enjoy? Or do you prefer to go back to being a maguey worm-eating mala vida?" *Low life*.

Cristobal enjoys the nutty taste and crunchy texture of maguey worms, but he knows the reference will trigger El Diablo. He will take it as an insult to his less than modest upbringing.

As predicted, El Diablo loses his temper. "Enough! I will not deal with Tovenaar's demented errand boy." He stands menacingly. "This one can stay," he motions to Ramirez, "but you can get the hell out!" He punctuates his final sentence with a middle finger directed at Cristobal's face. "Here's your f*cking maguey worm!"

Ramirez' eyes widen. He cautiously draws a cell phone from his back pocket expecting the situation may escalate.

"I don't have time for this," Cristobal calmly sighs. In response, he gestures four gnarly fingers back at El Diablo.

"What the hell is this?" El Diablo shrieks as his finger-flipping right arm deflates and hangs limp as a formless sack of flesh and blood. He watches in horror as his arm, hand, and finger bones appear suddenly in Ramirez' hands.

Ramirez is freaked out by the bones and does a hasty juggle to avoid dropping them.

El Diablo grabs the nearest weapon with his left hand. Unfortunately, it is a pump-action shotgun that has not yet been pumped. He throws the shotgun aside and reaches for a pistol.

"I'll kill you, you motherless…"

Cristobal, Ramirez, and El Diablo's bones vanish.

El Diablo's curse-ridden tirade is wasted on an empty room.

*

An immense steel-reinforced concrete structure occupies an acre of land deep within a mangrove swamp somewhere in Karachi, Pakistan. Giant mangrove trees sprout from the water surrounding the compound, as well as the watery courtyards that exist sporadically within the structure. They provide a thick umbrella of coverage from possible curious planes and/or satellites circling high above the earth. Dense green moss thrives on the roof and brownish slime covers the small windows, further camouflaging the fortress from prying eyes.

Generations of locals have learned the hard way to avoid the area due to unexplained disappearances. Tall tales place the blame on ghosts and an assortment of unsavory creatures.

Inside the fortress, a sea of ornate gunmetal filing cabinets fills a room the size of a large warehouse. The cabinets move on an elaborate conveyor system at the command of a sharply dressed man with an imposing physical presence. He gestures elegantly with both hands, like a conductor leading his orchestra. Draws open and mechanical constructs deliver files with the grace of a server presenting a fine wine.

A shimmery aura swills about the man with his every movement. The world's magic is flowing through its conduit. The atmosphere around him vibrates and becomes clearer as the Prime Wizard of the Industrial Age wields his powers.

Huge, sliding reinforced steel doors line the back wall. One room is open revealing pallets stacked with bars of gold and currencies from all nations.

Familiars from various countries sit bored at their desks awaiting instruction for their next assignment. They come in all shapes and sizes. Their only similarity being the black scales that dapple their solemn faces. All are newbies learning from the ground up. A life of servitude is their "reward" for saving themselves by betraying their fellow adepts. The alternative being certain death. Maintaining their magical abilities was also a motivating factor.

Tovenaar is fluent in the world's languages, yet he is a man of few words. He drops a thick leather-bound folder labeled 'General Itzak Pfitzerol' next to another folder that already sits atop the desk of a hapless familiar named Ivan.

Ivan tightens his lips and glares at the two folders. *A freaking double shift.* He manages to keep his groan silent.

Tovenaar leans in, "Time to reward General Pfitzerol for a job well done. Bring him a 5/50…" he reconsiders, "scratch that, a 4/50 pallet of gold ingots."

"Prioritety pozhaluysta, ser?" *Priorities please, sir?* The Russian-speaking familiar asks, unsure of how the handle the double workload.

"The General will be delighted to see you. Take care of him first."
Tovenaar frowns. "Next, you will pay a visit to a certain oligarch
named Petrov Solokov. If he disregards my request once again, you
will bring me two of his front teeth. If he complains," Tovenaar taps
the oligarch's file with his index finger, "assure him that he will lose a
more useful appendage."

Ivan gulps audibly.

*

At the far end of the room sits a stout familiar. With a heavy French
accent he questions, "This would be more efficient with computers, no?"

The familiar at the next desk, who is of Japanese descent and
sports a man bun, nervously glances over at Tovenaar. Without turning
his head, he whispers, "Computers are kept at facilities throughout the
world, but not here."

"How are we supposed to do our jobs without computers?"

"Before you become a hacker, you must first work in the field and
learn the Tovenaar's requirements." He is already tired of this newbie.
"Be quiet before you get us punished."

The French familiar frowns. He did not expect his life to become
so boring. "So put me in the field already," he wishes aloud.

*

Cristobal appears next to Tovenaar along with an ashen-faced
Theo Ramirez.

Theo gingerly carries the arm and hand bones of an adult man. No
signs of blood or gore. Clean as any bone found in a museum, though
not yet dried out and yellowed.

The prime wizard grimaces at the sight. "I wondered if El Diablo
would be cocky enough to challenge me." He takes the bones by the

wrist and considers the four fingers. "And the middle finger?" He inquires, eyebrows raised.

"He pissed me off." Cristobal shifts his stance before further explaining, "I left him his middle finger."

Tovenaar sighs to conceal a smile. "El Diablo was and is still integral to my plans. The success of his coup d'état is crucial." He turns his attention back to El Diablo's bones. He gestures his free hand, and the bones take on an eerie metallic hue.

He wiggles the fingers of his own hand. The fingers of El Diablo's hand wiggle in a mimicking fashion. He returns the bones back to Theo and tells Cristobal, "Return this with my apologies."

"Spare the rod and spoil the child," Cristobal grins.

Tovenaar makes quick grabbing motions with his hand. The bones mimic his movements and grab violently at Theo's throat.

Theo struggles to keep the bones at arm's length.

"If El Diablo wishes to further resist my wishes, I will strangle him with his own hand." He turns to Cristobal, "Once his arm is whole again, return here. You will escort Ivan to Moscow for a double. Then you can prepare for tonight."

Cristobal exhales sharply at the thought of going back out into the field.

"What now?" Tovenaar growls impatiently.

Cristobal complains, "I'm getting too old for this shit."

"Patience, my friend. Once I am in possession of Llewellyn's soul stone, your longevity will become considerable." Tovenaar assures him.

Cristobal is not so sure. "That slippery little shit Archibald always manages to outrun me."

Tovenaar uncharacteristically lays a hand on Cristobal's shoulder. "Your little friend will not outrun *me*."

Cristobal smiles with anticipation before vanishing with Theo to return El Diablo's cursed bones.

Archibald rushes forward and grasps Lawrence's chin with his hand. "Show me your neck," he commands.

Lawrence obediently hooks his index finger to the collar of his tee shirt and pulls it forward exposing his neck. "What the hell?'

"Checking for black scales," Archibald explains. "You were at the ball field. How did you track us?"

"I saw a shimmer in the air that headed south."

"Yet you did not head south," Archibald points out.

"My mama didn't raise no fool, but if she did, it's my brother." He pauses for laughter but gets none. "A couple of dudes on motorcycles headed south, but then I noticed a tiny flicker in the air headed north. The best place north is the beach which led me here."

"You, my implausible friend, are touched with the craft," Archibald concludes. "By chance, were you in town yesterday?"

"He was there," Marion groans. "His name is Lawrence. He

stumbled into our energy planes causing the entire triangle to collapse."

"I didn't do shit…wait, what triangle?"

"That is indeed interesting," Archibald's eyes light up. "And I must take your word for it, because I did not witness this triangle." He regards Lawrence with renewed interest. "Your blunder may have rewarded you with a touch of arcane talent."

He continues, "It is possible Lawrence may be a suitable candidate to become a wizard's familiar. Perhaps one day become an apprentice, or a wizard, as I was meant to be. Anyway, for now, he could prove to be a disruptive force."

Lawrence asks, "Is a disruptive force good or bad?"

"Time will tell," Archibald smiles.

"I think it's probably good," Lawrence says proudly.

Shea grows impatient, "So what's our next move?"

"I believe Tovenaar's familiars are already working to convince Tonio to betray both you and Marion. Have you noticed anyone out of the ordinary?"

Shea wrinkles his nose, "That creepy principal gave me uncool advice about Marion."

"Same here. Skinner told me Shea is a perverted stalker," Tonio grins.

Marion's eyes widen. "She practically followed me into the locker room and told me I should…" She is too embarrassed to repeat what the principal said. "It's as if she was somebody else."

Shea has a thought, "Can familiars possess people?"

Archibald shakes his head. "Certainly not Computer Age familiars, as far as I have seen."

Marion pushes for an answer, "Then what else would explain Principal Skinner's bizarre behavior?"

Archibald considers, "I would not put it past Cristobal. He was well on his way to becoming a wizard when Tovenaar corrupted him, and he always preferred the unsavory aspects of the craft. But if that were the case, it would mean he is already here. And if he is already here…” He lets his voice trail off, rather than voice his fears.

“We need a plan,” Tonio steps up. “We need a computer.”

Shea says, “You can use your phone, dumbass.”

Tonio shakes his head. “I’m thinking we need a computer that is hardwired, and I am sure that if you’re creating a video game, you have a nice one.”

Shea is not warm to the idea and refuses to let this amateur anywhere near his computer. “Um, I don’t think so.”

“Self-centered much?” Marion chides him.

“If Cristobal is here, you have even less time than I thought. If he kills you, I guarantee you won’t even miss your computer.”

Strangely, Lawrence does not take any of this seriously, even though he saw the four of them disappear from the schoolyard, and just saw Archibald morph into a dog and back again. He pats Tonio on the back and jokes, “Nice knowing you, buddy.”

Archibald catches Marion’s eye. He ever so slightly tilts his head towards Lawrence and motions away with his chin.

Marion notices Archibald’s subtle intention. She flutters her eyelashes at Lawrence. “I wonder if you would be a doll and do me a huge favor?”

Lawrence’s eyes brighten. Without hesitation he is at her side, “Name it.” He secretly always liked Marion.

“I’m worried that Principal Skinner may be in trouble.” She downplays the fact that Cristobal may have possessed her. “She just doesn’t seem herself today.”

Lawrence nods. “You mean her slutty clothes and crappy attitude?” He pictures her in his mind. “Kind of hot though.”

Archibald winces at the thought of putting Lawrence in harm’s way.

"What?" Marion addresses Archibald in an annoyed tone.

"That is not exactly a safe errand to send him on."

Marion may be a shy young woman, but she does know how to get her way. She pleads to Archibald with her eyes.

"I'm on it." Lawrence assures her then looks to Archibald, "How about a lift, sport?"

Archibald sucks in a deep breath and shakes his head vigorously. The last place he wants to be is anywhere near Cristobal, but he concedes. "Sure, why not."

"Cool," Marion smiles coyly.

"Give us a lift to Shea's house on the way?" Tonio invites himself.

Archibald raises his hands and spreads them wide.

Whooomph, all five of them vanish.

*

The group materializes on the driveway at Shea's house.

Lawrence stumbles and flattens himself against the trailer to keep from falling.

Archibald cautiously scans the area. He places a hand on Lawrence's shoulder. "It's you and me, kid."

They both vanish.

Shea hears his father in the backyard talking to someone. He scrambles behind the trailer to avoid being spotted. He motions with his head for Tonio and Marion to follow him.

*

It is after school hours at Huntsport High. Archibald and Lawrence materialize in the now empty hallway.

"Lead me to your principal's office," Archibald commands Lawrence who is sprawled on the floor.

"Sonuvabitch," Lawrence mumbles under his breath as he

struggles to his feet. He glares at Archibald, not appreciating his bossy tone, but lets it slide this time. "Come along, Dog Boy," and leads the way down the fluorescent-lit corridor towards the administrative offices. "What if this Cristobal chump is still here?"

"Your only chance would be to play dead." Archibald half-jokes.

"What the hell does that mean?" Lawrence stops in his tracks.

"Just be careful." Archibald takes the lead. He pauses at the door marked Principal Skinner and looks over his shoulder, "Last chance to un-volunteer yourself, my sluggish friend."

Lawrence shrugs, "What the hell." He reaches past Archibald to bang on the door before impatiently swinging it open wide.

A mess of paper still covers everything.

Lawrence lets out a low whistle.

Archibald brushes past him and surveys the room. He morphs into a Foxhound, sniffs with his canine snout then returns to human form. "Cristobal *was* here."

Lawrence is curious, "What exactly did you smell to know this Cristobal creep was in here?"

"Farts and rum."

Lawrence wrinkles his nose, "Gross." A muffled sound catches his attention. He puts a finger to his lips signaling Archibald to be quiet. "Principal Skinner?" He whispers.

A heavy sob escapes from under the desk. "Go away, Lawrence. It is not safe here."

Archibald reassures her, "The familiar named Cristobal has left the vicinity. You are safe to come out."

Principal Skinner sniffles and loudly blows her nose. She meekly calls out from under the desk, "Are you, Archibald Abel?"

The question spooks Archibald. "How could you possibly know my name?"

She does not respond. Finally, a hand grabs the end of the desk and Principal Skinner pulls herself up. She looks awful. Her hair is disheveled, and her clothing is beyond wrinkled. Thankfully, she now wears the outfit she left the house in. Her face is red and swollen from crying. She is physically and emotionally drained.

"That beast has plans for you," she warns Archibald. "The Wizard he works for is eager to take possession of a stone that you carry. A soul stone."

Archibald's eyes widen, "He told you this?"

She shudders and squeezes her eyes shut. "When he took control of my body, he had access to my mind. I did not have access to his, but for one terrible moment, he opened his mind to plant a vile memory of his own into my brain." She hugs her shoulders and squeezes her eyes even tighter. "At that moment, I could read his thoughts and learn of his immediate plans. You are in grave danger." Her eyes snap open. "So are Marion and Tonio. And the new boy."

"They are aware," Archibald informs her.

Principal Skinner reaches out and snatches Archibald's wrist. "Will you be able to help them?"

"I will do my best." He looks apologetically from Principal Skinner to Lawrence, wishing he had a better answer. *I should leave them with something to give them hope. This woman needs a purpose. It may help her to forget the ordeal she just suffered.*

"Adepts I have helped in the past created traps involving computers. Many computers and computer telephones. In this I can be of little assistance to them."

"I have access to computers." Principal Skinner grasps an opportunity to be of use. She wants nothing more than to help the children and to get revenge on the filthy creature that violated her. "Lawrence and I will gather as many computers as possible and have them ready to help with their trap."

Archibald studies the principal. He can only imagine the ordeal Cristobal had inflicted upon her and feels guilty for giving her false hope. But false hope is all he can offer.

"Very well. I will leave the two of you to amass all the computers and phones as you can muster." He flashes a weary smile. "And power sources. I would imagine they would need large batteries or a power generator. I must go now to advise them the best I can."

Archibald bows slightly before disappearing into thin air. He can think of no set of circumstances that will require him to return.

Principal Skinner flops tiredly onto the leather chair only to quickly spring up, recalling what happened the last time she sat on it. With a scream of rage, she kicks the chair across the room.

Although he is unsure why, Lawrence also kicks the chair once for good measure.

chapter 17

Shea, Marion, and Tonio press their backs against the trailer hiding from Shea's father and uncle who are in the yard.

Shea whispers, "I don't think we have time for introductions and explanations with my parents. So, let's just keep our voices down."

Tonio is skeptical. "This is not a big house. They are going to know we are inside."

"C'mon. I will show you, my room." Shea swings open the door to his freshly washed trailer.

"This is your room?" Marion's eyes light up, "You live in a trailer?"

Shea corrects her as he climbs the steps. "It is not a trailer. It's a vintage 1951 Airstream Cruiser."

They follow him into his new digs. Shea's computer is already powered up and displaying a video game that is frozen on the screen.

Shea frowns, "My game must have encountered a glitch while rendering." He taps at the keyboard.

Marion persists. "So let me get this straight. You live in a trailer and your parents live in the house."

Tonio admits quietly to no one in particular, "Sweet deal."

Shea is surprised by Tonio's compliment. *Maybe he is only half a douche.*

Tonio notices Shea's choice of avatar for the game, "So you are playing the game as a chick?"

My mistake. Shea's rolls his eyes. *He is still a douche.* "When developing a game, you need to thoroughly assess every character for glitches." He types code to fix the glitch. "But I'm sure you already knew that."

The avatar in the game continues to walk into a dark corridor, guns ready.

Shea sees Marion studying his living arrangements with a blank expression. "I plan on adding some Christmas lights and speakers to vibe up the atmosphere."

She smiles into his eyes, "That would be cool."

Tonio sniffs noisily, "It would be a lot cooler if you opened a window and aired this place out."

Whooomph.

Archibald appears in Shea's overcrowded bedroom and looks around. "Charming little flat you got here, mate."

"I found your principal. It is as you predicted. Cristobal took possession of her body. He has since vacated her, and thankfully left her alive."

Marion is concerned. "How is she?"

"She's a mess," Archibald says bluntly. "Remarkably, she learned of Cristobal's immediate plans. Your foes will most likely be here tomorrow, or with any luck, the day after. Tovenaar's prime objective is obtaining Master Llewellyn's Soul Stone. That could be catastrophic."

He looks at them quietly for a moment, hoping they will understand the depth of what he must now tell them.

"Look guys, I do not know how to help you. You need a cohesive plan to stand any chance at all. Unfortunately, even if you concoct a plan, you do not have the skills to pull it off in time."

Shea is angry, "This is bullshit!"

Archibald continues, "I watched you all at the schoolyard. Tonio can kick a ball with stunning accuracy, but that is not enough to save you." He holds up a hand to prevent Tonio from interjecting.

"You, my lady, can execute an impressive vertical split, and are exceedingly kind-hearted."

He turns his attention to Shea. "And you, my well-read friend, know about computers, which may be helpful." He hesitates before continuing, "And you can lay down a line of horseshit like a parade of stallions. Tovenaar is not likely to give you a chance to speak a word of it."

Archibald paces as best as he can in the confined space before getting to the point, "I will admit that from what I've seen, your styles of computer magic are somewhat unique." He glances at Shea and Marion, "Well, for two of you anyway."

Tonio narrows his eyes at the dig.

"It's not enough for me to risk…"

Marion says quietly, "He's bailing on us."

"If I run and leave a trail or two, I might be able to lure Tovenaar away from you. Your odds will be better against Cristobal alone."

Tonio concedes, "He's right. The only thing we all have in common is that we have nothing in common."

Marion cannot believe that Tonio is ready to give up so easily. She looks at Shea with a wide-eyed silent plea for help.

Shea sees the fear in her eyes and takes a breath. He addresses Archibald, "The other groups you helped… what talents did they have?"

"They all were in exactly your circumstances. The triads that survived the longest and came the closest to succeeding had expert skills with motorcycles, for example. One group constructed elaborate traps in an abandoned neighborhood. There was a trio of West Point cadets who were skillful sharpshooters."

"Yet their special skills still didn't help them," Tonio adds dishearteningly.

"They at least had something to start with. An underdog's chance, a smidgen of hope." Archibald's decision to move on is reflected by his pained expression. "Look, I am sorry, but I am afraid you three will fall quickly with or without me. I mean, look at the two of you," he gestures to Tonio and Shea, "You would betray each other for the price of a donut. It is best if I get to another group earlier. Maybe then…"

Shea interrupts, "Maybe the motorcycles and rifles and stuff didn't work because they are all tools of the Industrial Age."

Archibald hesitates. His eyes flash with a glimmer of interest. "I'm listening."

"Tovenaar most likely is well-versed in everything the Industrial Age has to offer." Shea continues, "Nothing mechanical is going to take down that mother fuc…."

"Let me get this straight," Tonio chimes in. "In all these years, the best these potential wizards of the Computer Age could come up with is to turn cell phones into weapons?"

Marion points her phone at Tonio and makes cute shooting sounds to emphasize his point, "Ptui ptui."

"To varying degrees. Recently they have learned to create simple objects with the plasma," Archibald admits, "but yes."

Tonio furrows his brow. He turns to Shea. "Citifield…" He cuts himself short and puts his hands up. "Sorry. No more infighting. Shea, you read a lot of science fiction books. Is there anything in them that could help us? Did they ever do anything dope with computers?"

"Well, there is a series of books where these people could go into an actual computer and exist in cyberspace," Shea recalls. "They were able to accomplish incredible things."

"Like what?" All three ask expectantly.

"Well, they had to build elaborate machines first and then hardwire their brains directly to the hard drive to pull it off. Way beyond my skill set," Shea admits.

Archibald has heard enough. "I do not know what to say, but good luck to you."

"Archibald, stay," Tonio commands him. He holds up his index finger to signal just a moment.

Tonio has always opted for action over thought. His instincts cause him to lash out when frustrated. "I have an idea. Check this out." Wearing a reckless grin, he rubs his thumb and index finger together and approaches Shea's computer. A pulse of plasma suddenly hums and sputters from the monitor.

"Don't even think about it," Shea warns.

The plasma stretches out from the screen like saltwater taffy until it reaches Tonio's fingertips. It quickly travels up his arm and engulfs his body.

In a flash, Tonio is sucked into the computer.

"Holy shit!" Shea cries out.

Marion is annoyed. "That is so typical! He just rushes in and does things without thinking."

Shea agrees, "He didn't even stop to consider the consequences."

Marion considers, "I guess he made our choice for us." She cocks her head toward the computer, "C'mon." She follows Tonio's lead and places her hand against the screen. With a flash, she is gone.

Shea and Archibald exchange dumbfounded glances.

"Well, I guess I'm next," Shea says sheepishly. "You'll be here when we get back?"

Archibald nods as a digitally enhanced version of Marion's hand reaches out from the computer screen towards Shea's turned back. "I'll see you when I see you, kid."

Shea is yanked by his tee shirt into the computer.

chapter 18

Shea tumbles and flails desperately as he free falls through a storm of fractured imagery. A deafening roar of unfiltered sound resonates through his very being. He tries to break his fall, but there is nothing to physically grasp. His brain struggles to *get a grip*.

Billions of tiny swirling bits of shattered imagery further dissolve into binary numbers. His reality becomes nothing but zeros and ones until they explode back into shreds of every piece of data ever uploaded to the Internet. Fragments of televised sporting events, every TV show, every commercial, every movie, every still image, every meme, every social media video, and every song ever uploaded on the World Wide Web flash before him. He cannot filter the onslaught of data that saturates his brain.

Mismatched segments intertwine and merge haphazardly before him. *There, what is that?* A partial image of a race car bursts into flames before a crowd of cringing fans. All too quickly it morphs into an image of the puckered lips of a fashion model as the rest of her face pieces itself together, followed by black and white movie footage of a long-forgotten musical. Shea experiences all this multiplied by a trillion.

He squeezes his eyes shut, hoping it will all go away. He re-opens his eyes. To his dismay, the nightmare continues.

Am I dead? His mind races. *I never finished my computer game. I never finished high school. What will my parents think? Will they discover my browser history? What did Tonio get us into?*

"You don't need to yell."

Wait, who is that? "Tonio?" Shea never imagined he would be so relieved to hear *his* voice. "I just thought your name and here you are."

"That's how it works in here," Tonio assures him. "Think of jellybeans. You'll see."

As the word jellybeans grasps a synapse in Shea's brain, the random information focuses. Thousands of images of jellybeans in every color surround him like a sugar rush. He can almost taste every conceivable flavor of them. His mind nudges the mass of data to present itself in an orderly fashion. The images arrange themselves into a neat grid.

Already bored, he swipes his hand from right to left and they all vanish.

"Yes!" Shea feels a slight, but welcome sense of control. With renewed determination, he shifts his perspective so that he is in front of his computer rather than inside it. He imagines a search box and mentally types the word, *Marion.*

Enter.

The word MARION grows to the size of an apartment building before collapsing into a single musical note that perfectly represents Marion. Every photo of Marion ever uploaded, from social media selfies to yearbook photos scroll before him. He can also access her school, medical, and dental records. TMI.

"Hey! Stop perving on my intel," Marion's voice calls out playfully.

He sees her now off in the distance. She is wearing… he searches for words to describe what she is wearing. *Flowing sails of…an ever-changing kaleidoscope of…?* He quits trying.

Shea calls to her, "Marion!"

Marion appears in front of him, face to face, but from his perspective, she is upside down. She grins at him with a smile that could only be possible if she won a beauty pageant and the lottery on the same day.

"How are you doing this? How did you learn this so quickly?"

Marion senses the apprehension in Shea's voice. She rotates her orientation to that of his. "Don't worry, you will get used to it. I have already been here for quite a while, and you only just got here." She points over to Tonio off in the distance performing multiple back flips through a vortex of data. "Tonio has been in here for so much longer than I."

Shea is puzzled, "I was only a few seconds behind you guys."

"Maybe time is different in here." She pirouettes perfectly and stands inches from Shea's face. "Just imagine anything you would like to learn, and you will learn it." She smiles into his eyes and challenges him, "Make it happen. Do the Dew. Make us proud." And with that, Marion disappears like a shooting star.

Shea ponders for a moment. *Where to begin?*

He selects a topic. "Teach me about fighting!" Shea's mind floods with data and images of pistols, shotguns, nun chucks, F-18 fighter jets, street riots, baseball bats, Bruce Lee, war footage, two scorpions in a brandy glass, mushroom clouds, WWI, WWII, WW… "Whoa! Too broad a search."

He reconsiders. "Martial arts. Search disciplines of martial arts."

A detailed list appears before him.

Karate, Jujitsu, Akido, Judo, Hapkido, Kung Fu, Capoeira, Krau Maga, Tai Kwon Do, Tai Chi, Nguni Stick Fighting, Collegiate Wrestling, Wen-Do, Bokator, Banshay, Muay Thai, Kurash, Savate, Fencing, Bare Knuckle Boxing, Quarterstaff, English Long sword, Shin Kicking, Glima…

"What the heck is Glima?"

A computerized female voice informs him. "Glima is a type of Nordic folk wrestling practiced both as a sport and a means of combat. In one form of glima, players grip their opponents by the waist and try to throw them to the ground using technique rather than force. Other variants allow for more aggression."

Glima could be cool. I guess. He considers the possibilities. *I suppose I should begin with karate.* He hesitates. *Screw it.*

"Download all!"

Shea's mind becomes a vessel of knowledge that soaks in every technique of every martial art form that has been uploaded onto the web. Texts. Photos. Video instruction. All sense of time vanishes from his consciousness as data floods in. Shea instantly has the intellectual ability to perform thousands of martial arts moves to perfection. He can expertly execute all offensive and defensive maneuvers from dozens of disciplines. Shea learns every pressure point on the human body and how to use that knowledge to his advantage. Skills that ordinarily would take lifetimes to master. Psych!

"Shea!"

That's Marion's voice. It feels like it has been hours since he last spoke with her.

"Shea, we are going back."

"Okay. Give me a second."

Shea intends to get in one more download, and to delete all his personal data from the internet.

chapter 19

Archibald stands alone in Shea's trailer. He is exhausted and looks longingly at Shea's bed. A rare opportunity to take a nap. Archibald tentatively sits on the edge of the bed and lays back. As soon as his head hits the pillow, an unexpected noise startles him.

He jumps to his feet.

Plasma and pixels spill from the computer and gracefully morph into Tonio and Marion. They are giddy from their experience.

"We just owned the mother-loving internet." Marion wraps her arms around Tonio's neck and hugs him with sheer exhilaration.

Tonio returns her hug and lifts her off the floor.

"Where is Shea?" Archibald asks casually, concealing his fear that the two may have betrayed their friend.

"Making up for lost time." Shea finally spills out from the computer and back into his room. He pats his legs and chest to confirm his physical form is intact.

"I'm going back in," Shea laughs. "Screw the real world." He invites himself in on the hug with Marion and Tonio like teammates winning a championship.

Archibald watches the trio with a bemused expression. He is especially surprised by the new dynamic shown between the two boys. *Have they forgotten their animosity towards one another?*

Marion has changed from a quiet, self-contained girl to a young woman teaming with confidence. He clears his throat to interrupt the celebration.

"That was an exceedingly appealing encounter with immense pedagogic erudition," Tonio exclaims.

Marion and Shea look stunned. "Huh?"

Archibald's jaw drops, "Tonio?

"You can call me *Antonio* now," Antonio addresses the group. He lightly punches Shea's shoulder. "I perused your sci-fi and fantasy novels. Many proved to be enjoyable."

"Oh yeah? Which ones did you read?"

"All of them, I think," Antonio shrugs innocently.

Marion laughs with whole-hearted delight. She warns him, "Dude, your vocabulary is off the charts. You may have to dumb it down a couple of notches or your old man is going to have a coronary."

"Darling, I can dumb it down in seven languages." Antonio is thrilled with his vast new intellect and enjoys being the smartest one in the room for once.

The ramifications of Antonio's learning curve intrigues Archibald. He is curious if the other two had similar upgrades. "And yourself, milady," he asks Marion.

She smiles. "Let's just say that I will have no problem acing every class I take from now on." Her smile is quickly replaced with a look of concern. "Did either of you notice all the falsehoods, deceit, and misinformation that lurks on the World Wide Web? It's going to take someone a lot of work to clean house. Oh, and there is no information on anyone named Tovenaar."

"Tovenaar is a Dutch word meaning wizard," Antonio offers. "The bastard doesn't even have a real name."

Archibald points to Shea. "And you, my friend, what have you learned?"

Shea grins. "I wasn't in there for long, but I learned every martial arts discipline in existence. You might be looking at the most dangerous man in the world." He executes a move with his arms. "Ouch," he rubs at a pulled muscle in his shoulder.

Everyone but Shea bursts into laughter.

Marion massages Shea's shoulder. "Your body needs to get in shape first, I think."

Archibald ponders, "But how did you three learn all of this in such a short span of time?"

"I too am curious about the real-time to cyberspace-time ratio." Antonio questions Archibald, "By your estimation, how lengthy was our computerized excursion?"

"I watched as the three of you entered the computer. I, um, I sat down for a moment and here you are again." Archibald estimates, "Certainly less than a minute."

"I lost track of time but felt like I was in there for many hours," Shea surmises.

"Felt like a full day to me," Marion speculates.

Antonio admits, "My experience felt like two days. I even took a nap."

"I knew I heard snoring," Marion teases.

"I'm calling it the Hyper Realm," Shea announces. "Cyberspace doesn't do it justice."

Archibald is curious. "More importantly, do you now feel that you are better equipped to deal with Tovenaar and his familiars?"

Antonio answers first. "The familiars will be a breeze but--"

"--Tovenaar is still an unknown," Marion completes his sentence. "I mean, why isn't his power waning by now? The Industrial Age has been in decline for quite some time. We need to figure out just what is keeping him going."

"Perhaps Tovenaar is half bionic by now?" Shea theorizes. "Is he replacing his failing body parts with mechanical alternatives?" He contemplates. "Or, maybe that is why he so desperately wants your Master's soul stone."

"Buddy, you did more in there than just watch The Karate Kid." Antonio slaps Shea on the back in a congratulatory way.

"After you guys left, I studied critical thinking and..." Shea taps his temple with his finger, "I downloaded The Art of War."

The intensity in Shea's eyes makes Marion's stomach flip. Her attraction to him, and to Antonio, *OMG*, is even more intense.

"Maybe he is using his new familiars as living soul stones." Antonio's mind races ahead. "I'm ready to make the first move in this chess match against Tovenaar."

"Let's do this," Marion states with a spirited aggression that quite becomes her.

Archibald is apprehensive. "Wait. Do you wish to go on the offensive so soon without a plan of attack?

Antonio argues. "We need to prove a theory before we can concoct a viable plan. I say we bag a pair of familiars and drag them into the Hyper Realm, surround them with a dozen firewalls, bind them with infinite security apps, and leave them to languish. The Industrial Wizard will be hard-pressed to find them. And if my theory of the familiars being living soul stones proves correct, Tovenaar's power will diminish exponentially as we take them off the board. If not, we will know that some other force is extending the life of his crusty old heart." He smiles, feeling satisfied with the simplicity of his plan.

Shea challenges Antonio's line of reason. "I don't like it."

Though Antonio is no longer smiling, the old Tonio that existed only minutes ago would have taken quick offense. The new Antonio simply nods to Shea to express his opinion. His powerful intellect now gives him the confidence to entertain opposing ideas.

Shea argues his point. "We could secure these familiars with a million security apps and a million firewalls making the odds of them ever escaping unlikely. However, we would still be introducing them as potentially dangerous 'viruses' to the internet."

Antonio admits, "Point taken."

"What about external hard drives?" Marion suggests.

Antonio asks Archibald, "How many familiars are we talking about?"

Archibald guesstimates. "Hundreds, a thousand, maybe more."

Suddenly from outside the window, Lawrence's voice chimes in, "The school has a ton of thumb drives. They are in a box labeled 'Regents Test Primers.'"

"How is he able to sneak up on me like that?" Archibald wonders aloud. "We may as well let him in." He throws open the door.

Lawrence wedges himself into the confined space. He checks out every corner of the room and concludes, "This is bad-ass."

"Are we really going to imprison people in thumb drives? We don't even know if they can survive like that?" Marion is concerned.

"We will just have to learn by trial and error." Antonio shrugs.

"But…"

"They are no longer people. They are familiars." Antonio reminds her.

Shea adds, "Familiars who want to hurt us."

Marion frowns at them. "Whatever happens during the next twenty-four hours, I would like to at least maintain some moral integrity."

Shea backs her up. "Yes, of course. I, for one, am glad you still have a good heart and would hate to see it tarnished." Marion's smile sends a thrill up his spine. "Maybe we can upload music or movies on the drives to keep them entertained."

Marion considers, "I'm thinking more like self-help books, or the Bible. Buddhism for Dummies, perhaps. Something new-agey. You know, give them a shot at salvation."

"Sure, why not?" Shea pauses. "But will a familiar even fit on a thumb drive?"

"What the hell are we talking about here?" Lawrence has just caught up with the conversation. He looks at his friends like they've lost their minds. "You can't put people on thumb drives!"

"Why not?" Antonio grins.

"Duh!" Lawrence rolls his eyes. "Because first, it's against the law of physics. And even if it were possible, I'm sure it would be against the Geneva Confection or something."

Antonio places an index finger on Shea's computer monitor. Instantly, an image of the Geneva Convention fills the screen. He informs Lawrence, "There is nothing in the Geneva *Convention* against imprisoning enemy combatants on thumb drives. And whether it is possible to do so, I know of two nefarious-looking familiars on motorcycles who shouldn't be too difficult to locate. We will quickly learn if it is indeed possible."

Lawrence's eyes bug out, "What the hell did you just say?"

He looks to Archibald for logical support but is met with a shrug and a weak explanation. "Magic."

"I have two empty thumb drives we can use for now." Shea grabs a mismatched pair from his makeshift desk.

"Wait." Marion takes hold of Shea's hand that is holding the thumb drives. She touches Shea's computer monitor with her other hand. A tiny spark of plasma arcs to the thumb drives.

"What was that?" Shea asks.

"I just downloaded the self-help literature onto the thumb drives."

"Sweet. I'll bring external hard drives for a backup. In case we need more gigabytes to store them. He searches through a cardboard box that is labeled 'computer stuff' until he finds two external hard drives. "One hundred gigs each should be plenty." He looks around the room and under the desk. "Does anyone see my backpack?"

Archibald replies, "You don't need a backpack. Just stash the computer drives in your wizard's cupboard."

"What the hell is a *wizard's cupboard*?" Lawrence snorts.

"A wizard's cupboard is one of the few things that every magical being from every age has in common, whether they are aware of it or not." Archibald snatches a bag of gummy candies from the small kitchen counter and pushes his left hand so that it disappears into thin air in front of him. When he pulls his hand back out, it is empty. "And just like that, my treats will always be with me until I am ready to enjoy them."

"My treats you mean," Shea grumbles.

Antonio snatches a fun-sized bag of chips and successfully stashes it into thin air.

"Hey!" Shea objects to the pilfering of his snacks.

Marion leaves Shea's snacks alone. Instead, she holds up her blinged-out cell phone and asks Archibald, "Will this cupboard ruin my phone?"

"The wizard's cupboard is an isolated space of neutral energy." He frowns, "I am afraid you will just have to try it and see."

Marion successfully stashes the phone into her own wizard's cupboard. She gives Shea a coy smile before grabbing a bag of chips for herself and stashes it along with her phone.

Shea accepts the inevitable. He reaches down and opens the door of his mini fridge revealing cans of soda. "Be my guest."

They all help themselves to a can of soda and stash them in their cupboards.

Shea reminds Marion, "Can you check to see if your phone still works?"

"Oh yeah." She reaches back into thin air to extract her phone. Marion then takes Shea's picture with it and studies the photo for a moment. "This one's a keeper." She takes a pic of Antonio and Archibald.

Shea smirks as he stashes away the two hard drives, chips, and a can of soda. "I must admit, it's a useful little trick. I'm calling mine a wizard's closet though."

"Let me try." Lawrence grabs a can of soda. He pushes with all his might, but only one inch of the can disappears. He finally gives up and pulls it back, but the bottom of the can is missing, along with all the soda. "That's not funny," he whines.

"I am surprised you had any success at all. So, atta boy." Archibald laughs along with the others. "Perhaps once your magic develops, your wizard's coin purse will grow to a useful size."

"Is there anything else you forgot to teach us?" Antonio questions.

Archibald puts a finger to his temple for a moment. "I think I've covered it all."

Shea asks his companions, "Where are we doing this?"

"The school parking lot, the one that is behind the building. It's mostly out of sight and should be empty by now," Antonio suggests.

Archibald is concerned. "Is it necessary to rush into this? It seems reckless."

"We need to make certain we can confine familiars onto thumb drives before we can concoct a proper plan of attack," Antonio assures him.

Lawrence adds, "Reckless times call for reckless measures, Archie."

Archibald grudgingly accepts when Marion calls him Archie.

Truth be told, he rather enjoys it. He will not, however, tolerate Lawrence abusing his name. He tightens his lips with a disapproving scowl before shrugging his shoulders.

WHOOOMPH.

Lawrence suddenly finds himself alone in Shea's trailer. "Oh, that's real nice!"

Mr. and Mrs. Blakely knock on the door before poking their heads in. Agnes carries a pitcher of lemonade. Carmine carries a stack of plastic cups and a sleeve of cookies.

"You just missed them," Lawrence informs Shea's parents.

"But we just heard Shea talking." Mrs. Blakely's goes up an octave, "We heard a bunch of people talking."

Mr. Blakely backs out of the door and looks down the street in both directions. He looks back to the strange boy who's alone in their son's bedroom. "Where did they go?"

Lawrence introduces himself, "Hi, I'm Lawrence Brown, but you can call me Lasagna."

He disregards the bewildered looks on their faces.

"Is that lemonade?"

chapter 20

Marion, Shea, Antonio, and Archibald materialize in the high school's back parking lot. This time the three adepts stick the landing like experienced professionals. Their new powers continue to have an intoxicating effect on them.

"Let's bag us some familiars!" Shea presents a fist to Antonio, who hammers back with force.

"Yeah, baby!"

Archibald watches them with concern.

Shea grins at Marion, then boldly scoops her up in his arms. He spins in circles as she clings to him, her arms wrapped tightly around his neck.

"Hey! Put me down!" She giggles.

Antonio's eyes narrow ever so slightly. "Dude put her down."

Marion shrieks with laughter when Shea tosses her in the air before gently lowering her to the ground. Although she has regained her balance, her arms remain draped around his neck. Her face is flush from their closeness. Marion pouts, feigning anger as she pulls away. She breaks a smile and lightly punches his arm.

"Ouch! You're stronger than you look," Shea teases.

He glances over at Antonio, who is eyeing him with disapproval.

"Dude, you're next." Shea walks towards him, arms extended for a bear hug.

Antonio can't help but laugh. "You are out of your league, Blakely." He takes a boxer's stance.

Shea puts up his fists and the two spar. "Are you ready to kick some old wizard ass?" Shea eggs on Antonio between swings.

"Bring it, bitch." Antonio shoves Shea away and does a freestanding back flip.

"Woo-hoo!" Marion cheers.

Archibald disapproves of their overt displays of drunken bravado. "You are not treating this moment with the gravity it deserves." He scans the area once more. "Are you certain you are ready to do this? There will be no second chances once you kick the hornet's nest."

The three quiet down and stare at Archibald with looks of feral amusement.

He swallows audibly, "The others never acted so impetuously."

"Ha! I know what that word means," Antonio jokes. "Tell me, just how did those well-thought plans work out for those cautious adepts?"

Archibald feels like he has lost all control over the situation. "Well okay, point taken," he stammers, "but that doesn't mean you should be so…"

"Dude, relax. When the time comes, we will have a solid plan in place for the big fish," Shea reassures him while resting a hand on Archibald's slumped shoulder. "We are just scrounging up some bait."

"Something to dangle," Marion adds with a playful smile and flirtatious wink.

Antonio adds, "If this doesn't happen like we are certain it will, you can take off to warn the next three adepts. No hard feelings." He rests his hand on Archibald's other shoulder. "Though we could use your help on this one." He leans in closer. "Are you in?"

"I'm in," Archibald agrees hesitantly. "Be forewarned, once you attack the familiars, Cristobal will be quick to their aid. Since he is not of the Computer Age, it is unlikely you will be able to collect him on one of your computer thumbs. My advice is to do the deed. If all goes accordingly, you should immediately vacate the premises. I will remain disguised as, I don't know, a squirrel perhaps, and will observe Cristobal's reaction and report back."

The three adepts exchange curious glances at Archibald's suggestion to flee the scene. They do not agree with his logic. There is a somber moment of silence.

Shea speaks first. "Yeah, okay. No reason for us to get cocky." He addresses Archibald, "When the coast is clear, meet us back in my room." He looks back at Antonio and Marion and subtly half winks his right eye.

Antonio catches on and pretends to agree. "Fine with me."

Marion simply nods.

Archibald also nods his head and exhales an audible sigh of relief. "When you are ready, I will enact a feat of Agricultural Age sorcery that will tip off Cristobal as to my whereabouts. He will surely send in his familiars to scout the situation."

Antonio takes an aggressive stance. "Let's do this."

"This is going to be fun!" Marion declares. The wild gleam in her eye is back. She asks Shea the unthinkable, "Would you mind sitting this one out and recording it? I have a feeling this will shatter all records on social media."

"I am really looking forward to some action," Shea protests. He doubts he can ignore his adrenaline level and sit this one out.

She pouts her lips at him.

Is Marion my kryptonite? Shea relents to her request. He takes a mental inventory of the security cameras that are mounted on the school building. "It shouldn't be a problem. But next time, you can sit it out and do the recording."

Marion smiles into Shea's eyes. "Thank you, darling."

His heart skips a beat.

She grins at Antonio. "Are you ready?"

He returns a mischievous smile.

Shea holds out his cell phone. The screen brightens as it comes to life.

Marion and Antonio point their index fingers at the phone. With a flash of plasma-charged energy, they are pulled through the screen and into the Hyper Realm.

Shea warns Archibald, "Do your conjuring, but nothing too crazy. We don't want to make them overly suspicious." He tosses a cell phone onto the grass behind a tree and instinctively holds his breath as he jumps into the phone.

Alone now, Archibald spreads his arms overhead with a sweeping gesture as he rotates a full 360 degrees. He kneels and hovers the palms of his hands over a patch of grass near the school's back entrance. Ever so slightly, ripples of energy radiate from beneath his hands. The waves grow stronger, and the ground below begins to vibrate.

A flourish of green sprouts bursts from the dirt alongside the perimeter of the building. The sprouts grow at a rapid pace and ascend the brick wall of the school's back entrance. They thicken into vines multiplying and intertwining. Climbing up and over the doorway, forming a dense archway. The vines populate themselves with fresh leaves. Buds appear and fully bloom into an array of pink and white flowers. The unnatural growth spurt continues until the archway completes itself. A beautiful creation that would fit gloriously in a tale of knights and fair maidens.

*

The low rumble of approaching motorcycles alerts Archibald that his efforts have paid off. He vanishes and at once reappears as a squirrel in the maple tree between the lot and the building. He intends to stay out of sight just in case his squirrel disguise is less than convincing.

Terrence and Hans cruise into the parking lot and head to opposite ends. They circle the lot slowly, looking for signs of supernatural activity.

Terrence rolls to a stop. He holds up one index finger to get Hans' attention. He calls out menacingly, "Archibald Abel. I know this fancy flower shit is your doing!" He points his cell phone at the floral archway. With a single blast, he effectively shreds the beautiful creation.

Hans' hands are poised above the cell phones taped to his handlebars in anticipation of a response. He recalls Cristobal's instructions to contact him at the first sign of the infamous Agricultural Age familiar named Archibald Abel. *Oops*. He quickly peels a cell phone from his handlebar and speed-dials Cristobal's number.

"Did he answer?" Terrence hisses.

"It's ringing!" Hans flashes Terrence a grin that fades to a look of confusion when an image of Antonio appears on the screen.

Antonio springs out from Hans' phone like a demented Jack-in-the-box.

Antonio's head, arms, and shoulders solidify into flesh, but from mid-torso down, he is a culmination of electrically charged pixels. He yells triumphantly at the alarmed German in his native language, "Wer ist jetzt der kleine Fisch?" *Who is the little fish now?* Antonio punctuates the sentence by tapping Hans on his forehead with a thumb drive.

With barely a chance to shriek, Hans turns plasma-tic and is instantly sucked into the thumb drive. His clothing flutters to the pavement.

"Gute Nacht, Colonel Klink!" Antonio yells triumphantly as he jumps completely out of the phone in full human form and surfs the seat of the still-rolling motorcycle. He dismounts with a back flip letting the bike tumble to the pavement.

Terrence squints his eyes even tighter than usual. He cannot comprehend what he has just witnessed. Rage and fear cause his mind to go primeval. Fight or flight. He rolls back the throttle, causing his back wheel to spin out. He belts out a full-throated yell as he races across the parking lot at Antonio. His free hand flicks out blasts of plasma from his cell phones.

Antonio has already conjured a plasma shield to absorb Terrence's blasts. He casually tosses Marion's pink and bejeweled cell phone in a high arch toward the fast-approaching Terrence.

Marion propels from the airborne phone and solidifies fifteen feet off the ground. She grabs her phone with her right hand and performs a midair tuck and roll. Her left hand is armed with a thumb drive.

Terrence shields his face with his arm against the flying girl.

"Tag, you're it, sweetie." Marion presses the thumb drive to Terrence's arm. The thumb drive hoovers him in a flesh-colored blur.

"Hey, you forgot your clothes," Marion giggles with surprise. She stashes the drive into her wizard's closet before touching her toe to one of the phones taped to Terrence's handlebars. She disappears in a whirl of pixels.

Terrence's empty jeans remain seated on the unmanned bike as it wobbles across the blacktop and crashes into Hans' bike.

Antonio steps up to collect the dozens of cell phones that are taped to the handlebars of both fallen motorcycles, purposely leaving one behind. He stuffs the confiscated phones into his wizard's closet, then turns and performs a theatric bow in Archibald's direction. He touches the toe of his shoe to the remaining phone and sinks into the Hyper Realm.

Archibald, still disguised as a squirrel, stares at the now quiet parking lot. His little jaw hangs agape. For the first time, he has witnessed some of the real potential of Computer Age magic.

chapter 21

Shea sits in front of the computer in his trailer/bedroom. He has hacked into the school's security cameras and recorded the events as they unfolded. Two camera views occupy the screen. One wide angle shot of the entire parking lot, and a close-up camera that focuses on the downed motorcycles. "Pretty adequate for a first attempt," he mumbles aloud. The grin on his face belies his understated evaluation of Antonio and Marion's bagging of their first two familiars.

Marion, followed by Antonio, spill out from the computer monitor and reconstitute on either side of Shea.

"I may have been adequate," Antonio agrees with Shea's assessment, "but Marion was stellar." He drapes his arm around her shoulders and pulls her close.

"Tell me you got that." Marion is dying to know.

"I recorded everything," Shea reassures her.

Antonio questions Shea as he pulls a thumb drive from his

wizard's closet. "Why were you so quick to agree with Archibald regarding fleeing the scene?" He takes a black marker from Shea's desktop and writes "Hans" on the drive, then passes the marker to Marion. "Sweetie?" He references the name that Marion called the familiar.

"Do I detect a hint of jealousy?" Marion grins. "Should I have called him, Sucker or Boy Toy?" She furrows her brows. "Do I need to work on my trash talk?"

"Your familiar's name is Terrence," Antonio informs her.

Shea finally responds to Antonio's question. "Archibald's suggestion about fleeing the scene made me suspicious. But the good news is we now have an opportunity to see if good old Archibald is playing us straight."

"Smart," Antonio compliments Shea.

"Wait, you don't trust Archibald?" Marion looks up from her thumb drive labeling with a puzzled look.

Shea shrugs his shoulders. "It's not wise to assume anything. Seriously, how well do we know the guy?" He motions with his chin to the monitor. "Check this out. The squirrelly little bastard is so close to the camera that he strains the focus every time he wags his stupid tail."

"I think the real question here is whether Archibald is aware he is impeding our view." Antonio squints at the blurred footage.

"Come on, guys," Marion pleads. "Let's give him the benefit of the doubt. At least until..."

On the monitor, Cristobal flashes into existence beside the two abandoned motorcycles. He pulls the hood of his satin robe off his grotesque head.

"There he is!" Marion points to the screen. "Can you zoom in on him?"

Shea touches the monitor and splays out his thumb and index finger. The camera zooms in and quickly focuses on Cristobal's face.

All three adepts lean back in shock at his appearance.

Antonio cringes, "Whoa, not what I expected."

"So many scales!" Marion squeaks. "Look, his skin folds where there are too many to fit. Gross!"

"What the hell is he wearing?" Shea comments on Cristobal's odd attire as they watch his head pivot from one motorcycle to the next. The front tire on Terrence's bike is still spinning.

Cristobal pokes at the discarded clothing with his bare foot then abruptly spins around and studies the shredded vine archway that Archibald had created. Like a detective, he turns his attention to the black tire track on the pavement left by Terrence's bike. He whirls around once more, making certain no one is sneaking up behind him. He positions his hands, ready to ward off a potential attack.

"He is definitely afraid of us," Antonio points out.

Cristobal stoops down to examine the bikes closer and runs his fingers along the strips of tape that once secured the cell phones to the handlebars. He scratches his butt as he studies the wreckage before him. His other arm reaches out and disappears into the thin air of his wizard's cupboard. His hand emerges wearing a thick industrial rubber glove and holding a military-style radio walkie-talkie.

"It's a shame we don't have audio."

*

Across the parking lot, Archibald, is still in squirrel form. He strains to hear what Cristobal is saying but doesn't dare risk peering from behind the tree. He uses the reflection from a nearby window to keep track of his lifelong nemesis.

Cristobal tentatively turns a dial on the handheld radio. After a moment, he replies defensively, "It is important." He crouches down, arms resting across his knees. "No, not a trace of them." Then a wince of his facial muscles. "I *was* talking about your tracking devices. Not a trace." Cristobal is up and pacing again. "We have hundreds of teams out in the world. No. This is a first." He viciously shakes his middle finger violently at the radio. He presses the button to disconnect the call. "ARE YOU KIDDING ME?!" He yells to no one.

He slams the radio into his wizard's closet and swings a clenched fist at an invisible target.

Cristobal takes one more look around before cinching up his robe which has fallen open.

*

Back in the trailer, the three adepts have been studying the computer screen intently. All three react to the sight of Cristobal's wardrobe malfunction.

"Oh. My. Gross!" Marion quickly averts her eyes.

"You can't un-see that." Antonio can't help but laugh. "The poor scoundrel appears distraught." He directs his question at the computer screen, "What now, pajama boy?"

"Is he wearing that thick rubber glove to protect him from the radio or to protect the radio from him?" Shea wonders.

Cristobal vanishes.

A moment later, he returns. With company.

"Wait, is that…?" Shea peers closely at the monitor. "Oh, my god. The squirrel just peed himself." He watches as a wet spot spreads along the branch that Archibald is standing on. "That has to be Tovenaar!" Shea points a capped sharpie at Cristobal's accomplice.

Antonio chimes in, "The Great A-hole of the Industrial Age."

"That is the meanest-looking face I have ever seen," Marion offers.

They watch as Tovenaar takes it upon himself to study the "crime" scene. He suddenly stares deliberately at the security camera and gestures with his thumb and index finger, causing the image on Shea's computer to zoom in until Tovenaar's face fills the screen.

Marion and Antonio both step back from the monitor with a start.

"Relax," Shea says. "He can control the mechanical functions of the camera, but I certainly doubt he has the computer prowess that he would need to see us."

On the screen, the dark circles under Tovenaar's eyes are the only hint of his advanced age. Otherwise, he appears to be in his mid-forties. His eyes are pale, but their color is not determinable on the black and white footage from the security camera. His hair is as dark as the sharply pressed suit that he wears. He has good muscle tone and the confident gait of a young man.

"He looks good for a three-hundred-and-something-year-old psychopath." Marion says, admiring the image, "He must moisturize."

Antonio snorts, "We'll see how his looks hold up when we take more and more of his familiars off the board."

Tovenaar points three fingers, middle, index, and ring menacingly at the camera.

"He is smart enough to assume we are watching." Antonio feels an icy chill up his spine. "This creep is going to be a worthy adversary."

"Still, we now know something about Tovenaar that we didn't know a moment ago," Marion says with hope in her voice. "He does not have the power to teleport. He needs Cristobal to do his teleporting for him. Like Archibald does for us"

As if on cue, Cristobal and Tovenaar vanish from the screen.

chapter 22

Archibald materializes in Shea's trailer, once again in human form. He loses his balance and falls into Antonio. "That's the closest I have ever been to the Grand Murderer." He leans forward his hands atop his knees. "I nearly pissed myself."

"You did," the three adepts chime in unison.

Archibald looks puzzled. "How could you…? Why would you…?"

Shea explains, "We were watching you through the school's security camera." He finger-slides the progress bar of the security footage on his computer screen. The video resumes at the very moment Cristobal appears in the parking lot with Tovenaar. Shea spreads his thumb and forefinger to zoom in on the micturating squirrel.

Archibald is mortified. "I did not expect you would be watching me."

"We needed to be sure we could trust you," Antonio further explains.

"That you weren't with *them*." Marion drapes an arm around Archibald's shoulder and assures him, "You did good."

"That hurts more than I would like to admit," Archibald confesses. "But smart." He studies the faces of the three confident adepts before warning them, "This is going to happen by nightfall."

"If not sooner," Antonio surmises.

"Tovenaar is not likely to rush into a situation he is not in full control of." Archibald is silently crunching the numbers. "He will command Cristobal to gather his familiars who are scattered throughout the world. It will take some time to retrieve them all."

"All of them?" Marion asks. A look of concern creases her forehead.

"Most anyway, to be sure. You three have already taken the magic of the Computer Age to levels far surpassing any earlier adepts that I know of. Tovenaar will not treat this threat lightly. I believe his lust for Master Llewellyn's soul stone will no longer be his priority." He looks at them, his eyes filled with concern. "The three of you have just become his primary targets."

"And he won't waste time trying to turn one of us," Antonio says bluntly. "He will go straight for the kill."

Shea reasons, "Unless he decides he needs an advanced Computer Age familiar who is powerful enough to work against future adepts."

"Listen to Shea," Archibald petitions. "Tovenaar always has a plan for all scenarios, and he certainly would have one for this situation. He is already three or four moves ahead of you." He then recalls, "Lawrence and your Principal are gathering computers. That will be useful for constructing a trap."

"We're good." Antonio casually dismisses the offer of help. "We are going to use his familiars' cell phones as our weapons. Tovenaar will not see that coming."

Shea and Marion nod in agreement.

"You three are not as worried as the situation calls for." Archibald persists, "Please do not underestimate the Industrial Wizard." He slaps the desk for emphasis. "For all our sakes."

Shea agrees. "We could use the extra computers as a distraction. Give the familiars something to occupy themselves with until we get around to thumb-driving them."

"Thumb-driving." Antonio smiles at Shea's invention of a new verb. "I like it."

"Do you mind picking up the computers, Archie?" Marion says with a hint of flirty charm in her voice. "Oh, and don't forget the thumb drives."

"Of course, it would be my honor, Milady, however, the last thing you need is a magical being from the Agricultural Age laying hands upon your computer drives. It usually has an undesired effect, like when Antonio sabotages his father's car simply for washing it."

"Do you know why that happens?" Antonio is intrigued. "Tell me."

"Your father's car is entirely a relic of the Industrial Age. It does not have a…"

"Computer." Antonio completes the sentence. "How did I miss that? It is so obvious."

Shea makes a mental note. *As smart as Antonio has become, a missed detail like one this could be fatal on the field of battle.*

"Shall we go to the school for the equipment?" Archibald is anxious to put the plan in motion.

"You're staying?" Marion is thrilled. "You're going to fight with us?"

"Reckless times, as they say." He raises his arms, and they all vanish.

*

Antonio, Marion, Shea, and Archibald appear in the hallway just outside the school's storage room.

Lawrence cracks open the door and immediately touches his lips with his index finger. He whispers to Archibald, "I smelt you coming," then turns his head and calls back into the room. "Um. I'm going to get a soda. Do you want one?"

Getting no response from the principal, he steps into the hallway and shuts the door behind him. In hushed tones, he tells Antonio, "She is intense. Keeps talking about murdering Cristobal."

"With good cause," Archibald remarks.

"I hear her talking. Is someone else in there?" Marion asks.

Lawrence shakes his head. "She has been talking the entire time and I don't think she said a dozen words to me. Bat shit. That's the worst one, right? Bat shit crazy. We loaded three carts with what must be a thousand pounds of computers on each of them." He looks amused. "This isn't petty theft, it's a full-blown heist."

Marion is concerned. "What can we do to help her."

"Do you know a psychiatrist?" Lawrence grins.

Shea glances at the time on his phone. "Do we really have time for this."

Marion slides her phone out from her hip pocket. She places a finger on the screen, causing plasma to sizzle. Her face relaxes into a trance-like state. Her eyes reflect faint traces of digital data. Five seconds pass.

"What the heck is this?" Lawrence snaps his fingers in front of her face but gets no reaction. "Someone snap her out of it."

"Relax Lawrence." Antonio restrains Lawrence's finger-snapping hand.

"Is Chainsaw possessed?" Lawrence is alarmed.

Another five seconds pass.

Shea grows concerned, "She's been in there a long time."

"Everyone's crazy," Lawrence's face reddens.

Suddenly, Marion eyes clear up. "We need to snap Principal Skinner out of her emotional psychosis." She purses her lips. "After that, it is up to her to commence with the healing process."

"What the hell just happened?" Lawrence demands.

"I just completed an on-line degree in psychology," Marion explains.

"You what?!" Lawrence barks, then raises his hands palms out. "Okay, it's cool. I will do my best to catch up. No, it's cool. Really. Chill. What did you do in the last ten seconds, Lawrence? Nothing," He answers his own question. "But Chainsaw got herself a freaking bachelor's degree."

"Doctorate."

"I got this." Antonio wants to hurry this along. He takes charge of the situation, swings the door open, and steps into the room.

The others follow him in, curious to see what Antonio plans to do to *snap her out of it.*

Principal Skinner is securing computer equipment onto a six-foot-long steel cart with bungee cords. "Oh, there you are," she says tiredly as they enter the room. The dark circles under her eyes hint at how mentally haggard and emotionally drained she is. She motions to two more carts stacked high with computers. "This is every computer in the building. I hope it is enough to kill that vulgar reprobate."

"Are you going to get in trouble for taking all of this?" Shea asks with concern.

Principal Skinner snorts back a cynical laugh. "What are they going to do? Fire me?" She reaches for another bungee cord. "I am no longer fit to be a principal, anyway."

"Your ordeal has adversely affected you," Antonio says in a calm voice as he approaches her. He is aware of feeling compassion. He has never felt the need to console someone, let alone a need to help Principal Skinner, a person he recently considered an adversary. *Is this a side effect of having an increased IQ?* He wonders.

"You don't know the least of it, Tonio," Principal Skinner says with a bitter expression on her face.

"It's Antonio now," he corrects her. He tells her in Spanish, "Estoy listo para mi examen final de español. *I am ready for my Spanish exam.* He smiles as Principal Skinner's eyebrow lift in surprise.

He switches to speaking French. "Ou si la demoiselle préfère, je pourrais passer le test en français?" *Or if the young lady prefers, I could take the test in French.*

Principal Skinner looks skeptical. "When did you learn two languages?"

He answers her in German, "Zwei Sprachen? Du musst mir mehr Anerkennung zollen." *Two languages? You must give me more credit than that.*

"How is he doing this?" she asks the room and is answered only with three knowing smiles and one equally baffled look from Lawrence.

In Russian, with a perfect accent, Antonio says "YA byl ochen' zanyat s momenta nashey posledney vstrechi."

"I don't understand Russian," she confesses.

Antonio translates, "I've been very busy since our last meeting."

In a half-hearted attempt to crack a joke, she says, "That is all very well and good, but if you can't speak Dutch, I cannot grade you above a C."

He replies, "Ik verwacht niet minder dan hoge normen."

"Are you messing with me?" she exclaims in a shrill voice.

It means, "I expect no less than high standards."

Principal Skinner cannot wrap her mind around Antonio's one-day transformation from problem child to prodigy. Antonio's display is enough to distract her from the recent torment she suffered. Her face relaxes slightly.

Antonio smiles, and says in Chinese, "Wǒ xiǎng, wǒmen dōu yǒu xīwàng." As her jaw drops incredulously, he translates, "There is hope for us all, I think."

Principal Skinner wraps her arms around Antonio and bursts into heaving sobs. She hugs him fervently and buries her face in his chest.

Antonio's arms float awkwardly as he is unsure how to handle this situation. He makes pleading eye contact with Marion.

Marion silently expresses a hugging motion with her arms.

Antonio clumsily returns Principal Skinner's hug and holds her until she is cried out and pulls away, embarrassed. "I am still going to call you Tonio."

"Not a chance," he teases.

"Get a room, you two." Lawrence chides them with an inelegant and inappropriate attempt to keep his own eyes from welling up. "Don't we still have to take all these computers someplace?"

"Oh, shush up Lasagna," Principal Skinner grins. She is far from being one hundred percent, but her emotional release has at least begun the healing process.

While everyone else was distracted by Principal Skinner and Antonio's heart-clenching moment, Marion took it upon herself to load up the computer equipment. She is low to the ground and uses all the strength in her legs to get one of the carts to roll forward. Once it is up to speed, she runs in front of it and motions to open her wizard's closet. The cart, with one thousand pounds of equipment, rolls in and vanishes.

Lawrence calls out, "Marion Grey, you're my hero."

Principal Skinner stares at Marion in disbelief. Yet another shock to her already strained mental fortitude.

"Shea and I will take the other two," Antonio offers as he looks around for the other two carts but cannot seem to find them.

"I already took care of it." Marion laughs, "Don't worry, you boys can practice being chivalrous later."

Shea questions Archibald, "Exactly how much stuff can these wizard closets hold?"

Archibald has a perplexed look on his face as well. "I never thought to carry more than a cupboard's worth. If I had thought to use it as a warehouse, the last few hundred years would have been far less complicated."

"So where are we doing this?" Marion wants to know.

Archibald advises, "I always encouraged the other adepts to stage their traps at secluded locations. Somewhere far from authorities and innocent bystanders."

The three share a knowing look. They just figured out why the earlier groups of adepts may have failed. They followed Archibald's advice.

Antonio has his own ideas. "Anywhere with 5G network capabilities suits me. We will need to access Wi-Fi networks."

"That would exclude a secluded area, but to Archibald's point we could use a little elbow room." Shea includes Archibald's suggestion as if he values his opinion, even though he is beginning to believe they might be better off without him.

"I would like to avoid innocent bystanders," Marion adds softly.

Lawrence offers a suggestion. "The neighborhood surrounding the Crab Meadow salt marsh has 5G. When we were there earlier, I hacked into the Wi-Fi of a house on Waterside Drive. The password was *password1*."

Marion places her index finger an inch from the screen on her cell phone and launches the weather app. She reports tonight's weather forecast. "Mostly cloudless sky with a full moon. High tide isn't until midnight."

Antonio grins. "Perfect. It will be dark at nine and we will not have to worry about the high tide turning the marsh into a virtual lake while we are thumb-driving familiars."

"Speaking of familiars, we need to remember to deposit the thumb

drives into our wizard's closets before we re-enter the Hyper Realm,"
Shea adds. "We can't take the risk of spreading a familiar virus
across the Web."

"I like it." Marion giggles as she pictures in her mind how
tonight's events are sure to unfold.

Principal Skinner is more than a bit troubled by Marion's
transition from being a reserved student to a dangerous young woman
with disturbing abilities. She steps back to distance herself from her.

Marion steps forward and drapes an arm around the principal's
shoulders and squeezes tight. "Don't you worry, Ms. S. We are going to
deliver a monumental ass-kicking."

"You are talking about putting people in thumb drives," she frowns.

"Familiars," Antonio clarifies.

"Can regular people be thumb-drived?" Lawrence inquires.

Antonio reaches out with an empty thumb drive and presses it
firmly to Lawrence's forehead leaving an indent. He does not get
sucked in. "Question answered."

"Don't you ever… I am not even kidding." He massages his
forehead with a knuckle and snaps at Antonio. "That was SO out of line."

Archibald assures Principal Skinner, "In many ways, their magic
already rivals my own."

"You are capable of vanishing at will. How is any of this
possible?" Principal Skinner sounds like she is going to lose it again.

Archibald smiles. "Earlier today, Lawrence eavesdropped on my
conversation about how this all began. He will get you up to speed."

"Okay, we should begin setting the trap," Shea interrupts. "Then
I would like to have dinner with my folks before going back inside the
Hyper Realm for a little pre-battle preparation."

"Dinner with our folks? Do we have time for that?" Antonio
questions the need for it.

"Just in case." Marion reads his blank stare. "Just in case it all goes wrong, and we don't win." She turns away to conceal the tears brimming in her eyes.

"We have this. What can possibly go wrong?" Antonio throws it back at her.

Shea steps in, "Let's not get cocky. When we are back inside the Hyper Realm, we can put a plan through a million scenarios. Let's not mess this up with a stupid mistake or unforced errors." He raises his clenched fists, one each for Marion and Antonio. They don't leave him hanging.

chapter 23

Except for the occasional paddle-boarder people respect the 'nature preserve' aspect of the Crab Meadow Salt Marsh and stay out of it. Being this late in the day, the odds of being spotted by a casual observer is slim to none.

Not taking chances, Marion and Lawrence stand partially concealed behind a dense cluster of tall grasses. Marion reaches her hand into her wizard's closet to expose the rail of one of the carts that is loaded with computers.

Lawrence grabs hold of it and plants his feet in a determined stance on the soft ground.

Marion slowly backs away until the full length of the cart slides out with a thud. Its caster wheels sink into the marsh floor.

All three piles of decoy computers are now in place. Marion shields her eyes and gazes across the marsh at Shea. He stands beside the westernmost group of computers that she deposited ten minutes ago and gives her a thumbs up. She returns the gesture.

Marion looks towards the third point of the triangle of computers.

Antonio sees her looking and speaks through her phone. "Not much of a decoy unless we figure out a way to power them up." He wasn't keen on this idea from the beginning. "Maybe Christmas lights and tiki torches will give the appearance they are powered up," he adds sarcastically.

Lawrence looks doubtful. "So, Chainsaw, what are we going to do with three piles of computers and only one generator, huh?"

Marion quickly swipes her thumb across the screen of her phone. A quarter-sized glob of pink plasma shoots out and hits Lawrence in the chest, where it spins wildly before fading away.

"Hey! What was that for?"

Marion scolds him sternly, "Don't call me that."

Lawrence looks down at the pinkish stain on his dark blue shirt. "You're malicious."

Marion frowns. "These computers are essentially decoys, so they need only to look like they're working."

Still rubbing his sore spot, Lawrence mumbles, "It would be cooler if they worked, though. We could put on a real show for the dumb chucks."

"You make a valid point." Marion ponders for a moment. She reaches into her wizard's closet and pulls out one of the black cell phones they collected from the motorcycles. She uses it to scan the web for an answer. "Not any actual solution to our dilemma on the internet, but I have a hunch." She grabs a power cord from one of the computers on the cart. "The internet is pure, boundless energy," she explains her theory as she moves the three prongs of the power cord closer to the phone. "Let's see what happens if I…"

With a plasma-tic slurp, the chord gets sucked into the phone. The computer on the cart chimes as it powers up.

"You did it!" Lawrence is amazed.

Marion is as surprised as Lawrence that it worked.

"But that's not possible."

"Until it is," she smiles. Marion scowls at the number of computers that are still waiting to be powered up. To save time, she hands Lawrence another power cord. "Archie said he thought you have an ability for magic. Do you want to test that theory?"

"He said I *might* have some potential. Nothing to brag about." Lawrence swallows anxiously as she hands him the cord and an extra cell phone. "What if I get sucked in?"

"Just let go of the plug if you feel it pull." Marion shrugs innocently. "Don't worry. I'll come to get you."

Lawrence tentatively touches the power cord to the phone and shrieks as a surge of plasma swallows the cord, then surges up his hand and forearm. He panics. "It burns! Get it off!"

Marion snatches his wrist and pulls Lawrence's hand away from the phone. "Are you okay?"

Lawrence wipes his hand frantically on the grass. "It won't come off." He runs to the closest stream of water and reaches down to scrub the plasma off.

Antonio and Shea flash in from the live computer next to Marion. They both ask in unison, "What just happened?"

Marion is embarrassed and shameful for not consulting with anyone before trying her experiment. She stammers, "I, well, I had an idea to power up the computers, and I…Oh Lawrence, I'm so sorry." She feels terrible he is injured.

Antonio kneels beside Lawrence who is lying by the stream with his arm outstretched in the water. "Let's see it, Buddy." He uses his phone to 'vacuum' the remaining plasma from Lawrence's arm.

Lawrence gets back onto his knees and holds out his hand. His entire forearm, hand, and fingers bare dark purple bruises. "It doesn't hurt anymore," he lies and wiggles his fingers to prove it. "Hey look. My hand is like tattooed with computer stuff."

The bruise fascinates Shea. "It does resemble the random data in the Hyper Realm."

Archibald appears. "What on earth did you do? I sensed a non-magical being trying to wield raw magic." He is concerned and angry.

Marion defends herself. "But you said he has potential abilities…"

"Potential abilities. This level of sorcery is only for a true adept, or an apprentice, or a wizard, or at the very least, a familiar." Archibald lectures her. "And as an adept, you cannot bind a familiar."

"Wait. I wasn't trying to…" Marion's face grows hot. She looks away, not wanting anyone to see the tears welling in her eyes.

Archibald's voice softens, "It was an innocent mistake, my dear, and Lawrence is reasonably robust." He wants to put a hand on Marion's shoulder to comfort her, but refrains. "Do not allow this incident to let you second-guess your resolve. You must be sharp and decisive against Tovenaar."

Marion swipes her eyes and forces away any feelings of self-doubt. "Do we have enough time to put all these power cords into the internet and still have time to visit our parents? Maybe for the last time…" her voice trails off.

"I got this." Lawrence kindly offers. "I will plug the computers into successive power strips. You know, like a pyramid. Then, when you return, all you will have to do is plug one chord into a cell phone." He smiles proudly at his wise idea.

"Don't you want to go home and eat something?" Antonio eyes Lawrence suspiciously. He is aware of Lawrence's relentless appetite for food.

"Tonight is my parents' bowling night. A PB&J is all I have to look forward to. Now go do what you gotta do." He turns his back on the group and heads over to the cart to gather the power strips.

Antonio examines the power cord that Marion had plugged into the cell phone. He quietly confers with Shea. "Do you think this is a good idea?"

"It appears to be working." Shea shrugs his shoulders. "I doubt I would have thought to do this."

Marion continues to struggle with her poor decision. *Not my best moment. I will be focused tonight, and I will not make another mistake like this one.*

Antonio notices the sad look on her adorable face, and assumes she is worrying about the possibility of never seeing her mom again. He calls out to Lawrence, "Hey Lasagna, we won't be long."

Antonio, Shea, and Marion simultaneously dive into a computer and are gone.

Archibald disappears as well.

Lawrence smiles briefly at being called by his self-appointed nickname, but winces. He shakes out his bruised hand and massages it exhaling a sigh of relief. He wasn't sure if he could hide his pain from Marion for much longer.

A moment later Archibald returns holding two deli bags. "You should eat." He offers Lawrence both bags.

"Thanks, dude." He snatches both bags. "One would have been plenty."

"Only one is for you. Your principal is on the way. Please convince her to leave the premises once the skirmish ensues. Escort her safely away if you must."

"But then I won't be here…"

Archibald exits before Lawrence can argue.

chapter 24

A small bedroom with gray walls and a well-worn hardwood oak floor stands empty. A surfboard lies on a rack above the twin-sized bed. Skateboards with varying degrees of scraped paint from rough use are thrown in a corner. Dirty clothes are strewn about the dusty floor. The bed is unmade. Three cluttered shelves display tools, skateboard paraphernalia, and a scattering of old-school CD music discs.

A laptop computer plastered with skateboard brand stickers sits upon a foldout table that serves as a desk. The computer powers on.

Antonio spills out of it and onto his bedroom floor. He stands up and looks around as if seeing his room for the first time.

"Gross."

The bell at the front door rings.

*

Marion, now wearing jeans and a hoodie, smiles and waves a little wave when Antonio's father answers the door.

Mr. Marcantonio still wears his mechanic's coveralls and an old school pocket protector with one pen in it. "Hello, Marion. I'm guessing you're here to see Tonio?" He grins. "I always knew you two would end up together. The way you were always teasing each other. Childhood hatred has a way of working itself out. It was like that with Tonio's mother and me." He touches his hand to his heart. "God bless her."

Marion smiles at his logic, and replies jokingly, "Can you tell Antonio that his childhood bully is here to smack him around?"

Mr. Marcantonio laughs. "Tonio's not here, but I'll tell him…"

"I'm right here, Dad." Antonio walks up behind his father.

Mr. Marcantonio is startled. "When did you…? I didn't know you were home. I didn't hear your crazy music blasting."

Antonio looks past his father at Marion. "Are you staying for dinner?"

Marion simply smiles and nods.

Mr. Marcantonio offers. "It's still nice enough to eat outside. You two make yourself comfortable and I will be out in two shakes."

*

The sun is low enough in the sky to cast golden rays before the official sunset.

The garage door is open showing off Mr. Marcantonio's Roadster.

Antonio and Marion sit on foldout lawn chairs, quietly sipping root beer from cans. Antonio breaks the silence. "So, that was a quick visit."

Marion watches a bunny hop across the driveway. "She wasn't home. I tracked her cell phone to a bar that is hosting a speed-dating event. She seemed happy, so I didn't want to bother her." She looks at Antonio and quickly turns away. "We'll make it home tonight," she barely whispers. "I'll tell her I love her then." She bites the bottom of her lip to prevent it from quivering.

Antonio takes a moment before responding. "When Shea finishes with his parents, we will meet in the Hyper Realm. We can use all the time we need to perfect our battle plan." He takes her hand in his and gently squeezes it. "I cannot fathom how we can possibly screw this up."

Marion cheers up slightly. "I think the universe is ready to get the Computer Age started already."

Mr. Marcantonio kicks open the screen door while balancing a tray of reheated leftover pizza slices on tin foil sheets. He serves Marion first. "Careful, they're still hot."

Marion gently takes two edges of the foil and places it on her lap. "Thank you, Mr. Marcantonio."

"And one for… Antonio now, is it?"

Antonio takes his slice. "Ah, a true gastronomic delight."

"Now I know you're just being a smart-ass." Mr. Marcantonio takes his seat on a chair and places the tray with a remaining slice and a can of beer on his lap. He pops open the top of the can and looks at Marion. "I'm guessing all these big words and fancy talk are your influence."

"I wish I could take credit," she replies through a mouthful, "but Antonio has far exceeded me in knowledge." She challenges Mr. Marcantonio. "Ask him anything. I'll bet he has the answer."

"He always has an answer," Mr. Marcantonio teases.

"Easy, Pops," Antonio warns.

"I think he's smarter than he looks." Marion giggles and tickles Antonio under his chin.

Mr. Marcantonio's sudden laugh causes him to choke a little on a bite of pizza. "I like this lass." He crushes his empty beer can and tosses it toward a trashcan. "Okay then, smart guy, give me an example of your newfound brain power. Tell me something I don't know," he challenges his son.

Uncharacteristically, Antonio is feeling guilty for giving his old man so much grief these past few years and decides to use this opportunity to help him out. "For starters, the reason you are having recurrent engine problems with your Roadster is that the spark plug gap should be .035 and not .027, as the poor-quality Xerox copy of a user manual that you purchased at a car show would have you believe."

Mr. Marcantonio swallows his bite of pizza before asking, "How do you know about spark plug gaps?" He is unaccustomed to his son schooling him about matters on a combustion engine. "Okay, smart guy." He presents his son with a mathematical word problem that auto mechanics often use. "A pair of gears has a velocity ratio of 3.20. The pinion has twenty teeth, and its circular pitch is 78.54 mm. What is the number of teeth on the driven gear?"

Antonio answers almost before his father finishes the sentence. "Sixty-four. There are sixty-four teeth on the drive gear."

Mr. Marcantonio is at a loss for words. He slides the pen from his pocket protector and double checks the math on a scrap of paper. "Son-of-a-"

"So, I expect the old girl will be purring smoothly by the time I get back," Antonio challenges his dad.

"If you're right about the spark plug gap being 035, I might just get you two Christmas presents this year." He hurries over to pop the hood on the Roadster.

While his father has his back turned, Antonio tosses a black cell phone onto the lawn and steps onto it. He enters the Hyper Realm.

Marion calls out, "Bye, Mr. Marcantonio. Thanks for dinner!" She touches her toe to the phone and flashes out.

Antonio's father looks back. "You're leaving?" He looks around for his son and *future daughter-in-law*. He stretches his neck to peer down the street wondering where they went.

*

The porch light flicks on at the Blakely residence. Shea's parents see him to the door. They are both dressed in vintage cruise wear.

"It's a school night," his mom reminds him. "Don't stay out too late."

"I won't be late, but don't wait up," Shea says hopefully and turns to leave. He pushes open the screened storm door but hesitates. "If I haven't mentioned it before, thanks for moving us to Huntsport." He hugs his mom and pulls his father in with his free arm.

"Of course, honey." Mrs. Blakely is relieved that Shea may finally be snapping out of his teenage funk.

Mr. Blakely awkwardly returns Shea's hug.

Just then, Marion and Antonio flash in from a cell phone that Shea left hidden behind the trailer. They step around the camper to make their presence known.

Mrs. Blakely notices them. "Are these your new friends, dear?"

Shea looks over and back to his parents. "If one of them brings up snowmobiles, just play along." A quick wink to let them know they are in on a joke. He trots over to greet Marion and Antonio.

"Guys, can you just meet my parents for a minute?"

"Of course," Marion waves in their direction.

The Blakely's step outside as Marion and Antonio walk up the path to greet them. Marion extends her hand and introduces herself. "Hi, I'm Marion. It's nice to finally meet you."

Shea's parents look at her with puzzled expressions.

As soon as she hears herself say the words, she realizes that she must sound like a real ditz. She has only known Shea for less than 48 hours.

Antonio comes to her rescue. "Hi, I'm Antonio. I love what you have done with this place. It will surely increase the property value for the entire neighborhood." He shakes Carmine's hand heartily.

Carmine instantly takes a shine to Shea's new friends. "Well, thank you. I realized its potential the moment I saw it. What do you kids have planned for tonight?"

Marion looks down at the ground, unable to respond truthfully.

Antonio once again steps in. He recalls Shea's smart-ass remark on the school field earlier and uses the opportunity to deflect the question. "Shea promised to show us his Like a Boss move."

"Snowmobiles and roman candles, I believe is what he said." Marion cheerfully joins in. She is all too happy to play along and put Shea on the spot.

Mrs. Blakely entertains Shea's earlier request and says with an exasperated tone in her voice, "Again, with the snowmobiles."

Mr. Blakely also takes part in the farce. "There isn't even snow on the ground." He taps on the side of his head with his index finger and informs Marion and Antonio, "Sometimes you gotta remind him to think."

This gets a delightful squeal from Marion.

Antonio expresses a look of amused surprise. He knows full well that Shea does not have a move involving two snowmobiles and a Roman candle. But the fact that Shea expected this scenario and conned his parents into going along with it, is nothing short of masterful.

"Well, it was very nice to meet you both," Marion extends her hand once again.

"The pleasure is all ours, honey," Mrs. Blakely smiles warmly.

"Have fun, kids," Mr. Blakely offers as he turns to open the screen door for his wife. He hesitates, then looks back, "Where did you kids say you were …?" His voice trails off.

The three have already vanished.

Mrs. Blakely turns to hear the answer and exchanges a stunned look with Carmine. She shrugs her shoulders, "Kids these days. They come and go so quickly."

<h1 style="text-align:center">chapter 25</h1>

Lawrence and Principal Skinner sit on the grass beside a stack of computers. Principal Skinner is busy inserting the plugs of six power strips into yet another power strip, as Lawrence does his best to retell Archibald's story.

"And there you have it. A familiar from the Agricultural Age is here to help three almost wizards of the Computer Age, to take down a wizard of the Industrial Age."

"That is some tall tale, Lawrence." The principal stands to stretch her legs. "I am supposed to believe that Archibald is two hundred years of age."

"He is more like three hundred years old," Lawrence corrects her.

"And that Tonio--"

"Antonio," Lawrence corrects her once more.

"And that Antonio, Marion, and the new boy…"

"Shea." Lawrence rolls his eyes.

"And that Shea, Marion, and Antonio are going to fight this wizard of the Industrial Age and his familiars, who he has corrupted from Computer Age students." She sits down on the grass. "It really is a lot of BS to swallow in one sitting. I mean…"

"It doesn't really matter if you believe it, or not. It's all happening anyway." He stares again at the picture on his arm that has come into focus. "I knew it. Look at this." He shows her his bruised forearm. "The bruise keeps changing. Ten minutes ago, it looked like a weirdo with crazy hair and his tongue sticking out. Now it's a…Whoa!"

Principal Skinner glances at his arm. The random pixel-looking bruise seems to have rearranged to bear the image of a woman, naked from the waist up.

"Lawrence! Shame on you!"

"Whatever," Lawrence says, admiring the image before continuing with his self-interrupted conversation. "You saw for yourself, Antonio speaking in six different languages, not including English. You watched as Marion made three carts full of computers disappear into thin air. And Shea, well, we haven't seen him do much of anything yet, but I am sure he has some tricks up his sleeve."

Principal Skinner must admit, "I think somebody will need to rewrite the history books when this is all said and done."

"I think you and Archibald should rewrite the books," Lawrence suggests. "He has a ton of firsthand knowledge."

"Archibald doesn't think we should be here," she reminds him.

"That's another problem." Lawrence stands back up. "But what's really bothering me is how are we going to be of any real help?"

The principal considers. "Antonio seems to think you are an agent of chaos."

Lawrence laughs aloud at a thought that just came to mind. "Every good battle I have ever seen, in the movies anyway, had a wicked soundtrack. I will create a score so intimidating that our enemies will soil their knickers."

"Lawrence Brown, what do you know about composing music?" Principal Skinner asks in a cynical tone of voice.

"Not enough," he admits. "But I do pay attention in music class." He holds his elbow out to Ms. Skinner. "Shall we?"

She graciously accepts and lets him lead her to the live computer.

chapter 26

Marion, Antonio, and Shea are back in the Hyper Realm. They have learned how to filter out the onslaught of data that incessantly bombards them. Each of them has created their own happy place.

Marion lays prone on a sun dappled, grassy hillside dotted with craggy boulders. Large puffy clouds float overhead.

Streaks of random data scratch across the idyllic scenery disrupting its chill sense of serenity. Marion reaches up and sweeps her hand across the blemishes. A cool breeze gently caresses her face as the scenery becomes flawless.

"Castle images," Marion commands. Random images of castles appear in front of her like a slideshow. She swipes to the right before selecting a large stone castle with spire roofs. It materializes in the hazy distance.

Something is missing. "Puppies," she calls out gleefully. All at once, a hundred puppies of different breeds appear and frolic in the surrounding meadow. Her virtual worldview is complete.

Marion turns her attention to her clothing. Her apparel morphs through a variety of contemporary military styles. The designs and colors of her outfits change from colored fabrics to darkly colored leathers and plastics. Elements of armor and chain mail incorporate themselves into the apparel.

More aggressive, she thinks.

Blades, spikes, and an assortment of weapons adorn her outfits in an endless sweep of options. The continual morphing settles on a final ensemble.

A mirror image appears before her. She strikes a fierce pose, then breaks into laughter. She looks dangerous, sexy, and insane.

"Pllippptttt." She blows a raspberry. The mirror image disappears, and her clothes become once again jeans and a hoodie.

She lays back onto the grass and agonizes. "I still can't believe I caused Lawrence to get hurt."

"I wouldn't worry about it," Antonio's voice reassures her.

From Antonio's perspective, he is lying back on a long wooden surfboard which comfortably rides the swells of turquoise Caribbean water. Occasionally, a flying fish will break the surface. He soaks in the sun, wearing nothing but colorful board shorts.

"Dude, why are you in space?"

Shea floats in a vast expanse of blackness populated by planets, galaxies, and stars. "I've always wondered what zero gravity felt like." He reaches out and flicks a star against a planet's surface, creating small circular ripples at impact. "I have been contemplating perspective and whether we are viewing everything as we should."

Although they exist in their own virtual realities, their positions create a perfect triangle with their heads at the center and their feet radiating out to be the three points.

Antonio yawns loudly. "Enlighten us."

"Tovenaar, for example. We view him as a dangerous adversary, a monstrous sorcerer. In his retelling, Archibald insinuated that Tovenaar's influence affects everyone from bankers to crime lords. Considering that there is no historical evidence that Tovenaar even exists, how do others perceive him?"

"That is interesting." Marion perks up. "Is he seen as being a god or a devil or a dictator, or something entirely different?"

Antonio opens his eyes. "The tricky aspect of your question is that every person Tovenaar has ever crossed paths with could potentially see him differently. An enemy, a criminal, an authority figure, a business executive, a drinking buddy…"

"A husband, a father," Marion chimes in.

Shea continues, "I'm thinking that very few people are aware he is a wizard, and he uses an elaborate web of aliases. But how does he keep track of them all for so many decades? Or worse yet, he extends his influence by magic alone and never needs to even interact with mere mortals."

"He definitely interacts with mere mortals," Antonio stipulates. "If not, he would have no reason to dress as sharply as he does."

"Good point. So, we need to figure out, what exactly is his motivation for getting up in the morning?" Marion poses the question.

"I don't give a shit." Shea flicks at a star causing it to ricochet through space. "We just need to figure out how to take him down. We can fill in the blanks at our leisure after we have nullified him."

Antonio closes his eyes again. "We also need to figure out what it will take for us to become wizards."

"All while thumb-driving a horde of familiars." Marion still feels overwhelmed despite her new powers. She adds under her breath, "Should be a cinch,"

Antonio senses her anxiety. "Don't forget, we can meet back here to review and update our game plan, as necessary. As far as Tovenaar and his creepy minions are concerned, they will perceive us as waging a relentless attack from every corner of the marsh. No matter how long we spend in here."

Shea grins. "Here's an odd question. Why is it when we thumb-drive familiars, their clothes don't get sucked in with them?"

Antonio chuckles. "And how is it that *our* clothing and phones accompany us into cyberspace?"

"Didn't Archibald mention that nothing happens without intention?" Marion asks.

"I like that theory." Antonio sits up on his surfboard and stretches his arms out. He's getting bored with this conversation. He's ready to kick some familiar ass.

Shea continues the conversation. "Can they even survive in the Hyper Realm? Or on thumb drives for that matter?"

Marion suddenly sits up. "We should make sure."

Antonio raises an eyebrow. "Do you want to try entering a thumb drive to find out?"

"No, thank you very much," she shudders at the thought.

From a distance, a voice calls out to them. For Marion, it echoes across the rolling hills. For Antonio, the voice is louder each time his surfboard crests a wave. And for Shea, it is cold and clear as a laser through the vacuum of space. The message is the same for all three.

"Hey guys, we are ready when you are." Lawrence has figured out a way to communicate with them in the Hyper Realm.

"Questions to ponder at another time." Antonio allows the seascape he was happily relaxing in crumble back into a chaotic storm of pixels and data.

Marion and Shea appear beside him.

They all flash out of the Hyper Realm.

chapter 27

The moon is not full, but it casts more than enough light to illuminate a silvery maze of waterways that meander throughout the marsh. Occasional rushes of wind blow across the tall grasses creating an eeriness of sea-like movement. Flashes of heat lightning flicker randomly across the night sky.

Lawrence tries yet again to lighten the somber mood with a lame joke. "Why was six so upset?"

Archibald and Principal Skinner groan.

With a flash of light, Marion, Antonio, and Shea burst from Lawrence's phone.

"Hey!" Lawrence complains. "That is sensitive equipment."

Principal Skinner starts defensively and raises a spade shovel to strike. "There is no getting used to all this. It still freaks me out," she says apologetically and lowers the shovel.

Only Archibald seems unperturbed by the trio's brusque arrival.

"Where did you get a shovel?"

"The janitor's closet."

Lawrence checks his phone and scrutinizes it for damage.

"Principal Skinner, you should not be here when this transpires," Antonio advises. "The same goes for you, Lawrence."

"Don't worry about it," Lawrence replies. "We are going to hang back in that neighborhood across that street over there. We will spot their moves for you. Oh, and we produced an ass-kicking soundtrack for when the battle goes down. It's a file labeled 'Choke out the Mofo's. The Principal and I put it together. It will get you pumped." He smiles proudly. "I suggest we blast it through all the computers and even on all the scumbags' phones."

"That reminds me," Marion pulls a thumb drive from her wizard's closet. With a snap of her wrist, the familiar named Terrence flows out in a pixel stream from the drive and onto the ground where he solidifies. He is still naked. Terrence lets out a shriek and covers himself with his hands.

Marion reaches down and taps his forehead with the thumb drive, sucking him back in. "He seems okay," she announces.

"Oh snap!" Lawrence's eyes bug out.

"Marion, you truly are beginning to frighten me." Principal Skinner can almost empathize with Terrence's dilemma.

"Lawrence, how were you able to call us just now?" Shea changes the subject.

Lawrence holds up his hand. "Check this out. The weird bruise changes every time I look at it."

Sure enough, along with the random code imprinted on his skin, there is a partial image of a motorcyclist jumping off a ramp over a line of school buses.

"I don't know who this dude is, but he looks pretty rad." The image mesmerizes Lawrence. "The crazy thing is it will be a different picture in a couple of minutes."

Shea's grimaces. "That still doesn't explain how you called us."

"So, check this out. I laid my hand on the computer screen the way you do. I concentrated in my head that I wanted to get your attention and let you know we were waiting for you, and *viola*."

"I feel a little better about getting you hurt," Marion laughs with a sigh of relief.

"It's cool," Lawrence assures her. "My hand can access the internet now. It's like I have Braille or something."

"I look forward to considering how that works later, but business first." Antonio looks at Archibald. "Please help me out here. I cannot, for the life of me, figure out what role you will play in our upcoming Mêlée. I'm thinking maybe you sit this one out with these two." He gestures to Principal Skinner and Lawrence.

The rest of the group looks visibly stunned by Antonio's cold-hearted suggestion.

Archibald is at a loss. He has finally committed to joining the fight. The last thing he expected was to have his value questioned. He stammers to justify his usefulness. "Who else is going to, I mean… someone has to… Cristobal, someone needs to counter Cristobal's malice."

"You told us yourself that you cannot harm Tovenaar or even Cristobal," Antonio counters.

Archibald grows defensive. "That was when Cristobal was an apprentice wizard. We are both familiars now, so..."

Antonio presses. "Cristobal has been a familiar for hundreds of years and yet you keep running from him."

"What is wrong with you?" Marion interrupts Antonio and comes to Archibald's defense. "Of course we need Archibald. If it weren't for his warning us what was coming, one of us would have black scales on their face and the other two would be dead, or worse."

Antonio raises his voice to make his point. "You heard what he said earlier. He is a jinx with computers. I just think he will be safer off the field with Lawrence and Principal Skinner."

Archibald tries to speak, but his words get caught up in his throat. He takes a deep breath before turning his back on the group. He walks dejectedly away and heads towards the neighborhood where Lawrence and Ms. Skinner plan to hide out.

"You're a jerk," Marion accuses Antonio.

He does not respond to her and instead looks to Shea. "Do you have an opinion on this?"

Shea exhales loudly. "I can't fault your logic," he frowns at the sight of Archibald walking away, "but a little tact, maybe?"

Marion purses her lips and glares at them both before chasing after Archibald.

After an awkward moment, a thought occurs to Shea. "Tell me, how are we going to invite Tovenaar to our little trap?"

Antonio considers. "We will simply…"

"Wait, I got it," Shea interrupts. "Tovenaar cannot sense when Computer Age magic occurs. That means using Agricultural Age magic to tip off his Agricultural Aged familiar to our whereabouts is our only workable choice."

Antonio rubs his face with the palm of his hand as he processes Shea's logic. He looks over at Lawrence and Principal Skinner, who are regarding him with disparaging expressions. "Okay, so I was wrong," he admits. "We'll give Marion another minute to console him and then I will apologize and convince him we legitimately require his help."

Lawrence's face brightens. "Maybe start with something like, I'm sorry for being such a douche bag."

"An inconsiderate philistine. That would be my suggestion," Principal Skinner chimes in.

"Or a slack-jawed dickhead," Lawrence continues.

"Churlish ingrate," Principal Skinner piles on.

Antonio is relieved to see Marion returning with Archibald, if only to put an end to this verbal assault. He extends his hand. "I am sorry Archibald. Of course, we need you. I was just being a churlish dickhead."

Lawrence and Ms. Skinner snicker.

"I'm not certain what that means," Archibald confesses, allowing Antonio to shake his hand, "but I accept your apology."

"Inconsiderate jerk, I meant to say," Antonio continues. "I am concerned that your presence on the battlefield may provide Tovenaar an opportunity to relieve you of your master's soul stone. That is a complication that may have dire consequences."

"I understand your apprehension," Archibald assures Antonio. "However, it is impossible to access another's wizard's cupboard. In case of my demise, Master Llewellyn's soul stone will be unattainable to everyone, including the Prime Wizard of the Industrial Age. It will be lost to history." He eyeballs the three adepts. "Good enough?"

"Maybe, but still, please don't get caught," Marion voices her concern.

"I would like to discuss the magic you are going to perform this time to lure the buzzards," Shea interjects. "Something more useful than pretty flowers, I hope."

Archibald grins. He can't help but be impressed by Shea's attention to detail regarding this trap.

"How about I grow a sharp variety of saw grass around your piles of computers? It will tear at their clothes and scratch at their flesh should they venture too close. Plus, it will blend in with the existing grasses."

Shea likes the idea but is concerned. "Do we want to infest this nice salt marsh with something invasive like saw grass?"

"I will give the saw grass a lifespan of one hour," Archibald assures him. "Afterwards, it will all crumble to dust."

"Sounds good." Antonio is eager for this battle to begin. He has a feeling of butterflies in his stomach, like a quarterback on game day. He addresses the group, "Is there anything else before we light this up?"

"I think we got it covered," Shea's voice cracks. He clears his throat in embarrassment.

Marion nervously twists her hair. "I'm ready."

Archibald remains stoic, his voice void of emotion. "Ready when you are."

Principal Skinner's lips are pressed as tightly as her white-knuckled fingers that grasp the spade shovel.

Lawrence has his hand patiently raised in the air.

"Yes?" Antonio exhales loudly through his nose.

"Is there a way you can get me access to their phones? I figure I can report on the familiars' movements."

"That won't be necessary." Antonio shoots down Lawrence's idea.

Lawrence tries again. "But I could, like, mess with their heads. Create cranial frenzy in their nasty little minds." He waits a moment and says pleadingly, "C'mon man, let me do something to help!"

"Consider it done," Marion promises.

"Okay, everyone, bring it in." Shea motions everyone into a huddle. "It is time to start up the Computer Age for real."

Antonio is getting antsy. "The quicker we do this, the less chance there is of making a mistake. If we must react to any sort of surprise threat from Tovenaar, we discuss it calmly in the Hyper Realm."

Shea and Marion agree.

"Let's do this," Antonio commands. He holds up his hand and makes a fist.

"Wait!"

All eyes turn to Principal Skinner.

"Successful battles in history often began with a prayer." She looks around at the group, "Unfortunately, I am not in a prayerful state of mind to say one, but I think that someone should."

"I'll give it a shot," Marion responds with sweeping arms to include themselves as well as their enemies. She utters a prayer that only a truly innocent soul would dare implore. "MAY WE ALL GET WHAT WE DESERVE!"

The group gasps.

"I don't think you're getting this whole pre-battle prayer concept." Shea grins.

"That is one reckless and alarming prayer, kiddo," Antonio remarks as he recounts a mental list of some not-too-cool acts he has committed over the years.

"It is pretty messed up," Lawrence agrees. "Some of us have pasts."

"Yesterday I may have recited that along with you, but today I feel I am a different person." Principal Skinner shakes her head.

Shea offers, "Maybe we should all just say our own prayers and get on with it."

Each takes a moment before reciting their prayers in turn.

Marion repeats her original prayer. "MAY WE ALL GET WHAT WE DESERVE!"

Shea follows next. "May our enemies get what they deserve."

Principal Skinner prays, "May we all get through this unharmed."

Archibald bows his head, "Bestow us the strength and courage to vanquish our enemies."

Antonio offers, "May our enemies underestimate us."

A beat later, Lawrence points his thumb at Antonio. "What he said."

The prayers end with a hammering of fists.

Chapter 28

The last golden rays of sunset fade to darkness.

Lawrence and Principal Skinner sit atop a small hill at the base of a neighboring backyard overlooking the Crab Meadow salt marsh. From their vantage point, they have a clear view of all three stacks of computers.

Both scan the marsh through night vision binoculars.

"Please explain to me how Antonio created these?"

Lawrence continues checking out the stack of computers in the distance. He is amazed by the clarity of what he sees. "Um. Well, all the specs for everything are accessible on the internet. And you know about 3D printers, right? It's like that, except Antonio doesn't need a stinking 3D printer. He just uses the schmutz that he squeezes out of his phone and makes it happen. Or so he says."

"But the textures and colors are exactly like they were created in a factory," Principal Skinner marvels.

"That's magic for you," Lawrence informs her nonchalantly. He pulls his face away from the lenses for a moment. "I've been thinking." Lawrence glances over at the principal, hesitant to share something personal with her, but he needs to get something off his chest. "Maybe I was supposed to be the third person with computer magic, but then this new kid moves to town and screwed up the calculations."

"What calculations?"

"I don't know. Mystical calculations or the divine calibrations or something." He frowns. "I can't stop thinking it should have been me."

"What's really bothering you, Lawrence?"

Lawrence exhales sharply before admitting, "It's Tonio. I mean, Antonio. Now that he's the smartest kid in the world and knows all this magic shit, why would he want to hang out with a putz like me?"

Principal Skinner forces back a smile as she searches for a flaw in Lawrence's reasoning. "Now, that's no way to talk about yourself," she reassures Lawrence. "You have many redeeming qualities."

"Maybe, but it still should have been me," Lawrence mopes.

"If you ask me, you should be thankful. I'm afraid the other three are in real danger."

Lawrence is already sorry he brought it up. To change the subject, he points across the marsh. "Check it out. Archibald is about to do his thing."

Principal Skinner brings the binocular lenses to her eyes and scans the bright green image of the marsh until she locates Archibald. He is standing approximately one hundred yards inland from the beach side of the marsh. She watches as he raises his arms high above his head. In one sweeping motion, he lowers them and falls to one knee. His hands hover above the ground. A burst of energy emanates from his palms creating a near-blinding flash of light. Principal Skinner squeezes the glare from her eyes enabling her to view Archibald in silhouette making subtle and elaborate gestures.

He then contorts his entire body. A bright crackle of energy surges from his fingertips towards the eastern cluster of computers to his left. Glowing sharp blades sprout and grow within the sea grass and spread into a twenty-foot-wide perimeter encompassing the school's computers. Before the surge of magic completely fades, Archibald redirects it. The radiant wave of energy sizzles across the marsh to the southern brace of computers.

"This is incredible!" Principal Skinner gasps in awe. "Shouldn't we be recording this?"

"I offered, but Marion said they have it covered," Lawrence sighs. "It would have been cool though if Antonio created video cameras for us." He pulls his binoculars away from his face to see the magic without the enhanced night vision, but notices nothing unusual. He quickly looks back through the lenses and once again spies the magic in the far distance, working this time around the third group of computers.

The task complete, Archibald Abel bows with dramatic flourish in their general direction. He instantly vanishes with a distant Whooomph.

Seconds later, a tricolored foxhound trots across the yard and makes itself comfortable between Lawrence and the principal.

Principal Skinner jumps up, a look of repugnance on her face. She takes a step back, putting distance between herself and the dog.

"What's up Miss S?" Lawrence inquires.

"I'm… I'm not a dog person." She wrinkles her nose. "And that filthy mutt better not lick my face."

The foxhound morphs back into Archibald Abel who chuckles, "As if. I should have figured you for a crazy cat lady. I'll let you know that cats make inadequate familiars. Aloof know-it-alls, always getting distracted and making a mess of things."

Principal Skinner opens her mouth for a retaliatory response but becomes distracted. "Do I hear a helicopter?"

A distant thudding whop-whop-whop-whop-whop-whop sounds from a high altitude.

"I don't see it." Lawrence tries again with his binoculars pointed upwards. He finally spots a faint glow that reveals a large military style helicopter with four distinct sets of rotating blades. It is painted black and displays no call letters or insignia. "There's the bastard!"

Lawrence grabs his phone with his thumb on the screen. "Hey guys, we have a peeping pervert in a black copter hovering high above the marsh."

Marion responds through Lawrence's phone, "We see it too. His familiars are already here." She hesitates for a moment, then adds, "Thanks Lasagna."

In the dark of night, Archibald is the only one able to notice Lawrence's cheeks redden.

Principal Skinner peers through her binoculars. She points to the right of the far grouping of computers. "There are people in the marsh!"

chapter 29

Four familiars tread brazenly across the marsh towards the eerie electric glow of the easternmost cluster of computers. They wear dark clothing with rows of cell phones taped in layers along each of their sleeves.

Each carry one phone in hand, ready to blast anything that moves. Their screens are dimmed so as not to betray their positions.

Black scales blemish their faces to varying degrees.

Dee Dee, whose full name is Deanna Davis, leads the group.

Dee Dee had fully embraced the punk rock scene back in the eighties when she betrayed her fellow adepts. She physically resembles the twenty-year-old she was when she became a familiar. Her street-tough expression enhances the beautiful features of her face. If it can be said, her scales have appeared in all the *right* places.

Theo Ramirez, a tall familiar with a lanky build, walks beside her. Two others follow from ten paces behind.

"This is a strange place to stage an ambush," Dee Dee quietly takes note. "So close to witnesses."

"Don't worry," Theo replies. "They are panicking just like we did when it was our turn. I can smell it." He looks over his shoulder and unnecessarily asks his companions, "Are you keeping up?" He has an obnoxious habit of running his mouth falsely trying to act like the leader.

They don't bother to answer.

Dee Dee comes to a sudden stop before accidentally stepping into a stream of water. She raises a fist to halt the others.

Ramirez does not think twice before leaping clear across the seven-foot span of water. He lands squarely across the other side. "What are you afraid of, Dee Dee" he mocks teasingly.

Dee Dee does not appreciate the lack of respect he shows her. She steps back for a running start and leaps across the stream, but stumbles to her hands and knees. She ignores Ramirez' outstretched hand to help her up. "They are not panicking." Dee Dee hisses. "And they are ignoring Archibald Abel's advice."

None of these four have crossed paths with Archibald Abel. They have only been briefed on his known habits and past performances. Capturing him is one of the main objectives of this mission.

The two shorter familiars are aware of their physical limitations. They look further downstream, scouting for a narrower section to cross, but see none.

"As I was saying, you should quit worrying. There is only so much that can be done with computer magic," Theo informs them loudly. "Shoot at shit and build simple shit with it."

He pauses to watch as Jean-Pierre takes a running leap. He makes it across, but his arms swing wildly as he tries to keep from falling backward into the water. Theo reaches out and grabs the front of Jean-Pierre's shirt, pulling him upright.

"Merci."

"Computer magic is pretty lame when you think about it," Theo continues, "I mean, compared to all the wicked shit that Cristobal can do."

Dee Dee murmurs under her breath, "Yet somehow these three adepts managed to get Tovenaar's attention."

The fourth familiar cautiously steps into the stream and finds it to be only knee deep. He wades across to the other side and shakes out his boots.

Jean-Pierre asks, "In America, does Tovenaar always bring these many troops?"

"I have never seen Tovenaar even bother to even show up for one of these," Dee Dee replies. "Cristobal has always taken care of it with only two or four of us." She has never been overly cautious but is spooked by the wizard's over-the-top reaction to tonight's operation. "Now be quiet."

Theo mumbles, "Why are *we* the only suckers out here?"

Breaking his silence, Bradley Owens, the one with the wet boots, informs him, "We are the bait."

Black scales mar Bradley's face, as well as scars from when he tried to cut the scales off with a camping knife. "The Prime Asshole is using us to determine what abilities these new adepts possess."

Bradley's assessment of their situation has instilled in them a new sense of caution. They crouch lower and tread more quietly. When they are finally close enough, they see that each computer is running different videos or self-browsing through an unrestrained montage of websites and random photos.

"Quést ce they use for energy?" *What are they using for energy?* Asks Jean-Pierre Luc in broken French. As a precaution he places his free hand over his cell phone, ready to fire.

Dee Dee commands, "Ramirez, move forward. Unplug their

power source if you can.

Ramirez moves in a few steps closer. "Sonuvabitch!" He shrieks in pain. He reaches down to check his leg. When he pulls his hand back, it is wet with blood. "There is something sharp in the grass." He spits on his bloody hand and wipes it across his chest. "It encircles the computers, I think."

Suddenly, their phones light up, including all the auxiliary phones that are secured to their sleeves. Lawrence's voice broadcasts through the phones. "We got us three orcs and one little pony approaching the eastern brace of computers."

"Orcs?" Ramirez questions.

"Did that sonuvabitch just call me a pony?" Dee Dee sneers.

Jean-Pierre scoffs, "I think he meant that Bradley must be le petit pony."

"Screw you, Pierre." Bradley retorts.

"Shut up. Shut up, all of you," Dee Dee warns. "Don't you see… they have hacked our phones!"

While they stare at their phones like deer in a headlight, all the computer monitors suddenly synchronize to one image of Shea, Antonio, and Marion observing them with shit-eating grins.

The familiars look up to see their enemies burst out from the stack of computers resembling pixelated riders of the apocalypse.

Antonio strikes first. "Looking for something, plasma boy?" He taps his thumb drive against Theo Ramirez's forehead. Theo gets sucked in, and his empty clothes crumple to the ground. Antonio thrusts the thumb drive into his wizard's closet and U-turns back to another computer to re-enter the Hyper Realm.

Shea charges straight for Dee Dee, "Whoa Nelly. Come to papa."

"Bite me, you mother…"

He lightly taps the tip of her nose with a thumb drive, cutting off her onslaught of obscenities.

Dee Dee transforms into a swarm of angry pixels and gets sucked into the drive. A pinpoint of energy sparks from Shea's index finger as he takes a moment to imprint the words Little Pony on the drive before tossing it into his closet. He feels exhilarated and does a roundhouse kick at no one before allowing the same computer that he sprang from to suck him back in.

In the same instant, Marion throws and bounces a thumb drive off the back of Bradley's head as he turns to run. It instantaneously hoovers him. Marion gracefully leaps into the air performing a grand jete and retrieves the thumb drive before it hits the ground. She secures it in her closet before diving headfirst into a phone that is taped to Bradley's pile of clothing.

Marion greets Shea and Antonio back in the Hyper Realm.

All three are on an adrenaline high.

"I feel stoked." Shea pounds his chest with his fist.

Antonio pounds his chest too.

Marion smacks a hand to her forehead. "Shoot, I forgot to trash talk. I gotta try again."

Before they can open their mouths to speak, she is gone.

*

Jean-Pierre finds himself all alone. This is his first time in the field. He had armed himself with an overabundance of phones secured to his sleeves as well as his pant legs.

"Fils de pute!" *Sonuvabitch!* In a panic, he shoots blast after blast of plasma at the computers, to no effect. He drops his phone and runs. "Aide-moi. Aide-moi." *Help me. Help me.*

The phones that are taped to him flash randomly like Christmas lights. He looks down and notices each one displays a different image of Marion.

Jean-Pierre stops running and frantically peels the phones off his clothing.

Each phone features Marion dressed in various attire including evening wear, a police uniform, a mermaid with a floppy tail, an inflatable sumo suit, and so on. She compliments each outfit with different hairstyles, yet her facial expression remains the same in all her variations. She winks maliciously at Jean-Pierre.

"Ca ne peut pas etre." *This cannot be*. Jean-Pierre whimpers.

Marion taunts him from a phone on the ground next to him, "C'mon sweetie, charm me with your world-renowned romance language."

Jean-Pierre leaps desperately into a stream. The water is up to his waist. He dips his arms and watches as the images of Marion go black in the dark water. "Haha!" he cries out in relief. "What are you going to do now, bitch? Les telephones are all dead," he jeers.

"Tu en as rate un, Petite Garce." *You missed one, little bitch.* Marion mocks him in French. She appears like a genie dressed as a harem girl from a cell phone that is secured at his shoulder. "Cest la vie," *That's life*. She mocks him one last time before thumb-driving him. Marion stashes the drive in her wizard's closet and sinks back into the phone before it and Jean-Pierre's clothing settle into the water.

The marsh is once again tranquil.

Lawrence pumps his fist in the air and rejoices, "That was so bad-ass!"

"I cannot believe what I just witnessed." Principal Skinner is in awe of these three students for the fourth or fifth time today. "They truly are magicians."

"Not magicians," Archibald corrects the principal. "Potential wizards. I saw them pull off a similar feat this afternoon in the light of day. Their powers are significant, yet they are still only adepts who only just became aware of their magic hours ago." He grins, "Imagine the possibilities if they can achieve full wizard hood."

"How does that happen?" Principal Skinner is intrigued.

"It will happen when they perform a feat so grand that the world's magic accepts them to be its conduits." Archibald pauses for a moment, "Or so I believe."

"When could that occur?

"It had better happen tonight if they plan to survive this." Archibald exhales sharply. "Only a wizard can destroy Tovenaar. We shall see."

The trio exchange sullen looks.

The owner of the yard they have made themselves at home in calls suspiciously from a sliding glass door, "Can I help you, folks?"

The three turn to see the homeowner dressed only in boxers.

Lawrence waves at the man, but whispers to Archibald, "You better do something quickly before that douche calls the cops."

Archibald responds to the homeowner in a cheery tone of voice, "I hope you don't mind, my good sir. We are just here to view the fireworks."

"Fireworks on a Monday? Hell, yeah! I think I'll grab myself a beer and a cigar."

"I'll have a beer too if you don't mind," Lawrence calls out.

As the homeowner heads back inside, Archibald wiggles two fingers in his direction before the glass door slides shut. "He will fall asleep in front of his television," he informs Lawrence. "Your beer will have to wait."

"A beer?" Principal Skinner lightly smacks Lawrence on the head. "I can overlook a lot, but underage drinking…?" She catches her reflexive outrage and lightens up. "If we all manage to get through this intact, I will personally buy you a beer."

"It's a date." Lawrence playfully drapes his arm around her shoulders, but quickly pulls it back when she gives him a stern look.

*

The black helicopter continues to hover high above the marsh.

Inside its dimly illuminated interior, the console is reminiscent of a WWII-era fighter plane due to its lack of computer technology. However, this chopper is an unmatched technological marvel with controls that emerge like liquid steel at the command of Tovenaar's Industrial Age sorcery.

Years ago, Tovenaar learned a costly lesson that computers and his age of wizardry do not mix. An arms merchant, in his debt, invited him to witness a demonstration of computer-guided missiles. His mere presence ignited a chain of mishaps that killed forty-eight people, including the arms dealer. The incident alerted him to the coming of the next age of humanity. The Computer Age. He has since purged all computers from his operations as a rule.

Tovenaar observes the current combat zone through a lens-based viewing device.

It has been decades since he has involved himself in such matters. Cristobal has proven to be quite exceptional at destroying Computer Age adepts with his unique blend of the craft, coupled with a keen understanding of human nature. But alas, it was inevitable that the day would come when a group of young adepts would take their skills to a threatening level.

Tonight, he wears a black woolen military-style overcoat bereft of symbols of rank and allegiance. He pulls his face away from the black rubber surrounding the periscope lenses. His expression is one of bewilderment.

"Give me your assessment on what I just witnessed." He glances over at the war hardened man seated across the cockpit who continues to peer through his own set of lenses.

"Their weapon emitted a prolonged flash that I have not encountered before. Very unconventional." Guy Fleet's face does not show any sign of black scales, but he *is* a familiar, nonetheless. In his case, he is a low-level demon who was ensnared by Tovenaar and was compelled to exist in a mechanized automaton.

Cristobal aided Tovenaar in erasing the demon's memory and rewriting its past. It now believes it is a human mercenary named Guy Fleet who was first employed by Tovenaar back in the 1930s. What he lacks in personality, he makes up for with a spirited lack of compassion.

From a distance, Guy Fleet can pass as a human. A closer inspection, however, would reveal metallic seams along his mouth and his eyes. Guy's serves primarily as an enforcer. He strong arms corrupt politicians who have re-found their conscience. His talent for changing their minds and/or offing them in a natural appearing manner is nothing short of masterful.

"From what I observed, your adversaries have figured out a means of converting their computers into advanced weaponry."

Tovenaar reasons. "Impressive, but not good enough to save them."

WHOOOMPH. Cristobal materializes in the cabin. His robe is matte black.

"Report!" Tovenaar commands.

"The adepts staged an ambush from behind a pile of computers and obliterated our advance squad. No trace of them. It's as if they never existed." Cristobal hacks to clear away phlegm from his throat. "I have never faced adepts as bloodthirsty as these. They have now eliminated six, if you include Hans and Terrence."

"What sort of weapons are they utilizing?" Tovenaar inquires, his eyebrows sharply raised.

Cristobal shrugs. "Beats the hell out of me, boss."

Tovenaar flashes a trace of annoyance from this response. "*You* initially surmised that these three were clueless imbeciles. *You* assured me they were underachievers, bleeding hearts, hapless losers." His voice simmers. "How would you assess their abilities now?"

Cristobal has been around long enough to know when to keep his mouth shut and when to speak. He decides against his better judgment and answers honestly. "Formidable. Their powers are formidable." He offers consolation, "Being that there are only three of them, surely we can overwhelm…"

Tovenaar growls, "After I lay waste to this stack of computers, send two battalions to advance on the other groups of computers." He considers, "The rest shall remain hidden in the tall grasses until I flush these vermin out."

"Affirmative." Cristobal tightens his robe before vanishing.

"You," he commands Guy Fleet. "Maneuver us into position. I will take care of the mini guns." He buckles his seatbelt. "I may not be able to kill them with sorcery, but I can annihilate their weapons."

"Shall I arm the missiles as well?" Guy asks as a matter of formality.

"Not necessary. There will be nothing left once I'm done." Tovenaar uses a thumb to crack the knuckle of his trigger finger.

"Aye." Guy Fleet starts the chopper's descent.

*

Shea and Antonio have settled down and are calmly discussing their first attack. "Not bad for a first strike," Antonio grins.

"I didn't expect there to be a chick," Shea marvels.

Marion pops in next to them. "If you're so smitten, you can just take her out of your pocket and buy her a latte."

"That's not what I meant," Shea responds sheepishly. "I just didn't expect a female would be the betrayer."

Marion informs him, "You have a lot to learn about women."

Shea changes the subject. "Whatever. We will need to be quicker at striking though. Before too long, the police will eventually show up. And the longer this confrontation drags on, the more likely innocent bystanders will get hurt."

Antonio has a suggestion. "Perhaps we could do with a little less taunting and concentrate a little more on strictly thumb-driving."

"But taunting is half the fun," Marion confesses.

"I taunted the punk rocker," Shea admits with a chuckle.

Antonio hesitates. He is suddenly unsure if it is wise to pursue this any further. "Sure, I mean Shea taunted the punk rocker and that's cool."

He carefully selects his next words, "But Marion, I am concerned that you are changing from a sweet, innocent…"

"Stop right there," Marion interrupts. "Sweet is not going to get us through tonight and no one survives a fight when worrying about shit like innocence. I am going to fight with everything I have and if that means talking smack to those jerks then you better get used to it." She looks Antonio dead in the eye, "So stop being a little bitch about it."

Antonio winces visibly and now wishes that he had kept his mouth shut. He realizes that Marion is intent on pulling her weight, but he is deeply concerned for her well-being. He throws his hands up. "You're right. Let's just get through tonight. We can worry about post-traumatic personality disorders later."

Marion flashes a fake smile.

For a moment, Shea finds himself pleased to see Marion angry with Antonio. He imagines what it would be like with Antonio out of the picture. To have Marion all to himself. Oddly enough, his first trip into the Hyper Realm has given him insight. Tovenaar needs one of us to betray the others. Like it or not, if one of us fails then we all fail. Shea wills all thoughts of petty jealousy from his mind and focuses on kicking Tovenaar's ass. "The familiars are working in groups. If we split up, we can each take out an entire squad per strike and speed things up that way."

Marion nods quietly. She still has a bit of a chip on her shoulder from her squabble with Antonio.

Antonio reminds them, "Remember, we discuss every move here in the Hyper Realm. An hour for us will seem like split seconds to our enemies."

"That helicopter is coming down over the Eastern set of computers." Lawrence's voice snaps Marion out of her brief funk.

"I have this," Shea announces and vanishes from the Hyper Realm.

"Wait…"

"Didn't we just agree…"

*

Wind from the powerful rotors blasts the sea grass, flattening them to the ground. Tovenaar's massive helicopter descends. It hovers forty yards off the cluster of computers. An intensely bright searchlight scours the area.

Guy Fleet surveys the target through his lenses as Tovenaar questions, "Do we have a visual on the little pricks?"

"That's a negative," Guy replies, but notices the footage from a World War II movie playing across all the computer screens. He pauses to watch a fighter plane in the movie take heavy rounds. He offers his professional opinion. "Likely they are wearing camouflage."

Tovenaar hovers both hands over the control panel of the console. The metal morphs and reforms into two handles, each with elaborate trigger mechanisms.

Outer panels located on either side of the helicopter slide open. Two mini guns roll out and click into position.

The guns come to life with a thunderous explosion and a sustained muzzle flash. Vrrrrmmmmmmmmmmmmmmmmm…

*

Mr. Blakely sits alone in the dark inside Shea's trailer. He sips at a can of warm beer that he has been nursing for the past hour. Shea and his new friends' disappearing trick has left a nagging itch in his mind that he just cannot satisfy. He checks his watch and yawns. "I guess this will just have to wait until tomorrow," he mumbles and stands up with a grunt.

Suddenly Shea's computer flickers to life. Seconds later his son spills out of the monitor and onto the floor.

Shea is initially unaware that his father is present and immediately reaches down to unplug the power cord of his computer. When he stands upright, he is face to face with his stunned father.

"What the hell is going on?" Mr. Blakely's eyes are bugging out of his head.

Shea calmly inserts the plug on the computer's power cord into a plain black cell phone and stashes them both in his wizard's closet. "I'll explain later."

Carmine's face is beet red. "You will explain now!"

Shea tosses another black cell phone onto his bed. "Love you, Pops." He smiles before diving headfirst into the phone leaving his flabbergasted father alone in the dark once again.

*

The mini guns are still blasting as Marion peeks out from Lawrence's phone. "We're going to join you for a sec."

Principal Skinner gasps, "No!"

"That is not a good idea," Archibald agrees. "Cristobal will spot your blue aura and give away our position."

"What's up?" Lawrence is thrilled to see Marion, "By the way, that dude is toasting the school's computers."

"We don't know where Shea is."

"Oh no," Archibald groans.

"He went rogue," Antonio calls out. "We need to see what is happening."

"Okay, no problem." Lawrence has a thought. "What if I videotape the copter with my phone? Will you be able to see it?"

"It will have to do." Marion's face leaves the screen.

Lawrence points his phone toward the helicopter and hits the record button.

*

Vrrrrrrrrrrm. The barrels of the guns glow red with heat from the continuous scorching blasts. Finally, the incessant roar ceases. The mini-gun's barrels continue to whirl with an electric hum, then click click click to a stop.

Tovenaar peers through the smoke and steam of the decimated target area hoping for confirmation of a hit.

"We probably should have left some DNA to identify the bodies," Guy Fleet jokes in his monotone voice.

Tovenaar frowns as he scans the area with his scope.

Twenty yards from the smoldering wreckage of computers, unattended cell phones from the ambush of the four familiars lay strewn about the ground.

One phone suddenly flickers with light. Tovenaar's eyes grow wide when he sees a computer-generated version of Shea flying towards him from a discarded phone.

In one blurry motion, he surges upwards at the helicopter.

Shea's body solidifies as he nears the copter.

"We should have armed the sidewinders!" Tovenaar shouts as Shea's grinning face comes into focus.

Shea looks every bit the heroic superhero he has always wanted to be as he hurls his computer, which is still plugged into a cell phone, at the base of one set of the rotating blades on the helicopter.

When the computer is close enough, it explodes into a considerable mass of plasma that smothers the blades and spreads out aggressively covering the remaining three propellers until they all freeze in place.

Shea drops back into the phone on the ground and reenters the Hyper Realm.

Tovenaar's helicopter falls noiselessly for forty feet until it craters the ground with a resounding impact.

chapter 31

Marion greets Shea in the Hyper Realm with an excited hug. "You did it! You destroyed Tovenaar's helicopter!

Shea plays it cool and concentrates on enjoying Marion's hug. *This would be so much better in the real world, but I'll take it.*

Marion pushes back and looks at Shea with concern. "But why would you do that without us? You could've been killed!" She pulls him in for a tighter hug. She pushes him away again. "And why did you sacrifice your computer?"

Shea shrugs. "After today's learning curve, I am going to require a much more powerful CPU. Anyway, I have an idea for a cooler game." He smiles a side wise grin. "I won't even need a computer now that I have direct access to the Hyper Realm."

Antonio waits on the sidelines watching the two hug it out. "Okay guys, break it up," he groans. He gives Shea a congratulatory back slap. "That was outstanding! Marion is right though. Why didn't you wait for us? You do remember that we agreed to discuss our plans before acting on them, right?"

"I felt left out when you two took down the motorcycles… I figured it was my turn to…" He feels his Hyper Realm face grow hot.

"Hold on a minute," Shea replies defensively. "You didn't think that I would betray…"

"Of course not," Marion lies, now that everything is okay. "It's just that for a moment we felt like…I don't know…"

"We felt vulnerable," Antonio finishes Marion's sentence.

Shea imagines himself in their position. "You're right. I'm sorry. It won't happen again. I promise."

*

Residents in the surrounding area gather in yards that face the marsh. Why does their quiet neighborhood suddenly sound like a war zone? They yell over the sound of incessantly barking dogs.

"What the hell is going on?"

"Did you see anything?"

"Did anyone call the cops?"

"Are we under attack?"

"Fred, put a robe on!"

Everyone with a cell phone tries to zoom in on the fallen helicopter.

The resident whose yard the trio occupy is still asleep in front of his television.

Principal Skinner throws her arms around Lawrence and hugs him. "That was so amazing! The new kid is a rock star."

"His name is Shea," Lawrence informs her, yet again. He quickly squirms out of her arms.

"Right, Shea." Principal Skinner regains her composure. "Shea is a rock star." She looks anxiously at Archibald. "So, is that it? Is the old wizard dead? Did the helicopter fall on Cristobal? Is Shea the new

199

wizard now?"

"I am going to answer all of your questions with a resounding, No." Archibald furrows his brow. "In fact, the situation has just become increasingly more dangerous for all of us."

"Shea!" Lawrence yells into his phone. "That was insane!" He looks through his night vision binoculars and sees troops break cover and rush the marsh. "Just a heads-up. The orcs are on the move. They are everywhere."

Shea's face appears on Lawrence's phone direct from the Hyper Realm. "Copy that, Lasagna." He sees the principal and waves. "Hi, Principal Skinner."

"Bring the heat, Shea," she encourages.

He asks Lawrence, "Hey, did you say you made some music for delivering a good ass-kicking?"

"Stay tuned, gangsta." Lawrence smiles mischievously.

Shea snorts out a laugh and disappears from the screen.

Tovenaar's forces split into squads of a dozen familiars each. All wear black clothing with rows of securely stacked cell phones affixed to their sleeves. In addition, some wear armored plates created from plasma. They do not understand what has just happened to their cohorts, but they are eager for revenge.

As the squads spread out, their running slows to a determined trot.

A lead familiar pounds his cell phone to emit an explosive pulse of plasma and an electric sounding BROOOMPH!

The others follow his lead and pound at their own phones until every one of them joins in. They quickly find a rhythm that results in a deafening BROOOMPH BROOOMPH BROOOMPH! Phones flash like repeated lightning strikes. Cheers and threats ring out in a chorus of sustained intimidation until Tovenaar's army presents itself as a cohesive unit of enthusiastic warriors.

One group of familiars cuts a beeline to the fallen helicopter. Like seasoned veterans, they do not pause as they approach a wide stream of salt water that stands between them and Tovenaar. The squad leader aims with his phone and expels enough plasma to generate a simple bridge. The familiars take the bridge in single file, then come to an abrupt halt when their phones cease to respond to their pounding.

The enthusiastic cheering simmers down as uncertainty replaces their bravado.

Suddenly, the glow of hundreds of cell phones light up from behind the tall grasses that surround the marsh. The positions of Tovenaar's reserve forces are revealed. Not only the phones they are holding, but every phone secured to the familiars' clothing lights up. Any chance of a surprise counteroffensive is thwarted.

Lawrence's cool voice reverberates from every phone in classic disc jockey style. "And by popular demand, we have a little dance music dedicated to our special guests at the Crab Meadow Salt Marsh."

The volume on every phone self-adjusts to maximum as a throat-rasping death metal growl kicks off Lawrence's composition. The music continues with every scream and every yell sampled from every genre of music, including rock, metal, country, and opera. Vicious pulse-pounding drums drive the beat while electric guitars, saxophones, and trumpets flesh out the rhythm. Lawrence's masterpiece is indeed chaotic, yet remarkably catchy.

Tovenaar's familiars scramble to turn off the loud music but find it impossible to do so. Panic spreads throughout the ranks.

Marion strikes first.

She spills out of the leader's phone, then disappears into the next familiar's phone until she weaves her way through the surprised line of elite combatants. Along the way, she effortlessly collects the familiars onto thumb drives then tosses them into her wizard's closet.

Marion has never felt so exuberant and confident and… crazed. She laughs wildly. "I love being a bad ass!"

It is suddenly clear to the familiars that the energy blur they saw earlier is in fact the enemy. Scores of familiars rush to the aid of their comrades, but the crazy flying girl is no longer there.

*

One beat after Marion's successful strike, Shea pounces on a squad of familiars who are gathered by the southernmost pile of computers. In seconds, twelve sets of clothing crumples to the ground. A glowing image of Shea stands atop one of the discarded phones as he surveys the marsh.

This is so cool.

He reaches down and peels a phone from a now empty shirt and tosses it at a distant group of familiars.

They seem perplexed by his intentions.

Once the phone is near enough, he springs out from it and sucks up a dozen more familiars. He reaches for another phone to throw at yet another distant group.

*

Antonio calmly strides forth from the western cluster of computers into the midst of sixty or so familiars.

When they finally realize their enemy is amongst them, they jump back in surprise before cautiously encircling him. "We're not taking prisoners," one of them sneers confidently.

"Oh, but I am." Antonio grins and multiplies into five thumb-drive wielding versions of himself. The clones spread apart and appear in various stances in front of and behind the group. "Let's not waste time on idle chit chat."

202

The five Antonios charge the familiars, each counting off in succession the current total.

"…fifty-eight."

"…fifty-nine."

"…sixty."

chapter 32

Cristobal crouches behind a tuft of sea grass to view the battle. He watches in horror as scores of familiars are swept off the board. He can only assume these adepts are killing them. *How can I have assessed them so poorly?* "They are savages!" Everything is happening so quickly. He has lost track. *Where are the other two?* He spins suddenly in case they are sneaking up behind him.

He sits down on the damp sand, succumbing to the physical exhaustion he has been trying to conceal.

By all rights, he should be long dead. But every fifty to seventy years, when his strength fades, Tovenaar recharges him with the soul stone of an Agricultural Age wizard. He fears that Flane's soul stone, which he is currently utilizing, is running on fumes.

After this, Llewellyn's stone will be the last. Fortunately, the soul stone of a former prime wizard should give him another hundred years, or so he hopes.

Today has been rough. It began with a full shift of running Tovenaar's errands. After learning of the demise of Hans and Terrence, Tovenaar sent him teleporting across the world to collect all the familiars. Now he is in the middle of a battle with these three blood thirsty adepts.

"I shouldn't be here," he says to no one.

Paranoia and a panic attack get the best of him. *What if Archibald Abel isn't here? What if he ran away like he always does? How much longer can I last with this depleting soul stone?*

Cristobal slaps his own face to pull himself together. He sniffs the air. "He's here," he reassures himself.

The battle erupts close to his position. Stray shots of plasma cut through the grasses. He shrieks as some of it grazes his cheek.

The empty clothes of a familiar fall at his feet.

Another shot of plasma soars just above his head.

Cristobal vanishes.

chapter 33

From his vantage point atop the small hill, Lawrence narrates the mayhem into his phone. "Whoa, doggie, we got us a stampede." His voice projects from all phones carried by every familiar in the marsh. He mocks them with a rude imitation of squealing swine. "Woink, woink, woink."

"It took milady 4.351 seconds to take one dozen familiars off the board," Archibald notes with an air of appreciation.

"This is epic!" Lawrence laughs with excitement. He broadcasts, "To the fool wearing the beret, you're next, sucker."

Throughout the marsh, at least a dozen beret-wearing familiars dive to the ground for cover.

Neighbors in the vicinity continue to capture video of the bizarre battle.

Lawrence notices the subtle movements of Archibald's fingers. "What are you up to?" He asks quietly.

"I am simply hindering any impulse these innocent bystanders may have of thinking they can do anything to help the inhabitants of the helicopter."

Suddenly, neighbors turn and walk quietly back to their homes.

Principal Skinner pulls the binoculars from her eyes to compliment Lawrence. "You did very well with your musical composition, Lawrence." She is half lying.

"I can't take all the credit. Somebody, maybe Shea, added many more layers to the mix, and don't forget it was your suggestion to add the opera." He shrugs, "Thanks though."

A shrill sound emits from Tovenaar's copter as a door panel spills open and cascades to the ground. A wave of elaborately designed mechanisms solidify forming a ramp.

As awed as Lawrence is by the action of Tovenaar's helicopter, he is having the time of his life. He whispers through the phones with a conspiratorial tone in his voice, "Wait 'til the bastards find out the helicopter IS the ambush site."

Every familiar approaching the helicopter hears Lawrence's whisper as it broadcasts through their phones. They stop progressing and look around nervously. More troops approach until a crowd quickly forms. Lawrence's mind games are having the desired effect. They argue in hushed tones deciding their next move.

In a fireball of blue and purple, Antonio springs out from a phone and takes advantage of their confusion. He wades seamlessly through the crowd. His arms are a blur as he moves at three times normal speed.

Familiars struggle to get a clean shot, but resort to shooting wildly at him with blasts that are absorbed harmlessly by the dome of translucent plasma shields that Antonio has surrounded himself with.

Phones and clothes litter the ground as their owners are sucked into USB drives.

Antonio's thumb drives drop into his wizard's closet like spent shells from a shotgun.

The yelling increases in volume and desperation as the troops charge from all directions only to watch their enemy disappear once again. *And that jerk will not stop playing that damn music over their damn phones.*

*

Tovenaar strides out of the wreckage of his helicopter with the bravado of a conquering hero. His mercenary follows him down the ramp with a noticeable limp. Tovenaar points menacingly at Antonio but takes no action.

*

Dozens of familiars shoot at the southern pile of computers. They plan to destroy the equipment from a safe distance while their enemies are busy fighting near the helicopter.

All at once, the monitors explode with a flash of random data as Shea bursts forth. He stands atop two computer generated snow mobiles, one foot on each seat. In his hands, he holds two Roman candles that spew forth thumb drives in all directions. Each shot bags a familiar and magically ricochets back to Shea's wizard closet.

"You snowmobiling sonuvabitch," Antonio calls out from across the marsh wearing a grin a mile wide. "You do have moves."

Shea allows his snowmobiles to dissolve gradually until he strides gracefully onto the marsh ground. He casually tosses the last of his thumb drives into his wizard's closet and salutes Antonio. Just then, he spots Tovenaar's lackey aiming a rifle at Antonio's back. "Watch out!" He yells.

Lawrence's voice simultaneously warns through all the cell phones, "Antonio! Bail!"

Antonio quickly steps onto a discarded phone and disappears a

208

second before the shot rings out from Guy Fleet's rifle.

*

Tovenaar studies the battlefield but cannot comprehend what is happening. He squints at Guy Fleet. "What am I looking at?"

Guy Fleet scans the marsh, "You are looking at a serious ass-kicking."

Tovenaar spots Antonio already attacking more of his troops two hundred yards from where he just disappeared. "Anything else?"

"Your adversaries appear to be enjoying themselves."

He frowns and looks to his right. "Ah, the female." He watches as Marion stages an attack on yet another squad of familiars. "Bring your weapons," Tovenaar snarls as he walks towards the action.

Guy slings the strap of an automatic weapon over each shoulder to complement the pistols holstered at each hip. He then takes up a long rifle with an attached sniper scope.

*

Marion now wears an adorable dress with a blue and white gingham pattern. She cradles in her arms a wicker basket that holds a computer-generated puppy. She looks innocent and nonthreatening, except for her eyes that glow with a static-like display of random computer data. She approaches her foes, no longer talking smack. Instead, she greets them politely.

"It is very nice to make your acquaintance."

Thumb-drive.

"Hi, my name is Marion. What's yours?"

Thumb-drive.

"I just love your hair."

Thumb-drive.

"We should get together for—"

Thumb-drive.

209

All the while, the animated puppy is trash talking.

"You want a piece of this?"

"Your parents must be so proud."

"Where do you losers think you're going? Get back here."

The effect is even creepier and more menacing than she intended.

Familiars turn and run away from her.

Marion giggles and steps into a discarded phone. She reappears in the path of the fleeing familiars. The first one screams as he runs into her thumb drive. She speeds up her attacks and disappears from one end of the marsh only to spring up wherever familiars have clustered. She bags dozens of them before they even think to fight back.

*

Principal Skinner can't tear her eyes away from the action.

Lawrence continues to mock the creeps through their phones. "Hey! You with your finger up your nose. Pick me a winner." He sees Principal Skinner staring at him with a deadpan expression. "Too much?"

The principal simply shakes her head.

*

The crazy music mercifully stops.

Rustling of dry grass is the only sound. A sudden lull in the battle has cast an eerie pall over the marsh. The remaining two working piles of computers pulsate between blue and red illuminating the empty clothing that is scattered everywhere.

The screens of deserted phones shine brightly creating an upside-down illusion of stars in the sky.

chapter 34

Tovenaar strides calmly across the field of battle. There is a solution to every problem, and he is confident it will present itself. All it takes is patience. Even an insignificant detail can be exploited.

Guy Fleet follows, scanning the tall grasses through the night vision scope mounted on his rifle. His torso and rifle barrel pivot quickly at every sound. He whispers to Tovenaar, "These three children certainly know how to throw a party."

"They are cocky and will make a grave mistake." Tovenaar takes a sweeping look around the circumference of the marsh before continuing his assessment. "This lull indicates they are wearing out or have used up all of their tricks."

"They don't need tricks," Guy informs him. "They are utilizing your familiars' very weapons against them."

"Are you telling me they are not teleporting as Cristobal does? That they are squeezing into the little phones like long-extinct genies?"

Guy offers his professional opinion, "Consider ordering your troops to destroy their cellular phones."

Tovenaar disregards his mercenary's advice. "My familiars are useless without their phones. We will stay the course."

Guy responds with an almost imperceptible shrug of his shoulders.

Tovenaar lifts his right hand. Shards of metal materialize from his surrounding energy and begin to self-assemble on his forearm. Metallic clattering continues until a steel gauntlet covers his forearm from elbow to knuckles. A missile lifts from the construct and clicks into place.

Tovenaar aims his magically created weapon at one of the remaining piles of computers. He shows little concern for the troops that are between him and his target. He squeezes the trigger on the hand cannon.

Familiars dive for cover as the missile shrieks past them leaving behind a billowing trail of smoke until it strikes the computers with a thunderous series of explosions.

The remaining troops aim their phones toward the shower of smoldering shards of plastic that flutter back to the ground. Surely their enemies will be forced to expose themselves.

*

Lawrence lets out a yelp. The brightness from the explosion is blinding through his night vision binoculars. When his eyes finally adjust, he notices Archibald is no longer with them. "Where's Archie?"

"I'm not his babysitter," Principal Skinner snaps. The stress is getting to her as well.

Lawrence nervously scans the marsh through his binoculars trying to make sense of things. He speaks quietly into his phone, "C'mon guys? Finish them already."

He gets no response.

"Where are they? It's been like ten minutes."

*

Marion, Shea, and Antonio stand in the parking lot of a local convenience store, casually sipping frosty drinks through straws. They are taking a break in real time.

"Your *Like a Boss* move was worth the wait." Marion's coquettish smile makes Shea's heart skip a beat. "I never doubted you."

"I bagged about fifty with that one attack." He tilts his head to the side and smiles back at her. "Making a total of two hundred and eight."

"Two hundred and twelve for me so far," she boasts proudly.

"Three eleven," Antonio adds displaying a toothy grin. His smile fades to a look of concern. "Does Tovenaar appear to be less vibrant, older, or even the least bit crusty after we took out seven hundred and thirty-one of his familiars?"

"No, but I'm not sure it really matters," Shea replies, his gaze still affixed on Marion. "What was going on with your eyes back there? You looked like a hot extra from a space zombie movie."

Marion flutters her eyelashes. Her intense eyes flicker with the chaos of data. "I'm trying out a new look," she winks at Shea. "You likey?"

"No, kind of psychotic." He scrunches his face. "Not a deal breaker, though."

"I think it looks quite becoming," Antonio compliments Marion. He feels the need to make up for his earlier comment about her losing her girlish innocence.

Marion grins at Antonio as she calmly slurps the last of her drink. Her eyes flicker back to normal.

Shea finally answers Antonio's question. "From a distance, Tovenaar does not appear to be weakened from the loss of so many familiars." He pauses and considers his actions. "He marches around like he's on safari, patiently waiting for an opportunity to get his shot at us."

"I may have been wrong about Tovenaar using familiars as living soul stones," Antonio admits. "Perhaps he *is* using bio-mechanical body parts.

Marion bites her lip in thought. "I'm thinking that the energy that surrounds him from being a prime wizard is more than enough to sustain him."

"Maybe. Let's clear the field of the remaining familiars. Then we can focus on what's keeping Tovenaar going." Antonio looks at the other two for approval. "Agreed?"

Shea and Marion nod their heads in agreement.

After a moment of silence, Antonio says conversationally, "Lawrence's music was a pleasant touch."

"I'd dance to it," Marion laughs and shakes her hips.

Shea smiles at her dance moves. "I liked it."

Marion grins. "I think we've given them enough time to sweat it out."

Antonio sums it up, "One last attack on the familiars. No need to waste time chasing the ones that run away."

"Let's take it up a couple of notches. Computer magic can be so much more bad ass." Shea looks at Marion. "You should… um, I mean all of us should still be more careful."

"They can't harm us if we remain pixelated," Marion reminds him.

"We have not fully proven that theory," Antonio counters.

The deep rumble of a powerful engine interrupts them. A red Corvette convertible pulls into the parking space next to them. An attractive man in a sports jacket and blue jeans exits the car and walks past them. He gives Marion a complete once-over and nods appreciatively.

"Say, that's a nice phone you have there," Marion purrs and smiles seductively at the stranger.

"Huh?" He glances down at the phone in his hand, surprised she is not more impressed with his fast car or good looks.

Marion approaches him.

He watches in awe as she slowly slides her finger down his chest. She hesitates just before touching his phone.

Marion leans closer and speaks in a breathy voice, "Let's get digital, baby."

Before he has a chance to process what she just said, Marion taps his phone and is instantly sucked in.

He gasps and drops it like it's hot.

"Marion is getting reckless," Antonio warns Shea. "We need to watch her. Make sure she doesn't get herself into trouble."

Shea does not necessarily agree with Antonio but keeps his opinion to himself. He disregards the dude and touches his foot on the phone and follows after Marion.

Antonio picks the phone up and uses his thumb to scan for data. "You should probably get back home to your wife, rather than cruising for underage girls." Antonio vanishes into the phone, letting it fall and clatter to the pavement.

chapter 35

Massive losses and a sense of futility has taken a toll on Tovenaar's troops. Their morale is toast. The eerie lull in the battle further frays their nerves. There is nothing to do but wait and wonder which of them will be next. The missile strike offered a brief sigh of relief. Finally, a successful counter strike, or so they hope.

Four *volunteers* move in to scout the area where the second pile of computers once stood.

The lead familiar cries out with pain. This sparks a flurry of panic fire which causes him to run deeper into the saw grass.

"Stop shooting, you assholes!"

"Cease," Tovenaar commands his troops. He does not particularly care about any of his familiars. Their lack of discipline irritates him.

The injured familiar calls out, "Medic?" He is hopeful his wound is severe enough for Tovenaar to excuse him from the field of battle.

The Prime Wizard knows he may require every last one of them to survive the night. He sighs and gestures with a flick of his hand at the familiar's bloody leg and torso. Liquid metal sloughs away from his aura and materializes into mesh bandages to compress the wounds.

A leg brace self-constructs over the bandages for added protection and lifts him to an upright position. This method stems the flow of blood but does nothing to alleviate the pain.

"Two down," Guy comments as he nods toward the last pile of computers. "An obvious trap, but…"

Tovenaar does not respond to Guy Fleet's assessment. He conjures his magic to fashion a rugged platform which quickly assembles into an oversized full-metal skateboard with tank-like treads. He steps onto it and heads for the last remaining group of computers, like a boss.

Guy Fleet trots closely behind.

*

The remaining cluster of computers emits a sinister red glow.

Overcautious familiars crunch through the grass from all directions, converging towards the eerie spectacle. The lack of action is nerve racking. They desperately want the next victim to be someone else.

A static *hisssssss* from their phones shatters the quiet.

Plasma-generated skeleton snakes slither out from the screens.

Familiars break any last appearance of order as they toss aside the phones to avoid the jaw snapping serpents.

Tovenaar's vehicle loses momentum when dozens of snakes entangle themselves in the tank treads. The prime wizard wields his magic to free up the treads, but it is no use against the plasma construction of the creatures.

Guy Fleet hops and back-peddles to avoid the angry reptiles that appear everywhere from deserted phones.

Tovenaar watches with narrowed eyes as five clones of Antonio and five clones of Shea materialize out from random phones across the marsh. Each clone is dressed differently and moves independently from its copies.

Shea's duplicates count off numbers each time a familiar is taken down. "Two hundred ninety-one." Another clone continues, "Two hundred ninety-two."

*

Marion surfaces quietly from an abandoned cell phone twenty yards behind the Prime Wizard and his mercenary until she is completely exposed. She calls out quietly in a childlike singsong voice, "Won't you help me Mister Mercenary man." Her voice is so faint that Guy Fleet questions whether he heard what he thought he heard.

He snatches a glance over his shoulder and spots the flickering image of Marion dressed in a short pink baby doll dress with a white bow tied around her waist. Each of her patent leather shoes rests upon a cell phone. He cannot fathom why she holds a large red lollipop.

Guy Fleet spins and draws the pistols at his waist. He shoots blast after blast at Marion. Bam Bam Bam Bam Bam.

The rounds leave quick dimples of impact on the pixels that make up her body and pass harmlessly through.

She now has Tovenaar's full attention.

Marion keeps steady eye contact with the Industrial Age Wizard. She touches her index finger just under her eye and pulls down an imaginary tear.

Guy Fleet has just proven that physical violence will not take her down. Tovenaar is also painfully aware that he cannot kill her with industrial magic. He does not attack.

Marion smiles coyly and swings her right hand back then forwards releasing a dozen pink plasma globes at Tovenaar's lackey. The globes sprout legs and develop large toothy voracious mouths as they charge.

Guy Fleet turns and makes a run for it.

218

The pinkies give chase. The first to reach him springs up and swallows his right foot. Others clamp down on his left foot and each of his hands, pistols, and all.

He collapses into a sitting position as the remaining animated pink nightmares pile on, effectively securing the mercenary in a blob of plasma from his feet to just under his chin.

"You are playing with fire, little girl," Guy Fleet warns. "None of this will matter in the end," he taunts Marion. "You are up against the one who invented *too big to fail*. He owns everyone that matters, and they in turn will do whatever he wants them to."

Marion accurately throws her red plasma lollipop into Guy Fleet's mouth which at once seals his jaw and shuts him up. She addresses Tovenaar, "Is it professional courtesy that you haven't taken a shot at me yet? Or is there another reason?"

Tovenaar stays silent. This is his first opportunity to study one of his enemies up close. *She is wise beyond her years. Her approach to magic has a playful innocence. Overconfidence will be her downfall.*

Marion's shines an arrogant smile at her adversary. "If I neglected to formally introduce myself, my name is Marion." She allows the phone she is standing on to slowly suck her back in.

Tovenaar finally understands what he is up against. What he doesn't realize is the significance of the image of Marion's face that remains on the phone.

Guy Fleet squirms as he tries to warn Tovenaar that she is still present, but the ridiculous lollipop gag will not budge.

Tovenaar considers the thousands of cell phones that glow on the battlefield like stars in the night sky. A plan of action comes to mind. "Destroy the phones!"

The familiars have already thrown down their phones in fear of the snakes but are reluctant to destroy their only source of magic. They are slow to respond.

"Cristobal, heed my call!"

Cristobal appears before his master. He stifles a laugh when he notices Guy Fleet's predicament.

Tovenaar commands him, "Destroy the phones. Now!"

"All of them?" Cristobal is dubious. "Sure boss, but I would have to touch each one and it might take—"

"Raise the tide!" Tovenaar simplifies his command. "Drown the damn phones and our enemies will have no weapons!"

Cristobal stares back in dismay. He fears that in his weakened condition, casting a spell of this size may exhaust his dwindling reserves of life energy. It is impossible, however, to refuse, or even to question his master's command. He cracks his weary knuckles and vanishes.

Marion's image disappears from the phone's screen.

chapter 36

Antonio and Shea persist in hyper-jumping from one phone to another in random areas of the marsh, further thinning Tovenaar's army. A beleaguered group of familiars close ranks to surround one of the Antonio clones from a *safe* distance.

"He can't get us all if we rush him," a familiar with a cockney British accent assures the twenty or so troops as they cautiously tighten the circle around their prey. "On my call…"

Antonio responds with a grin as more arms sprout from each side of his torso. Ten arms simultaneously reach into his wizard's closet and reappear, armed with thumb drives.

The familiars scramble back but keep their circle intact.

Their leader speaks, "Are those thumb drives? You are putting us on bloody thumb drives?"

"Pretty cool, huh?" Antonio spins into them like a mini twister taking a total of two seconds to secure all twenty of them. He scans the field for his next group to attack and sees something that excites him. He calls into a phone.

"Shea, I see a karate familiar." The five Antonio clones merge back to one before he jumps into the phone and lets it drop. He reappears thirty yards from a familiar who wears a black gi tied off with a black belt and carries a double-edged sword.

Shea sprouts from a nearby phone beside Antonio.

"You think your karate is good enough to take him?" Antonio challenges Shea.

"That's not karate," Shea explains. "It is Chinese Shaolin Kung Fu, and that is a Wushu Dragon Sword."

The familiar raises his sword and stands ready to face his enemies. A cell phone is mounted just above the hilt. He approaches them with intricate footwork and an emotionless facial expression.

Shea is intrigued. "He looks serious."

Antonio calls out in Chinese, "Rúguô nî dábaî wô de pengyóu wô jiu ráole nî." *I will spare you if you can beat my friend here.*

The familiar hesitates, surprised to be addressed in his own language. He yells, "Kiai!" and charges Shea with his sword held high for a downward slashing head shot. Red plasma glows along the blade.

Like a seasoned athlete, Shea deftly sidesteps and bends back to avoid the blade. He grabs his opponent's left arm and pulls it down while swinging his elbow upwards into the swordsman's bicep.

The familiar yells out in pain and drops the sword.

Shea lowers his hand with a thumb drive and touches his opponent's forehead.

The familiar is sucked into the drive minus his gi and sword.

"You *do* have moves, kid." Antonio nods approvingly before splitting back into five versions of himself.

Shea reaches down to collect the sword and the scabbard which he admires before depositing into his wizard's closet. He looks sideways at the Antonios with an irked expression. "By the way, I know what you said to him."

All five Antonios respond differently, but in unison:

"I needed to know if you really knew Kung Fu."

"That move was the bomb."

"Are you still my boy?"

"Dude, you won a sword."

"When did you learn Chinese?"

Shea can't help but laugh. "Let's finish this." He steps into a phone.

*

Lawrence and Principal Skinner stare through their binoculars as multiple Antonios and Sheas easily sweep through clusters of familiars. From every corner of the field of battle, Tovenaar's troops run toward him for his protection.

Principal Skinner questions Lawrence, "Should we be concerned the police have not arrived yet?"

"Antonio is blocking all calls from this area," Lawrence explains. He sniffs suspiciously then asks, "Where have you been?"

Principal Skinner reacts defensively, "Excuse me, but I was not privy to any conversation about blocking emergency calls. I would surely have recommended against it."

Lawrence smiles. "Sorry Mrs. S, I was talking to Archibald."

Whooomph. Archibald appears between them. "Do not tell me you smelt me approaching."

"Pickles and warm milk." Lawrence smirks. "No really, where did you go?"

"I almost forgot something," Archibald mumbles. "Mind your business."

Lawrence's phone lights up and Marion's face peers out from the screen. She looks concerned. "Please tell me Archibald is with you."

Lawrence points the screen to Archibald for a face time meeting.

"We need you, Archie. That creep Cristobal is trying to bring on high tide to drown the phones in the marsh."

The principal flinches at the mention of Cristobal's name.

So does Archibald. "You still require the telephones?"

"It will make things much easier," Marion explains. "We are so close to winning this."

Archibald hesitates out of habit. Until today, he never dared to join the actual fighting. It was unthinkable to risk his wellbeing by confronting Cristobal, or to be anywhere within ten miles of Tovenaar while still in possession of Master Llewellyn's soul stone. He knows full well that Tovenaar could easily torture the soul stone from him, despite what he told Antonio.

Today is a different story though. These three adepts are unconventional. Any one of them could be a wizard. They have proven themselves to be of superior ability. This is his best chance to destroy Tovenaar. Even if he is not likely to survive the next five minutes, he has decided that enough is enough. He is tired of running.

"I'm on it, Ms. Marion." He bows deeply.

Marion's eyes twinkle. "Thank you, Archie. Please be careful."

Whooomph. Archibald disappears.

Lawrence returns the night vision binoculars to his eyes and scans the marsh in search of Cristobal. He is curious to see how the scumbag will raise the tide. Without looking away, he informs Principal Skinner, "Things are getting lit." He gets no answer. "How did they say it in your day? Things are getting all Wang Chung?"

Again, no response.

Lawrence pulls the binoculars from his eyes to discover that Principal Skinner is no longer beside him.

*

Cristobal's face contorts from the physical strain it takes to raise the tide. His body trembles. Even if he were not already exhausted from a long day of fetching familiars from around the globe, and even if the soul stone he has been relying on wasn't almost completely depleted, this would be an arduous task.

He must practically raise the tide of the entire Long Island Sound for the tide of the Crab Meadow Salt Marsh to rise.

Beads of sweat trickle down over and around his black scales.

The narrow streams in the marsh begin to rise.

Cristobal is past the physical exertion part of his spell. It is now a simple matter of supporting the spell's momentum. He looks outward across the marsh and notices haggard looking familiars running like cowards from the spry adepts who give chase.

"Familiars suck," he mutters under his breath.

Before long, the water creeps onto dry land. The nearest cell phones short out and fade to black.

*

Archibald appears amongst the tall grasses beside the primary inlet of water that connects the marsh to the Long Island Sound. Where better to prevent the tide from rising and keep a safe distance from the fighting. No point in taking unnecessary risks.

His first plan is to synchronize his magic with the natural rhythms of the tide. He knows of such a spell. But even if he can pull it off, he will be severely drained. He thinks to himself, *How would Master Llewellyn handle this?*

Of course he would simply say, *"Cristobal, you vile creature, I reverse your spell."*

*

Cristobal gleefully watches the water creep along the grass and

225

swallow phone after phone. Tovenaar will surely be pleased. Maybe he will even allow him to take a vacation in the tropics. Cristobal has not had a day off since he betrayed Llewellyn and agreed to become Tovenaar's right hand man, so to speak. His days consist of waiting for Tovenaar's next command. He begins to hum contentedly.

Wait. Something is not right! The tide has stopped rising. It begins to recede.

"What!" Cristobal gasps and drops back to his knees, redoubling his magical efforts. The water level continues to sink. His filmy eyes scan the marsh to find the cause. He spies a pale greenish glow by one of the wider waterways two hundred yards away. *There he is, that wormy little turd!*

Tovenaar's voice assaults his eardrums. "The whole thing, Cristobal! Flood the entire damn marsh!"

Cristobal intensifies his efforts, but the water does not respond. *I do not need this!* His thoughts are illogical and scattered. *Abel cannot be doing this! The adepts must be helping him.* "He is cheating!"

Tovenaar's lips tighten as he watches his army dwindle. The smaller it becomes, the more his frustration with Cristobal's ineptitude increases. He roars, "Cristobal!"

Cristobal appears twenty yards behind Archibald. His barely contained rage is rivaled by the thrill that he will finally get to pluck this lifelong thorn from his side. Regrettably, Abel must remain alive long enough to remove Llewellyn's soul stone from his wizard's cupboard.

Exhaustion muddles Cristobal's mind. His thoughts waver between Tovenaar's urgency to drown the phones and deciding the fate of Archibald Abel. He wastes precious time considering which malady to inflict upon him.

I will root his feet into the sandy marsh and let the rising tide finish him once he no longer serves a purpose. No.

I will grant Archibald's body, from his scrawny neck to his oversized feet, the gift of its true linear age of three hundred and fifty-six years. No.

I will take possession of his body and use his own hand to extract the soul stone from his wizard's cupboard. Yes!

An eager smile twists across Cristobal's face.

"Raise the tide, damn you!" Tovenaar bellows once again.

Cristobal raises his arms and mutters an incoherent spell. Visible waves of energy gather in his arms. A filmy, black-scaled veneer sloughs from his body and extends toward an unsuspecting Archibald.

"Ooof!!"

Lawrence blindsides Cristobal like a linebacker sacking a quarterback and disrupts the spell. He turns and charges back to deliver the second strike of a one-two punch. His battle cry is, "Suck this, dickhead."

Still sprawled on the ground, Cristobal raises a shaky right hand toward his attacker. With barely enough time to cast a hastily reasoned spell, he splays his four fingers outward with a snapping motion.

A quick pulse of sorcery strikes Lawrence's right leg, shredding denim from his jeans. His leg shrivels to half its size. The skin turns an odd shade of pink and sprouts coarse hair. His foot becomes cloven hoofed, and when it does not reach the ground in stride, he face-plants into the mud.

"What the hell is this… a freaking pig's leg?" Lawrence scrambles for cover. He crawls to one of the now shallow streams and rolls in.

Cristobal sits up and twists his spine to pop his vertebrae back into place.

When he looks up, Archibald is staring down at him with a quizzical look on his face.

Possessing his enemy by stealth is no longer a possibility. Cristobal raises his arms and focuses a luminance of dark magic to amass at his hands.

He claps a powerful bolt of energy at Archibald.

chapter 38

Unaware of Archibald's predicament, multiple versions of Antonio and Shea flicker across the marsh as they collect more of the panic-stricken familiars. A single image of Marion joins them, now casually dressed in jeans and a hoodie.

"Do you guys have this?" She calls out sweetly while nonchalantly thumb-driving a tall lanky familiar whose dark complexion blends with his scales.

"We're good, babe," five clones of Antonio simultaneously reply.

"What's up?" One of the Shea's asks.

"Tovenaar's robot said something that gave me an idea." She wears a mischievous grin. "I need to go into the Hyper Realm and evaluate a theory."

"Maybe we should go with you," a different clone of Shea calls out over his shoulder while thumb-driving a screaming familiar.

"She has this," Antonio coolly assures him.

Marion smiles and gives him a slight nod, appreciating his confidence in her decision. She disappears into one of the discarded cell phones.

"It's not like we can't be in two places at once," Shea argues.

Antonio catches Shea's look of concern. "She will be safer in the Hyper Realm."

Shea still seems unconvinced.

"Don't worry, she'll be fine." Antonio playfully punches Shea's arm, "You breezy, my cheesy?"

Shea grudgingly goes along with it.

*

Archibald sighs ever so slightly as his chest absorbs the brunt of Cristobal's spell. The force shudders through his body then dissipates.

For centuries, he had been dreading the day he would come face to face with Cristobal. Now that the moment has arrived, Archibald is surprised to find himself feeling more puzzled than afraid. He has an epiphany.

*

Tovenaar assesses the situation. His remaining familiars are finally destroying the phones that are strewn about the marsh, but not quickly enough. He has seen the ones who have wizard's cupboards foolishly stash away a phone. He understands their reluctance to give up their only sources of power, but even one live phone could become catastrophic.

Thousands of phones continue to glimmer actively in a one square mile radius.

His mercenary is still useless under a pile of computer-generated plasmatic restraints.

Even Cristobal is failing him.

230

Tovenaar has not survived this long by relying on the competence of subordinates.

He gestures forcefully at the ground directing blasts of Industrial Age energy in pulse-pounding wave after pulse-pounding wave. A haze of molecular metal extracts from the earth. A mist of alloy pulls from Tovenaar's aura and proceeds to form into plates and rods and bars that self-assemble to construct a small launchpad. The metal continues to amass forming a trap door which slides open revealing a missile the size of a fire hydrant.

Tovenaar does not hesitate. He hammers down on a large metal button with his fist.

A low pitch rumble combines with a high-pitched squeal as the missile launches skyward. It explodes with an electromagnetic blast that radiates for miles.

The ground trembles from the explosion.

Every cell phone and computer in the marsh shorts out and fades to black. If not for the light of the moon, the marsh would be cloaked in complete darkness.

The concussion knocks everyone in the vicinity to the ground.

"What the hell was that?" Shea yells out.

"That, my friend, was an electromagnetic pulse," Antonio informs him. "The sonuvabitch came prepared with a freaking EMP."

The familiars stagger to their feet. They feel powerless without their phones but sense an advantage in numbers now that their enemies are also weaponless. They are eager for revenge and will settle for a good old-fashioned beat down.

"Of course, he did," Shea agrees in a calmer conversational tone. He taps the closest familiar with a thumb drive. The curly-haired familiar instinctively cringes back but does not get sucked in.

Curly sneers. "Guess you're not so tough now." He takes a

confident step forward.

"Don't forget our bodies are fully physical again," Antonio quietly reminds Shea. "And anything computerized that was exposed to the pulse is now toast."

Shea reflexively resorts to using his newfound knowledge of martial arts to his advantage with a roundhouse kick to his would-be attacker's face. The familiar falls to the ground with a thud.

Shea casually reaches into his wizard's closet and retrieves thumb drives that were not exposed to the EMP. He taps the backside of the downed familiar then kicks aside the remnants of the captured familiar's clothing. He faces the remaining group.

"Who's next?" Shea takes a step forward.

They all turn and run blindly into the darkness.

"Buh-bye!" Antonio calls out mockingly before directing his attention to locating Tovenaar. He spots the bastard in the distance riding a mechanical tank-tread device.

He is quickly closing in on Archibald who is facing off with Cristobal.

"Oh no!" Antonio says under his breath and runs at an angle to intercept the Prime Wizard. "Hurry before Archibald screws this up."

Shea gives chase. He felt invincible while his body was charged with Hyper Realm energy, but now that he is physical again, he feels sluggish and is already gasping for air.

As fatigued as he is, Cristobal throws everything he has at Archibald to the point of exasperation. He threatens, "I don't know how those little pricks are protecting you, but they will pay dearly."

He tries again with yet another supernatural assault. The ground at Archibald's feet steams and catches fire as molten lava oozes from under the bed of sea grass. Cristobal cannot believe his eyes when Archibald barely flinches and the lava cools and hardens.

Archibald steps up onto the newly formed lava rock and smiles down at Cristobal. "My turn." Energy crackles as he splays his fingers for a counter assault.

Two robotic orbs race past Cristobal and head straight for Archibald. Like liquid metal Pac-men, they swoop in and clamp down over Archibald's hands.

With a flick of his hand, Tovenaar releases two more grinning orbs that engulf Archibald's feet, pulling him spread eagle onto his back.

Tovenaar rolls in on his motorized platform stopping inches from Archibald's head. He hops off wearing an astonished look on his rugged face.

"A goddamned wizard of the Agricultural Age." He watches in amusement as Archibald struggles against the weight of the orbs. "How the hell did I miss *you* for all these centuries?"

"That's not a wizard!" Cristobal shrieks. "He's the familiar that carries Llewellyn's soul stone."

"A familiar cannot harm a wizard, as you have just demonstrated," Tovenaar smirks not taking his eyes off the struggling Archibald. "Be he a familiar or a wizard, it hardly matters now."

Centuries of justifying his decision to betray Llewellyn to save his own ass has falsely inflated Cristobal's ego. He had considered himself to be history's most powerful familiar and could live with that. But now, the little peon he once looked down on with contempt is a *WIZARD?*

Reality sets in. He is only just a lowly familiar. Cristobal's mind reacts like a tempest in an outhouse. His fingers clench into fists. A scream builds silently in his head before finally escaping his crusty lips.

He lunges at Archibald, who is restrained by Tovenaar's metal orbs.

CLANG!

The spade end of Principal Skinner's shovel strikes Cristobal's forehead so hard that his feet leave the ground.

He is unconscious before his back hits the dirt.

The principal promptly positions the blade of her shovel against Cristobal's chest. Revenge has focused her mind into tunnel vision. She raises a foot to stomp the blade deep into his degenerative heart. Regretfully, she does not see Tovenaar's orb until it clamps over her head.

Principal Skinner's muffled cries of rage echo futilely. She takes a blind step before stumbling to the ground.

Tovenaar stares down at the woman with a quizzical yet bemused look on his face.

"DO NOT HARM HER!" Antonio's voice commands with a tone of authority.

*

The Hyper Realm quakes violently tossing Marion like a rag doll. Every pixel of her digital self struggles to hold itself together. She spasms wildly as infinite torrents of data course through her very being. She feels her sense of reality fading and struggles to remain conscious.

One final panicked fragment of self-awareness confirms that her experiment went wrong, and she let everyone down.

She cries out silently, "I'm so sorry!"

*

Tovenaar turns his attention away from the implausible woman who just brained his most powerful familiar and regards Antonio with narrowed eyes.

"You've got some pair of balls for a delinquent with no weapons." Tovenaar has no way to know that his intel on these upstarts is vastly outdated. He watches with amusement as Shea slowly jogs over and stoops, resting his hands on both knees, trying to catch his breath.

"This must be the outsider with a distaste for sports. And where is the girl, I wonder?"

He motions with a head nod to his largest remaining familiar to attack Shea.

With an incoherent scream of pent-up vengeance, the familiar charges Shea.

Shea doesn't bother to stand up for the attack. He reaches out a thumb drive, which the familiar runs straight into and disappears. His clothing flops to the ground.

Shea finally stands and questions Antonio, "Were we mistaken about how he keeps his youthful appearance?"

Antonio paces around Tovenaar. He speaks in a calm voice, "I had a theory that you created the familiars to use as living soul stones to bolster your longevity."

His confident demeanor and civil vocabulary take Tovenaar by surprise. "No, but I like the way you think." He turns as Antonio continues to circle him. Tovenaar has a sinking feeling that he critically underestimated these adepts but stays poised for any slip on their part.

Shea joins Antonio by circling the wizard in a counterclockwise direction. He theorizes, "A wizard from a preceding age cannot use sorcery to harm a magical entity from a proceeding age." He grins menacingly. "Isn't that about right, Old Man?"

Antonio grins as well. "This clown cannot use magic to harm us for the same reason Archibald cannot harm him."

Shea feels cocky now and points a finger at Tovenaar. "You cannot kill an adept from a later age of magic. But, if you can con one to betray his friends and pledge his servitude to you, that adept becomes bound to you while the other two…" He pauses for dramatic effect.

Still restrained and on his back Archibald finishes the sentence. "Become human once again."

"Rendering them defenseless," Shea adds.

"And easy to murder," Antonio concludes.

Tovenaar informs them, "And yet a lowly adept of any age cannot harm a wizard, let alone a Prime Wizard."

"The question before us is," Antonio addresses Shea, "how do we break the stalemate and rid the world of this sonuvabitch?"

Shea cannot stop thinking about what Marion said before she entered the Hyper Realm. *Something the robot said gave her insight about Tovenaar.* He wonders what's taking her so long. *Where are*

Antonio extends his hand towards Guy Fleet, who is still bound by Marion's pink plasma. The lollipop gag softens to a formless blob and floats to Antonio's outstretched hand. The plasma hovers for a moment between his fingers before separating into seven bullet-shaped pieces that align in a circle and rotate as if spinning in the barrel of a pistol. He wants to test the theory that he cannot harm the Prime Wizard.

Tovenaar faces Antonio's makeshift weapon stoically. He suspects a shootout will cause no considerable damage to either of them. His instincts compel him to be patient.

Antonio is riding a full-blown power trip while toying with the murderous wizard. He has never felt so in control. So powerful. So…dizzy.

The suspended pink bullets lose cohesion and splatter onto the dirt.

The world spins around him. His vision tunnels as he falls to the ground.

Shea feels it as well. He clumsily aims a cell phone at Tovenaar to blast him, but only a spurt of plasma spills out. "Did we screw this up?" He asks as he falls to his knees.

"I'LL TAKE IT!" Tovenaar rejoices with a humorless laugh. He magically propels a cluster of his metallic orbs to restrain Shea and Antonio. Just in case their moment of weakness passes.

"I don't know what just happened to you insolent bastards, but a win is a win."

The orbs swallow the hands and feet of his adversaries. He gestures his palms upward, causing the orbs to rise. Shea and Antonio float several feet above the ground as the orbs begin to pull their limbs in opposing directions.

It is Tovenaar's turn to taunt. He stands smugly between the hovering adepts. "Too young to understand the value of patience."

Antonio grimaces as the orbs apply more pressure. "This is not over," he threatens.

Tovenaar's voice is devoid of humor. "I will admit that it was the girl's magic that inspired these orbs, but do not expect to see her again. Even if she did not betray you and it was my EMP that drained your magic," he sweeps his arm in a grand gesture, "the nearest working computer is more than five miles away."

His eyes light up. "Let us suppose she is alive. Even if she manages to steal a fast car, a Bugatti perhaps, she will only get here in time to bury your corpses."

Guy Fleet is still bound by the plasma, but his mouth is now free for him to chime in. "You picked a fight with the wrong individual. Tovenaar owns the very people who influence your local police force. He will notify every squad car on the street to be on the lookout for your spooky little girlfriend if she dares to show her face."

Tovenaar feels tired and has an uneasy feeling about these adepts abruptly losing their powers. He decides it is best to finish this business and beat a hasty exit.

He assesses his captives and decides Shea looks like the more weak-minded of the two. He makes him an offer.

"You are once again only human, but someone with your knowledge of computer magic may be of use to me." He leans in uncomfortably close to Shea's face. "Join me and live on."

Shea is not about to betray his friends. "No way," he grunts as the orbs pull harder.

Tovenaar sweetens the deal. "Just give up on this one," he motions to Antonio, "and you and your girlfriend can live happily ever after."

He hisses through clenched teeth, "Not a chance, creep."

Tovenaar scowls with disappointment. He turns to Antonio and offers the same deal. "And you?"

Antonio's face drips with sweat from the pain he is enduring. He stares directly into the wizard's piercing eyes. "In your dreams."

Tovenaar must accept that he will not gain their extraordinary knowledge of computer magic. At least he will leave with Llewellyn's soul stone and Cristobal will live on and continue to be of use to him.

He turns his attention to Archibald. "You understand your time is short, so I won't insult your intelligence."

He wiggles his fingers while spreading his hands apart, causing the orbs on Shea and Antonio's limbs to pull more forcefully.

"Give me Llewellyn's soul stone, or I will draw and quarter your friends."

"Don't you dare give it to him!" Shea yells.

Antonio calls out through the pain, "Dammit, Archibald! I told you to not get caught!"

Tovenaar readies his hands to command the orbs to destroy the two adepts. "Give it to me," he repeats calmly.

Archibald has finally found his courage. He lifts his chin in defiance and addresses Tovenaar. "These two young adepts understand that the world will be a better place the quicker you wither away, even if they are not here to see it."

Tovenaar scowls. "Violence then."

Antonio and Shea continue to struggle against the incessant strain of the metallic orbs that pull on their limbs.

"Marion must be in trouble," Shea whispers painfully through gritted teeth.

"No shit, she's in trouble."

A familiar sucker punches Antonio in the ribs to shut him up.

"Fall back," Tovenaar commands his familiars. He wipes his damp forehead with the back of his coat sleeve. Tovenaar cannot recall ever feeling this weary.

The match up tonight was closer than he was prepared for. *I should have taken the field on occasion to stay in shape.* He has a sinking feeling that the next groups of computer adepts are likely to become more difficult to deal with. He frowns at his downed helicopter and wearily gestures a reconstruction spell.

His magic works to repair the damage, but at a sloth's pace.

Tovenaar checks on Cristobal, his other mode of transportation, who is in worse shape than the copter. Still breathing, at least, but he needs a new soul stone more than ever if he is to remain useful.

"You little bastards put up good a fight," Tovenaar commends Antonio and Shea. "I'll give you that."

He turns his full attention to Archibald Abel. "I'll have Llewellyn's soul stone now," he demands.

Archibald shakes his head. "The stone will follow me to the grave."

Tovenaar doesn't wish to waste time torturing Archibald. *Perhaps this woman who knocked out Cristobal means something to these belligerent fools.* He relaxes the intensity of the orbs that are straining to dismember the two adepts. He needs them focused.

Antonio, Shea, and Archibald watch helplessly as another orb self-assembles around Principal Skinner's feet. The orb around her head lifts her off the ground. Her muffled screams echo from inside the metal chamber.

"Leave her out of this!" Antonio threatens.

"Why do you care about her?" Tovenaar addresses Antonio. "Is this your mother?

He cocks his head in Shea's direction. "Your mama, is she?"

He gets no answer from either of them, so he kicks Archibald in the ribs.

"Will her torso split at the midsection, or will her head simply pop off first?" Tovenaar questions. "Heads or tails?" He gets right in Archibald's face. "Or will you suffer her to live?"

Tovenaar is growing impatient. He gestures to add more tension to the principal's orbs. Her muffled screams grow louder.

A tear runs down Archibald's cheek. He offers Tovenaar a desperate counteroffer. "Everybody lives, and you get the soul stone."

"I could just as easily make do with *your* soul stone, wizard, as diminutive as it must be." Tovenaar spits with contempt.

Until only a few minutes ago Archibald did not realize he was a wizard and hadn't had the time to reason he may have developed a soul stone of his own. Despite this added complication, he tries again for mercy. "Everyone lives together in the shame of our failures, or we die together as heroes who almost took the throne."

Cristobal reveals he has regained consciousness and screams, "Kill them all." He cradles his head with both his arms to relieve his pain.

With his eyes, Archibald again implores Antonio and Shea to make the dreaded decision for him.

They both disregard his silent pleas.

He gives in and tells Tovenaar, "You will have Llewellin's soul stone in exchange for the woman's life."

"Agreed!"

One orb opens enough to allow Archibald's right hand to slide out. It continues to hover beside him, ready to encase his hand if he tries something foolish.

The orbs that constrain Principal Skinners' head and feet crumble to dust. She falls unceremoniously to the ground.

Tovenaar clears his throat to remind Archibald it is time to fulfill his end of the bargain.

Archibald usually accesses his cupboard with his left hand. He reaches awkwardly with his right arm down to his right side until his hand vanishes into his wizard's cupboard. He squirms clumsily, as if searching through the clutter of a junk drawer. A desperate attempt to delay the inevitable.

Tovenaar's eyes tighten impatiently. "Stalling will not make your deaths any more pleasant."

"I know it's here somewhere." He continues searching. "Here it is."

A bright glow radiates from Archibald's cupboard. In the darkness of night, it becomes almost blinding as Archibald draws it out.

When Tovenaar's eyes adjust to the glare, he realizes that Archibald Abel is not holding a soul stone. "What is this bullshit…?"

Archibald's right hand, protected by a thick ill-fitting left-handed yellow rubber glove, holds a blinged-out pink cell phone. Marion's face fills the screen. He shows the screen to Tovenaar.

With the chorus of a thousand angels, Marion explodes from the phone surrounded by veils of chaotic energy generated by the Hyper Realm.

Tovenaar is thrown back twenty feet into Cristobal.

Marion stands tall like an exquisite goddess. Gossamer robes of pure magic swirl about her. The air crackles with static electricity as the world's magic that once encompassed Tovenaar now flows through Marion. She moves her index finger with a slight downward motion which reduces the volume of the 'chorus of angels' audio.

Without so much as a gesture, a thin dusting of computer plasma swarms to the metal orbs that bind her friends and quickly dissolves the metal into crumbling cakes of rust.

Shea and Antonio drop gently to the ground.

Marion speaks her first words as the Prime Sorceress of the Computer Age, "Where is Lawrence?" Her voice resonates with power.

Lawrence calls out from the nearest stream of water. "I was waiting for my chance to jump this fool." He pulls himself out and hobbles awkwardly on his mismatched legs to join his friends in victory. "Nice touch with the celestial chorus. I could not have done it any better."

Marion smiles with relief.

Prime Sorceress of the Computer Age, Marion Grey, turns her full attention to Tovenaar, who is now just an ordinary wizard of the Industrial Age. "Your reign is ended."

Tovenaar scrambles to his feet and yells defiantly, "I may no longer be the Prime Wizard, but I still wield the magic of my age" he bluffs. "You cannot end me. I am powerful in more ways than just sorcery. More ways than you can even imagine, little girl."

Marion cracks an endearing smile reminiscent of the once human student she used to be. "You are destitute, sweetie." And with a sterner voice, "You are no longer able to pay off your debts to your corrupt leaders of society."

Tovenaar refuses to accept defeat. He argues belligerently, "I cannot kill you, but my influence is..."

"Ended." Marion cuts him off mid-sentence and explains. "I traced back every account in every bank in every country in the world to their account holders and I discovered hundreds of billion-dollar accounts with no name attached to them. I distinguished those as being your secret accounts. I have distributed the funds equally to every other account in existence." She adds, "A little extra for charities."

The color drains from Tovenaar's face.

"Milady," Archibald councils, "Now would be the time to kill him."

"Kill them both," Principal Skinner eggs her on while staring down Cristobal.

Tovenaar shakes Cristobal by the shoulders and commands, "Mangrove!"

Cristobal shrieks from the pain in his head caused by Principal Skinner's shovel.

"Get us out of here dammit!" Tovenaar yells and continues to shake Cristobal as he looks over his shoulder expecting Marion to strike.

Antonio informs everyone, "Marion is not going to kill them."

All eyes turn to Marion. She meets their surprised stares at once and explains, "I will not set the tone of my age with an act of murder."

No one tries to argue against Marion's logic.

"Mangrove. Mangrove." Tovenaar shakes Cristobal's shoulders. "Take us to the Mangrove, blast you!"

Cristobal draws deeply from his precious remaining power. Tovenaar and Cristobal vanish.

Guy Fleet calls after his master, "Wait! What about me?"

Tovenaar's remaining familiars flee into the darkness.

In a fraction of a flash, Marion stands before Guy Fleet, who is still bound from toe to chin in pink plasma. She presses her two hands to the automaton's temples and releases a surge of magic. "Do we understand each other?" She asks kindly.

"Yes, your grace."

The plasma dissolves and falls away from Guy Fleet in chunks.

"I am to follow Tovenaar and Cristobal to the Mangrove Swamp in Karachi, Pakistan, via this helicopter that you will restore. I will then attempt to relieve Tovenaar of his reserves of gold and silver."

"And?" Marion pushes.

Guy Fleet continues, "I will spread word that Tovenaar's reign is over and that he is bereft of funds." Before Marion can say go, Guy Fleet is trotting to the helicopter.

Marion dispatches a swarm of plasma, bolstered by the world's magic, past the running Guy Fleet to the damaged helicopter. It is repaired before he even reaches it.

She turns to her friends with a glorious smile on her face. "Tovenaar bound a minor demon to inhabit his automaton. I simply copied its personality onto a computer and replaced it. I can track him anywhere."

"And what of the demon?" Archibald asks.

"You don't want to know."

Marion approaches her friends. The shimmering magic that surrounds her dissipates.

"We did it!"

Marion drapes her arm over Archibald's shoulders. "Your acting is worthy of a freaking Academy Award!" She asks the others, "Wasn't Archie outstanding?"

She notices Shea and Antonio do not look as happy as they should. "What's wrong?"

"The magic has left us," Shea answers dejectedly. "We're back to normal again."

This momentarily surprises Marion, but she suddenly realizes that all along, only one of them would own the magic. She releases Archie from her hug. "Did you know that only one of us would retain the magic?

"I suspected," Archibald replies. "I couldn't think of a good reason to bring it up."

"Do you both still recall what you have learned?"

"Indubitably," Antonio smiles.

Shea flashes a strained smile. "A consolation prize, I guess."

"We'll figure something out," she promises them.

Lawrence uses Principal Skinner's shovel as a makeshift crutch while he balances on his normal leg. His new pig leg twitches incessantly at his side. "Yo, Archie…bald, when did you become a full-blown wizard?"

Archibald simply shrugs. "When did I even become an apprentice, for that matter?"

"If I had to guess," Antonio suggests, "it was when Llewellyn released you from his service as a familiar. It was then that you automatically became an apprentice, as per the original contract."

Marion answers with her opinion, "And it was when you accomplished a grand feat that you became a wizard. Perhaps when you conjured a means of finding Computer Age adepts." She smiles with pride at her friend.

Shea asks, "So when you traced every bank account in the entire world, it was a grand enough feat to make you a wizard?"

"As I was processing infinite amounts of raw data, I became one with the internet. That is when the world's magic embraced me."

She turns her attention to Lawrence. "Speaking of limits, it seems we have some pork in our Lasagna." She frowns sympathetically. "What are we going to do with you?"

"I've been wondering the same thing," Lawrence admits. "There's a girl in my math class that seems freaky enough to be into this." He jokingly motions to his pig leg.

Antonio has a thought. "If you were to bring him into the Hyper Realm, I surmise you could undo what has been done with a gradual pixel swap until his leg returns to normalcy."

"You do remember what happened the last time I exposed him to the Hyper Realm?"

Shea reasons, "It might work out better if you make Lawrence a familiar."

Lawrence is thrilled. "Please please please, Marion, I mean, your highness," he begs. "Please make me your familiar."

Marion hesitates. "I wouldn't even know where to begin…" She looks pleadingly to Archibald for a better suggestion.

"Well, my dear, you would simply make him the offer…"

"What like, hey Lasagna, do you want to be my familiar?" Marion wrinkles her nose.

"And he would accept." Archibald continues, "But…"

Lawrence jumps at the opportunity before Archibald can complete his sentence. "I accept!" He shakes his fist with delight. "Me and Chainsaw are going to bust a cap on the internet." He touches his hand to Marion's cell phone that Archibald still holds in his gloved hand and is instantly sucked into the Hyper Realm.

His empty clothes flutter to the ground.

Marion's jaw drops. She looks to her friends desperately. "How did I let this happen?" She turns to Archibald, "You said *but*."

Archibald smiles, "I was going to say, *but* since I am a wizard now, I can undo any of Cristobal's old spells." He reaches out a hand to Principal Skinner, "Ms. Skinner, I believe I can ease your mind."

Principal Skinner would give anything to not have to bear the burden of a sin she never committed. She gingerly takes Archibald's hand, hopeful he can remove the horrid memory that Cristobal placed in her mind.

A tiny crackling surge of green energy rushes from Archibald's fingertips. It courses up the principal's arm disappearing at her forehead.

She releases his hand as if zapped with a shock of static electricity. Principal Skinner exhales sharply. All lines of stress vanish from her face.

"You look ten years younger," Marion compliments. "How do you feel?"

Pamela Skinner cannot recall why she was so distraught all day. "I feel like singing," the principal admits in a falsetto voice. "I feel wonderful."

Marion regards Archibald with a beaming smile. "You are going to be a wonderful wizard, Archibald Abel." She considers. "You told us Cristobal put terrible spells on innocent adepts once they were betrayed."

"Yes, that is true."

"When you find those adepts and reverse Cristobal's magic, would you please put them in touch with me."

"I may have to travel the world to locate them." His eyes light up, "Perhaps it's even time to revisit England."

Marion motions to her phone then winks. "You have my number."

She turns her attention to the two boys she still has raging crushes on and gives them a bittersweet smile. "I better see to Lawrence before he does too much damage."

Shea hands her the pile of Lawrence's clothes.

"I'll be in touch."

Marion, the Prime Sorceress of the Computer Age gives them each a warm hug before allowing herself to be sucked back into the Hyper Realm.

Tovenaar's helicopter, piloted by the new and improved Guy Fleet, lifts swiftly above the marsh. He flies off in pursuit of his old master.

Archibald reaches out to shake hands. "It was an honor to join you both for a historical ass-kicking."

Shea and Antonio cannot help but laugh. They pull him in for a bro hug.

After a moment Antonio asks, "The phone in your wizard's cupboard… who thought to do that?"

"Miss Marion had me stash it when she came over to console me earlier. 'Just in case,' she said. I believe that she knew all along what she was doing." Archibald turns to Principal Skinner and offers his elbow. "Need a lift?"

She smiles shyly and reaches down to retrieve her shovel. She gives Antonio and Shea an approving head nod.

Whooomph. Archibald Abel and Principal Skinner vanish.

"Really?" Antonio says disappointedly. "I didn't expect the moment to end so abruptly."

"Everything happens fast in the Computer Age."

*

The boys walk quietly along a dark road.

Shea notices that Antonio seems lost in thought and hardly reacts to the police cruisers speeding past with flashing lights. To break the silence between him and the person he hated this morning, but now considers a good friend, he asks, "Are you still in love with Marion?"

After a moment, Antonio replies, "I am. Even more so."

Shea admits, "Me too. She is the coolest girl I ever met."

Antonio promises, "I will never again underestimate her."

They are still a couple of miles away from their homes. "Do we even know what time it is?" Shea instinctively reaches for his wizard's closet in search of his phone. To his dismay, he no longer has access to it. "This sucks," he huffs. "How is it that Lawrence is rocking the Hyper Realm, and we are stuck hoofing it down this road like a couple of regular shmucks?"

"If its bothering you so much, go ahead and tell Marion that you want to be her lowly familiar," Antonio remarks with an irked tone.

They continue walking, each pondering their own thoughts.

Antonio breaks the silence, "Marion is the Prime Sorceress of the Computer Age. What I am more concerned with, is how are we going to help her now that we are mere mortals again?"

Shea is painfully aware that while he is wallowing in self-pity for the loss of his powers, Antonio's main concern is Marion's wellbeing.

"I see what you mean." He frowns. "What's next?"

It has been three days since the battle at Crab Meadow and Angela
Grey is still getting accustomed to her daughter's long disappearances.
Now that Marion chooses to spend most of her time in "Computer
Land," Angela is doing her best to cope with being the mother of the
now famous computer queen.

Angela sits at her favorite spot in the kitchen, pursuing her favorite
activity, browsing on-line for dates. She clicks on the bookmark of her
favorite site.

The page loads fine, but something is wrong. All the photos of
the top candidates are identical. She scrolls down further, but all the
images are still of the same man. Mid-fifties, unkempt hair, seriously
out of style wardrobe.

"I'd rate him a six. Seven tops."

She closes the site and launches another. Every photo on the new
site is of the same man.

There cannot be the same glitch on two different websites, she thinks. Then it hits her. She yells at the monitor, "I know what you're doing, young lady!" Angela Grey accuses. "Just because you're the queen of the internet now, it doesn't mean you can mess with my social life."

"Prime Sorceress of the Computer Age," her daughter corrects her. She looks out from the monitor at her mother. "I crunched all the data, and this is the one guy who can make you happy. Better yet, he is the one guy who *you* can make happy."

"But look at him," Angela complains. "He has probably been wearing that same haircut since grade school, and he doesn't even know how to dress for an important picture. He needs too much help."

"And you are just the woman to fix him." Marion gives her mom a conspiratorial look. "His dating bio does not mention that he created two successful companies and sold them both for a nice profit. He is generous to a fault and gives to charities. The only thing he needs is the company of a woman who can help him with the details in life that he has been neglecting."

Angela Grey's attitude does not soften. "I enjoy browsing the sites."

Marion frowns as her face fades from the monitor. "Good night mom."

The dating site reloads with dozens of listings for single men.

"Good night, darling." Angela pours herself a glass of prosecco.

*

One week after the battle of Crab Meadow, two people sit behind computers in a dingy, windowless room. Plain metal shelves hold stacks of hard drives.

The woman speaks with an affected Southern drawl. She reads from a well-worn script. "I assure you, sir. You would not be in this situation if you had not ignored the three prior notices we sent you. If we do not receive your payment today, the authorities will be escorting you from your property tonight."

A flustered voice responds from the phone's earpiece. "But I didn't receive anything from the IRS."

The woman rolls her eyes. "I am going to switch you to my supervisor. Please hold, sir." She points to her cohort.

The man picks up a phone. He clears his throat and speaks with a fake Northeast American accent, "This is *Special Agent Daltrey*. Please confirm your name, address, birth date, and Social Security number."

Special Agent Daltrey's computer monitor explodes outward with a mix of plasma and Lawrence's face and upper body. "What are you chooches up to?" Lawrence grins ear to ear.

The two scam artists tumble out of their chairs and scramble back. A third person rushes through the door tugging at a pistol that is caught between his belt and waistband.

Lawrence vomits a torrent of plasma onto the stacks of hard drives that instantly break down and crumble to the floor.

"All my work!" The man with the pistol still stuck in his waistband yells. "Why do you do this to me?"

"You can have it all back if you answer this one question." He pauses dramatically. "Why isn't dummy spelled with a b?"

Daltrey's mouth drops open without an answer.

"You're banned from the internet," Laurence informs him. He stares menacingly as he slowly sinks back into the Hyper Realm. "I'll be watching you."

*

Four hours after the battle of Crab Meadow, Shea is too wired to sleep. He works on a series of Tai Chi moves in his backyard to burn off excess energy. His new plan is to get in shape as soon as possible, become insanely famous on the Mixed Martial Arts circuit, and then release the greatest MMA video game the world has ever seen.

*

Two hours and one second after the battle of Crab Meadow, Antonio sits slouched at the desk in his bedroom staring wistfully at his laptop. A ding alerts him of a new email. He clicks the link. An opening page shows four thumbnail images with titles.

Testing a Theory - Marion & Antonio Thumb-Driving 2 Motorcycle Familiars.

Battle of Crab Meadow - Shea Takes Down the Wizard's Battle Copter.

Battle of Crab Meadow - Archibald Beats Down the Evil Familiar Called Cristobal.

Battle of Crab Meadow – 5 Antonios Take on an Army of Familiars.

Battle of Crab Meadow - Marion Banishes the Industrial Age Wizard.

Antonio sits up in his chair, *how could Shea have posted these already?* He then notices that the videos were posted by someone identified as chainsaw_789. The videos already have millions of hits and have twice as many comments from users arguing about whether the footage is computer generated or authentic.

Antonio laughs. He touches his fingertips to the screen, without so much as a crackle of plasma, and whispers, "I miss you already, Marion."

A wave of energy ripples across the monitor

Antonio leans in for a closer look.

Boom!

Marion lunges outward from the screen and wraps her arms around his neck. Her hips and legs remain in the Hyper Realm. "I've missed you too." She gently touches his face.

Antonio has never seen her look so beautiful. His heart is racing as he pulls her close and kisses her perfect lips.

Marion hesitates for a millisecond before gently returning his kiss. Her first kiss.

After a moment she pulls back. "I have something to ask you."

She whispers a question in his ear.

Antonio nods and allows Marion to drag him through the laptop screen and back into the Hyper Realm.

Also by John Rafferty

Novel
Real Tales of Surf Arcana - A Perfect Wave

Childrens picture book
A Gift for Spigot Sloatwater

Comic strip compilation
The Beachiest Bits of Marooned on the Mainland